THE UNIQUE MAGAZINE   ISSN 0898-5073
WINTER 1990–91   Art by Thomas Kidd

Weird Tales® is published 4 times a year by Terminus Publishing Co., Inc., PO Box 13418,
Philadelphia PA 19101-3418 (4426 Larchwood Ave., Philadelphia PA 191014-3916). 2nd Class Postage
paid at Philadelphia PA & additional mailing offices. Single copies, $4.95. Subscriptions: 4 issues
(one year) $16.00 in U.S.A. & possessions; $20.00 in Canada & Mexico, $22.00 elsewhere, in U.S.
funds. Publisher is not responsible for loss of manuscripts, although publisher will take reasonable
care of them. Postmaster: send address changes to *Weird Tales®*, PO Box 13418, Philadelphia PA
19101-3418. Copyright © 1990 by Terminus Publishing Co., Inc.; all rights reserved; reproduction
prohibited without prior permission. Typeset, printed, & bound in the United States of America.
Weird Tales® is a registered trademark owned by Weird Tales, Limited.

THE EYRIE

Welcome to the tenth issue of *Weird Tales*® under the present management. Now, it's time for us to reflect what we've done right with this magazine, and what wrong. The most obviously right thing is that we are continuing. The real thrill for all of us came when we first held copies of the Spring 1988 issue in our (variously squamous or rugose) hands and realized that we had created, not a pastiche or a derivative anthology, but a genuine new issue of *the* classic American fantasy and horror magazine.

The most obviously wrong thing we've done was publish *Weird Tales*® in three different editions: magazine, trade hardcover, and limited-edition hardcover. More specifically, the trade edition was the mistake. The buyer psychology seems to be that anyone who wants more than the regular, magazine-format edition goes all the way to the more collectable, signed-limited edition. So we found the $50.00 signed editions were far outselling the $20.00 trade hardcovers. We have discontinued the latter, increased the print run of the signed, limited edition from one hundred to two hundred copies, and lowered its the price to $30.00 per copy. (You can subscribe in limited, signed hardcover: four issues for $100.00.) This is now the *only* hardcover edition. The irony is that the trade edition of #297,

the last issue to have a trade edition, actually had fewer copies offered for sale than the signed-limited edition of that issue, and is actually scarcer, but of course that trade edition isn't signed by anyone.

We are generally pleased by the appearance of the magazine, and by the mix of fiction and art. We admit we'd like to do *better*, of course.

Weird Tales® and the Small Press. We opened a twenty-year-old can of worms recently. Didn't smell worse than usual, though; and the contents still wriggled.

No — *I* did it, on a panel at NECon (the 1990 **N**orth **E**ast Regional Fantasy **CON**vention) this past July. For the moment, the mask of the editorial "We" drops off. This is Darrell Schweitzer typing.

Anyway, I said the Unsayable on the Start Your Own Publishing Company panel. The fact that it was an old argument, with nothing I hadn't written in the back pages of *Space and Time* twenty years ago, hardly mattered. What I said caused a certain stir, and the issues addressed are still relevant.

There exists almost uniquely in the horror field (definitely not in science fiction, except a little bit toward the extreme "New Wave" end of the spectrum,

4

and far less so in fantasy than ten years ago) a species of home-made magazine known variously as "semi-professional" or "small press," which are lovingly produced by one-man (or -woman) out-of-the-basement publishers more for love than profit. Some are excellent. Stuart Schiff's *Whispers* contains stunning art and important fiction, both by top names in the field and by promising newcomers. The magazine appears on no newsstand and has a circulation in the low thousands, but Robert Bloch and Fritz Leiber are not ashamed to appear in its pages with major new fiction. Paul Ganley's *Weirdbook,* now in its twenty-first year of publication, is also outstanding, the one place you can reliably turn for ichor-dripping Cthulhu Mythos fiction in the traditional mold that isn't, if you will excuse the choice of words, *moldy. Weirdbook* also publishes a wide variety of fiction by new and established writers. Brian Lumley is one of its regular contributors. And there are many more than we can hope to list.

So what was the argument about? Well, there also exist many small-press magazines that do not pay even approximately what the professional magazines do. Some pay only in copies. All have very low circulations, often only in the hundreds.

The crux of the matter, which caused such a controversy at NECon, is that magazines which can pay authors as much as 24 times as much for fiction and offer professional credits and as much as one hundred times the readership will naturally attract the better material. It's in the authors' interest to submit their stories to the bigger magazines first. When I said that, I wasn't trying to set up *Weird Tales*® as "better than those little guys" either. These figures apply just as well to *Fear, The Magazine of Fantasy and Science Fiction,* or several original anthologies, such as Thomas F. Monteleone's *Borderlands.*

You may well imagine that none of the small-press editors and writers present

Editors & Publishers:
John Betancourt
George H. Scithers
Darrell Schweitzer

Assistant Editors:
Leslie Smith
Dainis Bisenieks
Diane Weinstein
Michael W. Betancourt
Don Keller
Carol Adams

Circulation Manager:
Richard Kabakjian

Computer Consultant:
David J. Williams III

Of Counsel:
Yale F. Edeiken

Photographer:
Advanced Litho, Inc.

Typesetter:
Campus Copy Center

Printer & Soft-Cover Binder:
Malloy Lithographing, Inc.

Hard-Cover Binder:
Hoster Bindery, Inc.

Mailing:
Unit Packaging Corporation

Unsolicited Submissions?

Yes, we read unsolicited submissions — but only if they are in standard manuscript format. We survive, as do other editors, only by insisting on these Rules. Each submission must include a return envelope with your address and enough postage to bring the manuscript back to you. Postage must be affixed to the envelope, not loose. Or tell us to discard the manuscript if not bought and include a business-letter-size envelope, stamped and addressed to you, for our comments.

This proper format appears in many reference works. Some of us have even written one: *On Writing Science Fiction: the Editors Strike Back!* by Scithers, Schweitzer, & Ford; $19.50 in hardcovers from Owlswick Press, P.O. Box 8243, Philadelphia PA 19101-8243. Another good reference is Barry B. Longyear's *Science-Fiction Writer's Workshop,* also available from Owlswick Press at $9.50 in trade paperback. These prices include shipping and handling; but in Pennsylvania, add 6% sales tax.

We cannot be responsible for manuscripts in transit or in our hands; you **must** keep a copy of every manuscript you send out, and you **must** put your name and address on every manuscript. Please: no padded envelopes, and no registered nor certified mail.

agreed with me. Many seemed genuinely to believe that because small-press magazines are freer of commercial constraints, they can foster more original and creative talents than the professionals can — that the story published at a quarter of a cent a word is just as good as one published at six cents a word, and not, by implication, a reject from professional markets. Indeed, the whole point of small-press publishing is that there *aren't* enough professional publications to accommodate all the new writers out there. "What chance," a small-press editor asked me rather testily, "does a story by a new writer have of getting into *Weird Tales*®?"

The answer is, about one in two. That is, of the perhaps one hundred manuscripts *Weird Tales*® receives a week, there will be three or four which we could actually buy. At a rough guess, we are getting twice as many good, publishable stories as we can print.

Yet the small-press writers would have us believe that their stories are rejected by the professional magazines because their editors are rigid in what they want. The professional editors insist they merely have higher standards and want writers who are not merely promising, but *delivering*.

The question is still open. A professional colleague typified one extreme when he remarked, "These people [i.e. small-press writers] are doing something terribly self-destructive, and it's not pretty to watch." He meant that by refusing to submit to the big markets and convincing themselves that the professional markets don't want them (or even aren't *good enough* for them), amateurs remain amateurs, never develop skills or discipline, and ultimately waste what talent and imagination they have.

On the other side, the small-press editors point to Thomas Ligotti, who did indeed develop his strange and unique style in the pages of tiny magazines, which he probably could not have done in a newsstand publication.

NECon had another panel which summed it all up in the title: *Small Press, Salvation or Swamp?*

My own feeling is it's a little bit of both. Even those very little magazines, the ones that pay in copies, are very useful. They are like minor-league baseball teams, training players for the majors. I wouldn't want to discourage any of them. Some of the better ones, such as *Whispers* or *Weirdbook*, do indeed supplement the professional field and publish excellent stories which require no excuses at all. Others, let's be honest, have lower standards. Not different standards, but lower. They, of necessity, can't demand quite the same level of originality or craftsmanship, for all that sometimes they get fine material which — let's again be honest — could probably have been published elsewhere for more money.

It's only when small-press publishing becomes an end in itself, a closed little world, that it becomes, as our professional colleague remarked, self-destructive. Anyone can start a small-scale magazine with patience and a few thousand dollars. Very possibly, that magazine will make a real contribution to the horror/fantasy field. But when a small club of amateurs starts genuinely believing that what they're producing is inherently better than the professional product, and that all the rejections they're getting from the big magazines are because of deference to big names, and conspiracies against new writers, then those folks are, quite bluntly, deluding themselves.

A writer like me, who isn't established as a major novelist, has to make every story count. You keep your reputation alive by publishing in the best and most visible markets you can. You can't afford to bury a good story in a 500-copy magazine for ten dollars if you could get several hundred dollars and reach 20,000 to 50,000 readers. Big-name novelists can afford to be more generous, and many will give perfectly saleable stories to little magazines for small sums, but it *is* charity; and charity, like miracles, is not to be relied upon.

So, *Salvation or Swamp?* Do I have any right to demand that every writer make himself a professional and go on to have a professional career? No, of course not, for all one does have a vague feeling that any artist, having created a worthwhile piece of art, has some duty to preserve and propagate it. As the Bible puts it, what good is a light if you hide it under a bushel?

Weird Tales® has never regarded itself as a small-press magazine, but we're fully as independent as one. Policy is set by the three editors. We are answerable to no one except the U.S. Postal Service obscenity rules — and of course to you, the readers.

We are happy to publish new writers. It's an amateur's myth that the bigger magazines won't "take a chance" on a new writer, since a magazine, unlike a novel — which is an all-or-nothing proposition — does not sell on the strength of any single item in it.

Weird Tales®, like all the other professional magazines in the field, tends to have one or two new (first-sale or nearly first-sale) writers in every issue. For a moment there we thought we had discovered Robert Sampson ("Magician in the Dark" in #293, "Sacred to Women" in this issue) and felt that very unique thrill an editor gets upon discovering a brand-new, possibly major talent. Certainly we didn't buy him on his name, since, before we discovered him in the pages of *New Black Mask Mystery Magazine*, we didn't know he'd ever sold a word.

Patricia Anthony ("The Deer Lake Sightings" in #297, "The Murcheson Boy" in #298) is not quite a novice. We've seen her science fiction in *Aboriginal SF*, but think we were the first to buy her horror. Other new or almost-new writers who have appeared in our *Weird Tales*® include Peg Kerr, Mark Noe, Kij Johnson, Ken Wisman, Robert Metzger, Rayson Lorrey, Mark S. Painter Sr., John Accursi, Mary Turzillo, Michael Rutherford (whose novella in #296 was only his second published story), and Valerie King.

So we're doing it. As the magazine prospers, particularly as we grow from quarterly to bimonthly, we'll be publishing even more new writers, as the need for material increases.

Next time you get worried that the pro editors disciminate against beginners, remember this: the big names are mostly busy writing novels. They cannot be relied upon to provide all the stories in an issue. And blank pages *just* don't sell.

Note: We've made some changes in the typography of *Weird Tales*®. With last issue (#298), we switched from outside typesetting to setting most of our type in house. For us, this speeds our publication cycle; but — how do you like the change?

Letters:

As if to amplify what our professional colleague said about would-be authors deluding themselves, the following missive from **Leon Monroe Frazier** came the very hour this Eyrie was being typed:

Where on Earth did this piece of junk mail come from? Thank you for soliciting me to re-subscribe, but I believe I explained, quite clearly to you, long ago, that I send you potential submissions, wanting to be published in your magazine — but you rejected them, while publishing what I regard as inferior fiction instead.

Well . . . enough of you. Bye.

Mr. Frazier, you've *got* to be kidding.

On a happier note, **Harlan Ellison** writes from California:

I am enjoying the magazine. The love you put into it, every issue, is apparent. Keeping WT *alive and kicking puts you squarely on the side of the angels.*

Two small matters.

First, even if the fiction were not good (and much of it seems to me considerably better than just good), you would be on the roster for plaudits in that you have brought Kelly Freas back to us with his best work in more than twenty years. There is clearly an affinity; him for the magazine and its bent, the magazine for him and his winsome ways. The spreads on pp. 100–101 and 142–143 in the Summer 1990 issue near brought me to misty-eyed with joyful memories of Kelly working in this style in his best days. Thank you. Again, thank you.

Second, John makes a small misrepresentation when he writes in "The Den" (p. 13, same issue) that the magazine Midnight Graffiti *"is a delightful fan-produced magazine." The perception of its quality is accurate, but the suggestion that it is* fan *produced is dead wrong, and might inadvertently cause those who are unfamiliar with the magazine to think that it's a slick, well-produced fanzine of semi-professional intent or quality. In fact,* Midnight Graffiti *is produced by people no less professional than the three of you. Their staff may be smaller, but as one who was paid $3,000 for an original novella, and $2,000 for a novella-length essay, I can assure you* Midnight Graffiti *is as pro-driven as* Playboy, Omni, F&SF, *and* Weird Tales. *I'm not chiding, just trying to correct a misperception.*

Keep 'em howling, boys. Youse is doing a good job.

To which we can only say (*sigh*) we wish *we* could afford to pay that kind of money for *anything.* Presumably John came to his conclusion about *Midnight Graffiti* because the magazine seems to be irregularly published and sold only through SF/horror specialty outlets. But we must stand corrected.

Edward W. O'Brien Jr. of Trenton NJ writes:

I thought the hero-worshipping profiles

of David J. Schow were a bit much, and I am distressed at the four-letter words now appearing in Weird Tales. *Your magazine does not need four-letter words. Good writers like Lovecraft, et al., did not rely on them for their literary effects. It seems that you permit dirty words in order to show that you're modern, liberated, and sophisticated. But the use of those words only shows that you are afraid not to use them, afraid to appear unliberated.*

David J. Schow's well-written tale "Monster Movies" disturbed me because George Scithers recently rejected a story of mine and he turned it down by saying it was "preachy." Yes, it was preachy in having a Catholic tone to it. There were other reasons why Scithers rejected it, but my point is this: Don't tell me I can't preach in Weird Tales *and then allow David Schow to do just that. On pages 58, 59, and 60, Schow preached a digressive sermon against conventional Christian faith, and supporting atheism. So you can't preach in* Weird Tales? — *It all depends on what you're preaching! Okay for Schow to launch an extended attack on Christian doctrines, and to characterize the only two believers in the story as bigoted, cruel dolts. But not okay to defend or support faith.*

And it doesn't seem to me that Schow's preachments in "Monster Movies" advanced the plot very much. Anyway, one can see that the pulpit is permitted in Weird Tales, *as long as the sermon has the approved orthodoxy: agnosticism, atheism, and a rather harsh, even ugly anti-Christian sneering. Is it any better if such things are said in dialogue? Of course not.*

You raise two important points here, both of which have to do with battles we'd thought finished decades ago.

The fight for more and more explicit dirty words in literature and performance surely ended with Lenny Bruce, or else William Burroughs, or at the very least Harlan Ellison's *Dangerous Visions*

(1967). No, we don't feel any obligation to insert such language in order to show how liberated we are. We are in the "post-shock-effect age" and no longer impressed by profanity for its own sake. There *are* times when profanity or explicit sexual material or any other formerly taboo matter still belongs in a story. Particularly, a string of profanity can work in a story by its *lack* of continued ability to shock — to show a character's mental exhaustion. This can be simple realism: an illiterate character with the brain of a peanut is going to talk that way, as will a bored yuppie when he runs out of anything real to say.

As for the allegedly anti-Christian tone of Schow's story, you are confusing the character's opinions for those of the author. Maybe they are the same. Maybe not. But if the story had made this opinion its main focus, rather than an incidental aspect of one character, *then* we would have regarded it as a preachment.

Bruce Moffitt of Brookfield MO :
My vote for Number one in issue 297 goes to Thomas Ligotti's "The Lost Art of Twilight" — a genuinely weird tale! It actually had this jaded old stomach turning, and I have been enjoying offbeat fiction for fifty years.

Number two honors go to Nancy Springer for "#20," which is not a weird tale. In fact, I consider it realism. Paul Harvey recently spoke of a florist whose business was destroyed (financially) because he lost weight. Rumor said he had AIDS. He had himself tested, was found HIV-negative, and posted the results in his shop window. This failed to convince some of his detractors and at last report he had been assaulted. So I consider "#20" to be unhappily true-to-life. A minister's wife knows whereof she speaks. Mrs. Springer is, or was, I should say, unknown to me, but I will watch for her work in the future.

Certainly a *horror* story can be realis-tic, as is the whole tradition of the French *conte cruel*, and the same applies to many of Poe's most celebrated tales, which have no overtly fantastic elements, but deal memorably with bizarre situations and mental states.

As for the florist, the whole point about a rumor, and the reason Mrs. Life's rumors were so devastating, is that as soon as you have to deny the rumor, the rumor-mongers have won.

George Baker writes from Fresno CA:
There are two nasty little items boring into my brain:

1) The constant badmouthing Fantasy, Horror, and Science Fiction receive is nothing less than pomposity at its worst — pomposity for pomposity's sake. The critics and readers who expend so much time assuring us that the three genres are nothing more than hopeless hackwork are the same goons who have bookshelves full of John Updike, Kurt Vonnegut, Jr., and Anthony Burgess. They legitimize themselves by claiming, "Well, they're doing more than writing about bizarre realities; they're prose stylists and they're making observations about the human condition."

Not long ago I worked as a columnist for an Alternative (also known as Underground, Left-wing, or Pseudo-Hippie-Antisocial-Chickenshit) newspaper. Ray Bradbury came into town and was to be speaking at a nice hotel down by the beach. After some car-salesman-like negotiations, I finally talked my editor into letting me cover the event.

After Bradbury had finished, and was talking with the crowd, I ran into someone I know who worked for the local press — a Good Ol' Boys' network if ever there was one, and received a "Bradbury has always been more than an SF writer."

Somehow the conversation between this man and myself came around to, yes, Updike, Vonnegut, and Burgess. And, of course, I was given the old "Prose stylist, important writer" *run-around.*

Asks I, "Ever read Brian Lumley?"

"No."

"Clive Barker? Tanith Lee? Paul Hazel? What about C.J. Cherryh?" (I was enjoying this.)

"No," said the schmuck.

"Well," I said, "they are all wonderful prose stylists, and, in their own way, have made some rather remarkable statements."

His response was brilliant: "Yeah, well ..."

So what's with all this nonsense about SF, Horror, and Fantasy not being worth much? Come on. The way I see it, the most delicate handling of words, the most precise definition of "prose stylists" is to be found in the bizarre. I'm putting no one down — I happen to love, with a passion, the works of Joseph Heller, and especially John Irving. Both mainstream writers. But then again, a fine jaunt into lands where a man can stretch his "Soft" wife out of wack (and have the favor returned), where "Fruiting Bodies" destroy people, where the characters of a movie called Boiled Alive *telephone an innocent man, is more than a pleasant diversion; it's a Hell of a way to spend an evening.*

Who is F. Gwynplaine MacIntyre? Since issue 290 I've been following his poetry with great admiration, and more than the occasional laugh. Where's he from? How old is he? Is he planning any novels or collections of his verse?

Please, more MacIntyre.

We are reminded of an observation once made about academic English teachers: their problem is they don't know much about literature. Surely, when anyone tells you that a whole field of writing is no good, no matter what that field may be, this claim must be regarded with the deepest suspicion. Those ferocious English teachers of yore who tore up any science fiction they caught their students reading, while delivering impassioned lectures on how this evil, subliterate pulp stuff would stunt one's aesthetic growth, cause hair to grow on the palms of the hands, etc. etc. were almost always speaking from a position of *total ignorance.* Similarly, the mainstream critic who insists that only realistic fiction constitutes "real literature" is similarly ignorant — of the fact that most literature, in all cultures of the world, is fantasy.

But some people within the field of fantastic literature don't seem to have learned *a thing* from such persecutions. So we have science-fiction writers producing such articles as "Fantasy as Cancer," horror writers regarding all science fiction (and fantasy) as junk, fantasy writers sneering at horror. The more things change, the more the stay the same. It's enough to put the *sigh* back in Sigh Fi.

As for F. ("Froggy" to his friends) Gwynplaine MacIntyre, he has published some of the best fantastic light verse we know in *Isaac Asimov's Science Fiction Magazine, Amazing Stories,* and now *Weird Tales®.* He has published occasional short fiction, and *does* have a quite good novel making the rounds of publishers. He is, by his own account, Australian by way of England, and now resides (some of the time) in New York. Beyond that, he is (jokingly) a Man Of Mystery. When we recently suggested that he might be the illegitimate son of B. Traven, he *didn't deny it!*

We think a volume of MacIntyre verse would be a good idea too.

The Most Popular Story

The most popular story for issue 297, Summer 1990, was by a close margin, "#20" by Nancy Springer, followed by "The Pronounced Effect" by John Brunner (second place), "The Lost Art of Twilight" by Thomas Ligotti (third), and an honorable mention to "The Deer Lake Sightings" by Patricia Anthony, which made an unusually strong showing.   Ω

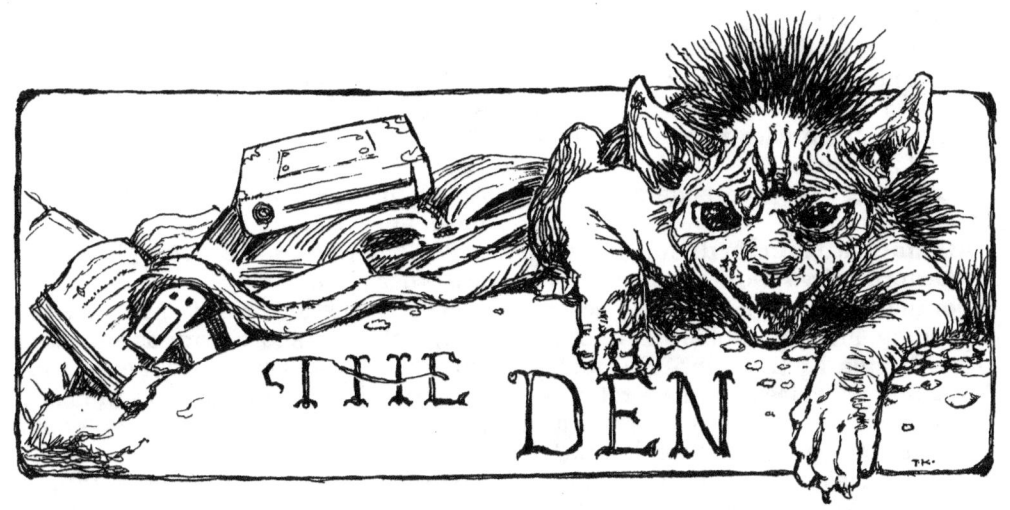

by John Gregory Betancourt

The Horror Writers of America recently held their annual get-together, which concluded with their Bram Stoker Awards Ceremony. This year's winners were:

Best Novel: *Carrion Comfort* by Dan Simmons (Dark Harvest).

Best First Novel: *Sunglasses After Dark* by Nancy A. Collins (NAL/Onyx).

Best Novelette: "On the Far Side of the Cadillac Desert with Dead Folks" by Joe R. Lansdale (*Book of the Dead*).

Best Short Story: "Eat Me" by Robert McCammon (*Book of the Dead*).

Best Collection: *Collected Stories* by Richard Matheson. (Scream/Press)

Best Nonfiction (tie): *Harlan Ellison's Watching* by Harlan Ellison (Underwood/Miller); and *Horror: The 100 Best Books* by Steve Jones and Kim Newman (Carroll & Graf).

It's hard to argue with a line-up like that. Karl Edward Wagner's "At First Just Ghostly" was the only story from *WT* nominated this year; but then competition was tough. The market for short horror fiction is probably better today than it's ever been, considering the number of fine small-press and professional magazines using it, not to mention all the original anthologies!

Who will make it big next? I enjoy watching award nominations, best-of-the-year anthologizations, small presses reprinting paperbacks into hardcover, specialty dealer catalogs, and trying to guess.

My picks for the next few writers to make it big:

#1: **Joe R. Lansdale**. His writing is brilliant, as fans have begun to realize. I've seen Lansdale's out-of-print paperbacks priced as high as $10.00 per copy at conventions . . . and dealers are getting it. Mark V. Ziesing is reprinting two of Lansdale's suspense novels; British publishers are putting the rest into hardcover.

#2: **Thomas Ligotti**. Anyone who's read his stylish horror stories knows what a master of the genre he is. He's just had his first hardcover (from Carroll & Graf): the revised and expanded *Songs of a Dead Dreamer*. Clive Barker has shown that short-story collections can still reach the masses in the horror field, and Ligotti may soon find a similarly large audience. Pick up the hardcover edition of *Songs* now, while you can still afford it.

#3: Alan Rodgers. See the review of his first novel below. He's probably going to be a cross-genre success like Koontz and McCammon with the publication of his next few books.

Other possible contenders, further down the line:

Michael Rutherford. Judging from Rutherford's first two stories, we have a major new fantasy writer here; I've been describing him as "Robert E. Howard meets Ursula K. Le Guin." He's one of those unique voices; if his first novel (currently in progress) is as good as I think it's going to be, who knows? It might be a major break-out book.

Nina Kiriki Hoffman. Her wonderful short stories have been appearing throughout the field for several years now; I understand she's finished seven novels, but never marketed them(!). If she gets her act together, the field will be richer for it.

Ed Bryant. He started as a science-fiction writer, and produced a number of interesting but commercially unsuccessful books. Recently he's turned to horror, and his stories have been excellent — see his contribution to *Book of the Dead*. When he finally gears himself up to do horror novels (which I hope is soon!), I know they're going to be something extraordinary.

So much for predicting the future of horror. On to the reviews!

Blood of the Children
by Alan Rodgers
Bantam, 299 pp., $3.95.

Those who have been watching Who Does What in the horror field for the last five or six years will probably recognize Alan Rodgers's name. He began as an assistant at *Rod Serling's The Twilight Zone Magazine* and graduated to full editor of *TZ*'s sister magazine, *Night Cry*. He discovered or developed many new writers, including A.R. Morlan, David Schow, and even our own Darrell

Schweitzer, to cite a few names *Weird Tales*® readers will recognize.

Rodgers brought that same creative energy to his writing, and his first story ("The Boy Who Came Back From the Dead," in *Masques II*) won a Bram Stoker Award in 1988. Since then his stories have appeared in *Weird Tales*® (Fall 1988), *Full Spectrum 2, Scare Care*, and a few other places.

Why is this important? After reading Rodgers's first short story as soon as it came out, I began seeking out everything he wrote. I've now read every published piece of his fiction, and I think he's going to be a major writer.

His first novel, *Blood of the Children*, is further evidence. It is in many ways a summation of his career thus far, a reworking at novel length of all the themes and devices that made his short fiction work so well.

The plot: Ben and Jimmy Tompkins move from New Jersey to Green Hill, a town somewhere in the Deep South. Ben's wife (and Jimmy's mother) had a mental breakdown, butchered the family dog, and sliced up Jimmy with a knife (leaving him scarred both mentally and physically). She's now institutionalized, and Ben just wants to get Jimmy to a safe, secure place so they can get about rebuilding their lives.

However, Green Hill is not the Shangri La it seems. The adults are good, kind, simple folk; but the children are monsters. A gigantic, otherworldly Stone is encouraging the children to do as much evil as they can. They worship the stone, of course, and mutilate pets their in sacrifices to it.

When Jimmy Tompkins first ventures out of his new home, he discovers four boys chasing a wounded dog that escaped while they were skinning it alive. Jimmy (of course) saves the dog and makes it his own — but he's interfered in the Stone's affairs, and the children aren't going to forget. What follows is a grim game, as the Stone's minions capture Jimmy and prepare him for sacrifice, and Ben Tompkins and the county sheriff desperately try to find him.

Rodgers's chief asset is his writing style: deceptively smooth, with a voice reminiscent of Ray Bradbury's. He shares Bradbury's ability to evoke emotional responses in his readers. It's chiefly this style which carries the plot — which is (admittedly) something of a cliché. But Rodgers looks dead-on where Bradbury might flinch, and the graphic violence is going to disturb some people. It isn't splatterpunk, but it isn't a cozy tea-room horror, either. It's an amalgam of the two.

Nor is the book flawless. Very few first novels are so perfect that they can withstand close scrutiny, and this one begins to unravel around the edges. A few plot devices are simply *too* convenient. But the fact that Rodgers can drag you into the story, and *keep you there* so long as well, is remarkable, and bodes well for future books.

And I hope he does continue to stretch and grow as a writer. Everything he's written thus far is about children, and it would be nice to see him give adults the same treatment.

Nightmare People
by Lawrence Watt-Evans
NAL/Onyx, 254 pp., $3.95.

When Edward Smith wakes up one night, he sees a creature at his window. He thinks it's a dream, until the next day, when everyone else in his apartment complex has disappeared. It turns out they've been replaced by vampire-like creatures who wear human skin to masquerade as people.

Of course, nobody will believe Smith, so he sets up a resistance band on his own, and begins killing the creatures, which reproduce at an alarming rate, and are taking over the world.

Lawrence Watt-Evans's first foray into horror is a mixed success. The writing is good and Smith is an interesting protago-

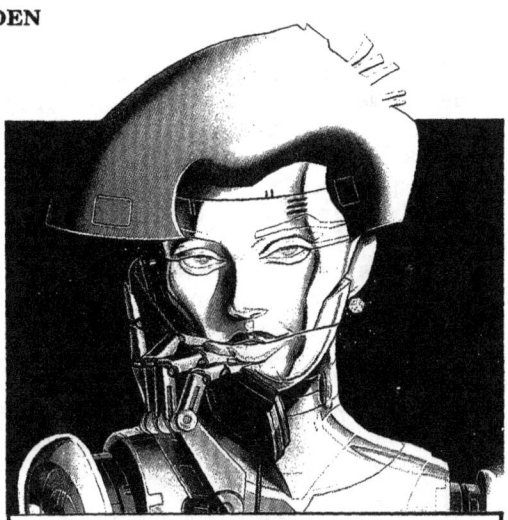
13

nist. However, that's not enough. What's missing is an understanding of what makes modern horror tick. Watt-Evans approaches horror from a science-fictional perspective, going more for action/adventure than emotional resonance.

It seems there is a vast evil Out There trying to destroy humanity. It comes up with a new monster every so often for this express purpose: werewolves, vampires, etc. were all past (failed) attempts. The nightmare people are sort of upgraded vampires: you can't kill them with bullets, knives, silver, fire, or much of anything else.

What *will* work? I'm not going to say, because it will spoil some of the story's suspense for those hearty (if you'll pardon the expression) enough to sample *The Nightmare People*. But it's so inane, I almost threw the book across the room when I read it. Be warned.

Seeing Red by David J. Schow
TOR, 268 pp., $4.95.

It took me a while to find *Seeing Red,* since TOR didn't see fit to send me a review copy. This is another one of those interesting books that get published with great stealth.

Seeing Red collects 14 of Schow's stories. Quality is somewhat uneven, since it includes a number of weaker, pseudonymously published works from early in Schow's career; but there are enough gems here to make it all worthwhile.

I think my favorite is "Lonesome Coyote Blues," about a phantom radio station which plays songs dead rock stars would have recorded if they'd only lived. But "Red Light" is also a masterpiece, about a woman afraid of being photographed, because she thinks her image is being used up bit by bit. And "Blood Rape of the Lust Ghouls" is fascinating for its title if nothing else, about a jaded critic of horror movies . . .

Take the time to hunt *Seeing Red* down. It's worth it.

Agviq by Michael Armstrong
Questar, 275 pp., $4.50.

Although published as a genre science fiction book, *Agviq* is packaged like a best-seller. It even has a couple of rave quotes from Whitley Strieber plastered prominently on the covers.

The story is simple enough: after a nuclear war, Alaska is one of the places mankind lives on. The Eskimos revert to their old ways, and Claudia (our archaeologist heroine who knows more about the old Eskimo ways than the modern Eskimos) must teach them to live as their ancestors did.

Armstrong glosses over the unpleasantness of death to get to all of the good stuff — surviving. It's a palatable survivalist story, I suppose; but when I want to read a post-nuclear-holocaust story, I'd prefer Nevil Shute's *On the Beach* or Pat Frank's *Alas, Babylon.* Or for survival, George R. Stewart's classic novel, *Earth Abides.*

Agviq is also a book out of its time. It should have been published at least a decade ago, when the threat of nuclear war seemed more real. These days, amidst *glasnost* and the dismantling of the Berlin Wall, not to mention the Soviet Union's relaxed grip on its satellite states, nuclear war just doesn't hold the same threat.

Night Things by Michael Talbot
Avon Books, 248 pp., $3.95.

Night Things has one of those garish covers I usually avoid because they look *too* trashy but when Kim, my wife, picked it up and began to rave about what a great story it was, I couldn't resist.

Lake House is a 160-room mansion in the Adirondacks. The woman who had it built was a bit odd, and Lake House has stairways that lead nowhere, rooms designed to distort the senses, and a series of mazelike halls — and a history of violent death.

When Garrett's stepfather, Stephen, rents Lake House for the summer, Garrett isn't thrilled with the idea. He doesn't like Stephen, and wants nothing more but for his mother to get a divorce. Soon a ghostly apparition visits Garrett; and there's a manlike creature with night-glowing eyes lurking outside. Nobody is quite what he seems. Even Lake House has secrets — which lead to a showdown between forces of good and evil.

Talbot is a great storyteller, playing games with reader expectations. *Night Things* has twists which will pleasantly surprise even jaded horror readers. I'll be keeping my eye out for Talbot's other books, *The Bog* and *A Delicate Dependency.*

It's Loose by Warner Lee
Pocket Books, 312 pp., $3.95.

It's Loose has an even more garish cover than *Night Things,* which just goes to show that good books can hide behind bad covers.

When Stephen Kesselring, a cop, kills a man who went berserk and shot up a supermarket, he sees a monstrous ghostlike creature flee the dead body. With a little research, he discovers that this creature has been hopping from body to body, possessing people and feeding on fear and death. Kesselring quits his job and begins a quest to find the creature and kill it.

Cut to the present. The creature (which Kesselring calls the Evil) has come to Ice Island, Michigan. Ice Island gets cut off from the mainland when the lake freezes or thaws, and it's isolated now for the duration of the thaw.

When people start committing gruesome murders, Don Farraday — Ice Island's only policeman — finds himself in over his head. The Evil's feeding frenzy makes it ever more powerful, and soon it's controlling dozens of people. Kesselring must persuade Farraday to overcome his doubts and help him kill the Evil.

Warner Lee has hit upon one of the successful formulas of horror fiction: isolate a group of people, have an outside force begin to kill and/or influence them to bad ends, and force them to join together to defeat the outside force. Lee hits all the notes right, producing a more than competent book.

In Short . . .
If you're interested in non-fiction about science fiction, fantasy, and horror, let me recommend two magazines. The first is *Afraid: The Newsletter for the Horror Professional.* It runs columns on horror writing, book reviews, professional news, and lots of opinion. Cost is $20.00 for 12 monthly issues, which is a good buy. Single copy price, $2.95, seems a bit steep.

The other magazine (and probably of more interest to the average reader, since it's not geared toward professionals or would-be professionals) is the revived *Science Fiction Review.* The old *SFR* was the premier critical journal in science fiction for many years, running interviews, reviews, essays, and lots of letters.

The first two issues of the new *SFR* contain work by or interviews with: Robert A. Heinlein, Ursula K. Le Guin, Roger Zelazny, Gregory Benford, Orson Scott Card, and many others. $18.00 for 4 issues from: SFR Publications, PO Box 20340, Salem OR 97307. Cover price on the second issue is $4.95; you might try $6.00 for a sample copy.   Ω

TIRED ANGEL

by Jonathan Carroll

You don't know me, but you will — soon. Give me an hour to introduce myself if you would. Less, if you're a fast reader. I imagine you're a fast reader. You read fast because you're a no-nonsense woman. Get up to change the channels manually on the television (despite having a little gizmo box to do it for you), know where your scissors are, as well as everything else in your desk. Fresh underwear every morning. Let me guess — white? With perhaps a pair of expensive black sexy ones in a drawer for special occasions? Am I right? I bet I am.

I thought of you today in a restaurant. Wondered if you would react the way that waitress did. You see, she was bustling by and dropped a water glass. It crashed on the floor, pieces flying everywhere. But she pretended nothing had happened! Kept going, even though she knew it had fallen. Didn't stop when it crashed, didn't clean it up. Minutes went by! Huge shards of glass lying in the middle of the floor for anyone to step on and she leaves them there. She didn't want it to happen, so when it did she just acted as if it hadn't. For a while her silly little planet could orbit around a sun that wasn't there . . . Anyway, I wondered if you'd act the same way when your turn came. Act like nothing was happening, despite crazy calls in the middle of the night or blood in your handbag, chewed gum warm on your pillow, things like that. Ignore it, leave the splinters on the floor and walk barefoot across them until glass is ground so deep into your feet that . . .

I'll call her Toni. That wasn't her name, but I love women who end their names with 'i,' as if it were exotic and Italian, rather than stupid and about as cute as a bum's asshole.

My Toni was a plain-looking woman who, with a bit of taste and money, had made herself into a nice-looking woman. Her nose was too small and her forehead too high to help out the roundness of the rest of her face. When she made love, that round came up and became more childlike and interesting. That's probably why she wished for a larger nose. To put a real feature on her otherwise nothing-special face.

I knew that face so well because I studied it through my binoculars for some months before doing anything. They're not especially strong glasses, 7×21; the kind you use at the opera to look down some fat singer's throat, but they do the job.

I discovered Toni in her apartment the night I bought them. Calmly scanning the building across the street, lo and behold there she was, one floor lower. I could look right in through her transparently white curtains and watch her watching television. Naked! Really, she was naked the very first time I saw her. Little breasts, little hips . . . Adorable. Every man's dream — a naked woman he can spy on and charge his lonely nights. The nudity didn't excite me but rather made me like her a lot. At home this woman did just what she wanted — watched TV naked in January with a cup of cocoa in one hand and the other stuck under her bum. Sometimes I'd turn on my television and try to guess what she was watching. News in the nude? Did she strip for her favourite talk shows? Get down to the essentials when she knew Mel Gibson was on so she could pretend to show him what she had?

It seemed like she enjoyed being naked all the time. I particularly liked watching her walk from room to room, so often restless late in the night with nothing to do and the morning creeping up on her, the moment when she'd have to put the clothes back on and go back out into the world to whatever job waited. I guessed she was a business woman from the taste and expense of objects in her apartment, or the ones I could see. There's only so much you can see from the one dimension of your two windows. I'd often spend whole evenings in the dark, walking slowly back and forth from window one to window two, watching Toni live her evenings away. She had a fake antique spinning wheel in one corner, a comfortable-looking couch with an unforgivable floral pattern. The back of her television was almost against the window so I sometimes fantasised she was watching me from her easy chair and not Channel Two.

One night when she wasn't home I took out my pistol and fired several shots through her window. Not from my apartment, of course. No, I went up on the roof of the building next door and did it, so if the police came and checked they'd think it was just another lunatic taking target practice at unknown black windows. I never asked her about it later, but am sure that came to her mind when the other events started happening.

Everything was spontaneous. I didn't decide I wanted to sleep with her until I saw her in the corner market one morning buying grapefruit. Suddenly the thought of sitting across the breakfast table eating grapefruit with her seemed a wonderful, fulfilling idea and I wanted her very much for the first time. So I moved in the same direction as her through the market, allowing her to catch glimpses, letting her know I was looking at her. At the checkout counter she stood in front of me, as planned. When she put down her grapefruit I groaned and said I wished I'd picked that one and not the ugly, small thing I had in my basket. This didn't endear me with the grocer but it made her smile and we began to talk. That was it. We walked out of the market together and into each other's lives.

The first time I was ever in her place I went to the window, looked out and waved at my home. Hello there!

That was also the first time we ever made love. Borrrrrring. Who would have thought that someone who loved to walk around naked would turn out to be so dull in bed? She thought moving her hips a little and mouse squeaks at the end was La Dolce Vita. She told me I was the only man she'd ever slept with who made no sound or move when he came. Then jokingly she asked if I *had* come. I said "Yes." Her smile fell and she said "Oh," as if she'd walked into a room that was off limits.

She had.

So the first thing I taught her was how to make love and she became good at it but that wasn't enough. In bed, in conversation, in life, my Toni-lover wasn't nearly as interesting as my Toni through my binoculars. Looking through them, I could imagine anything. In her bed, or eating what she cooked, hearing what she said, no matter how interesting, was only so much and not more. There wasn't anything to imagine. How often I fled her house, her arms, her dreams and rushed back to my place where I'd grab up my glasses and cock at the same time and watch her, naked, emptying the ashtray I'd just filled, taking off the album we'd danced to before going into the bedroom an hour earlier.

On her birthday I did something that bound her to me forever. As a child, her favourite story had been *Peter Pan* and jokingly she told me she often wished Peter Pan would come now and take her off to Never-Never Land. I rented a big green elf costume and that night, with the help of a thick rope I'd used years ago when I was mountain climbing, lowered myself off the top of her roof, in costume naturally, and tapped on her window. I'm here! I've come for you, Toni! When you wish upon a star . . .

That's how I got my nickname. When she opened the window and I swung in, she embraced me and asked hadn't I been scared out there, thirty stories up.

I said no, just a little tired from all the manœuvering.

"Oh, my wonderful Tired Angel. I love you!"

After that, I could have put a leash around her neck and told her to heel.

Instead I started to call her. There is an art to that kind of telephone call which is much like the art of making a perfect soufflé. Without the best ingredients the thing never rises. You can always tell someone over the phone that you're going to kill them, but that is cheap eggs. Triple A jumbo eggs is sending a funeral director to Toni's door to talk to the "bereaved" about "the recently deceased." Only the deceased in this case is the same as the bereaved. Imagine the consternation of the funeral director. Better, imagine Toni's fear. I called ten times a day. I told her I knew the colour of her best bra, the colour of her bathroom. I told her I was in love with her. That I hated her. Etcetera.

I would stand at my window with the lights out, pick up my binoculars with one hand, the telephone receiver with the other, and call. To see her face when she realised who it was! Often she'd hang right up. Or I'd hang up, just in case she was having the line tapped. One can't be too careful. I watched her cry. I watched her throw down the receiver and shake. I watched her cover her head and fall to the floor, scared as a human being can be.

The astonishing thing was she didn't tell me about the calls until a month after I'd begun them. What courage she had! I was outraged. Call the police! Who does this pervert think he is! I had many good suggestions. She was calmed and heartened by what I told her to do. She was sure one of my ideas would work.

But they couldn't because I knew what they were and was always watching. When she put the whistle in her mouth and blew as hard as she could into the receiver, I took the phone away from my ear and laughed. When she had blown herself out, I put my whistle in and, tooting, broke her eardrum. Things like that.

I would call in the middle of the night and tell her terrible things. Then she would call me minutes later and say I'm so so sorry, but he called again and please talk to me.

Talk? I would rush over and hold her in my arms, the best friend she ever had. Peter Pan, lover, no fair-weather friend here! Sometimes the phone rang when I was there but she would never answer. I would, and twice pretended it was HIM. Cursed and screamed, "The police are after you, you fucking creep!"

What I would have done next I have no idea because one night in April I called, watched her walk by the telephone and jump out the window. Zoom! What a surprise.

Not much more to tell you. Here's a hint — maybe I'm someone you already know. Maybe not. Maybe I'm looking at you right now.

Have you ever thought about how many people look at you that you don't even see in a lifetime?

Soon,

Your Tired Angel   Ω

JONATHAN CARROLL SPEAKS

from an interview on Austrian National Radio (ORF)

conducted by Walter Gröbschen and Wolfgang Ritschel

transcribed and edited by Darrell Schweitzer

Three times in my life I have been faced with death, once when a guy put a gun to my head and pulled back the hammer, and he was in the mental state in which he could easily have done it. And I'll tell you something: there's nothing, *nothing* more frightening in the world than knowing that you're going to die [snaps fingers] *now*.

The Russian writer Gurdjieff says we're literally asleep all the time. Only at certain moments in our lives do we wake up.

So there have been moments in which I was utterly happy and there was a *light* that went on in my head, denoting: this is what reality is. That's the good side. The bad side is the guy puts a magnum pistol to your head, you hear *click! click!* and you say, "This is *it*? This is all there is?"

To me, the three greatest fantasists — not artists — who ever lived are in the Germanic tradition. You have Hoffmann. You have the Grimm brothers, and you have Kafka; and you have some of the other boys thrown in for good measure.

For example, Günter Grass. Günter Grass to me is a fantastic novelist — I don't mean fantastic in the sense of *good*; he is good — but he is one of the great fantasy writers of the 20th century. But people talk about him more as a political writer and exclude what I think is most wonderful. A friend is reading *The Tin Drum* now and says what's so wonderful about it to her is the fantasy element. The hero Oskar is not of this Earth. That's where fantasy begins, when your main character or your main environment is not of this Earth. I don't care what kind of fantasy you're talking about, whether it be spaceships or Kafka. Gregor Samsa woke up one morning and he was an insect. He is not of this Earth.

These great, great writers are of the Germanic tradition, but they were a long time ago. We look at them and go *mon chapeau*; my hat is off to you (in respect); because it's just not being done today.

I remember being most frightened by books in which the character asks the same questions that I do but they're never answered.

A very simple example is, oddly, a book I don't like very much but which comes quickest to my head: *The Castle (Das Schloss)*. If you're going to look at that book as a metaphor where the character is trying to find God, so he keeps trying

21

to get to the Schloss but never can — I've been thinking about God all my life, and if that's what it's all about — you can see Him but can never get to Him, which makes it even more frustrating — *that* really frightens me. That really frightens me a lot.

At the one pole you have the inescapable existential doom of Kafka. And at the other there are the dramatic bestsellers of Stephen King. Now I think that anybody who's *that* popular must be doing something right. I haven't read all of King's work, but I've noticed this about his success. King draws his horror out of everyday things. He uses such devices as a refrigerator and a cheese sandwich. That's miles away from what the typical horror industry grinds out — full of fake blood, and in the end completely trite. King is often both moving and profound.

I don't generally respond to horror novels or horror movies because I don't particularly believe in monsters. The greatest monster I know is death.

I just wrote a scene in my newest book, just half an hour ago, in which a dog is killed. Now, whether you like animals or not, that's, as Richard Pryor would say, the *real deal*. If you've ever picked a dog that you love up off the road that's been run over, and you don't know what to do because it's dead, and you start to think of things like "What do I do with the body?" All of a sudden this animal that which had all this meaning to you twenty minutes ago has now become this *thing*. You're thinking, "What am I going to do to get rid of it? Am I going to burn it? Am I going to bury it? What do I owe it?" That's real horror.

At one point I taught Creative Writing for a year. The students were crazy about writing brutal, frightening stories, full of decapitations and rapes and drug overdoses. But at the end, they often couldn't think of any other way to get out of the morass of blood that they'd called into being, than to write:

"Kate turned over in bed and touched the hair of the sleeper beside her. Thank God, it had been nothing but a bad dream." Their horror was conveniently controllable. In real life, after a rape or death, it isn't. It never ends. In *Voice of Our Shadow* I wrote a line in which the guy said, "Somebody's death is like walking down a staircase you're used to going down, but then suddenly there's no step there." **Boom.** You just keep tripping on it for the rest of your life. *That's* horror. The staircase without the step. And as Calvino said, you reach a point in life where more of your friends are dying than are alive. If there are ten steps when you're young, when you get older you're having to take these increasingly large steps to get up the staircase because all these in-between ones have been taken away. *That's* horror.

My father died a year ago after two years of absolutely agonizing pain. That's *horrible. That's* horror. The only real horror is the pain or death of loved ones. Period.

Very often people who read my books say, "I *loved* the first half. It was wonderful. The romance was just great, but when the crazy stuff started, you lost me." That is certainly a valid criticism, but what happened was they were expecting a romance or a realistic novel, and they got dogs talking.

Inside their brains they went, "No, this is not possible. In a realistic novel dogs do not talk. Therefore it's a fantasy. I don't like fantasy, so I put it down."

When you read a book, basically what you're doing is giving up your own world and taking on the world of the book. You cannot apply rules that have got to hold in the book, because the book creates its own reality. Whether that reality is Tolkien with hobbits, or Tolstoy with Anna Karenina, you've given up your world, so you can't bring the rules of that world into the book.

So, if you read one of my books and children fly out the window, and you say "But children *don't* fly out the window," I say, "Stop. We're not talking about your world. We're talking about the world of this book, and *that's* what matters."

Now, I may not have those children fly out the window well. You can criticize me for that, but don't criticize me for the fact that they can fly.

I am also often criticized for being trendy. One person said a line that makes me smile. It should upset me but it makes me smile. He said I write yuppie horror novels.

A friend of mine once said something which has always haunted me. I asked him, "Are there people who can walk on water?" He said, "Sure." I asked, "Are there people who can fly?" He said, "Of course." I asked, "Why don't they show us?" He said, "Why would a person so advanced give a *shit* about showing you that he can walk on water?"

Sleeping in Flame is set in Vienna but it's based on a story that happened to me. Someone saw a picture on a gravestone in Russia, and took a photograph of it because the original photograph looked *exactly like me*. Very strange. It really gave me a little chill up my back. Only in *Sleeping in Flame*, the picture is seen on a gravestone in Vienna, in the Central Cemetery.

I think that whether you believe in spirits or ghosts or not, there is absolutely no question that people live on, if only in other people's memories. That's one of the things that we have — I mean, if we have children, long after you're dead they remember you. My books basically take that one step further, where often people literally do come back from the dead.

I have not seen ghosts and I have no idea what happens to us after we die, but I think that trying to understand what death is is probably the equivalent of one cell in our finger trying to understand what our entire body is.

When I was living in America, I was offered three jobs as a teacher overseas. One was in Beirut, one in Tehran, and one in Vienna. Thank God, I chose Vienna.

As, basically, an *extremely* private person who does not like to be bothered by outside influences, I found it more and more comfortable for me to live here. Interestingly enough, the more well-known I have become, the happier I am that I am here because other friends of mine who gained a certain notoriety as writers have great difficulty functioning within cultures that will not leave them alone.

If you live in America, Americans have a very bad habit of thinking if you're well-known, you belong to them. So if they see you on television or read a magazine article about you, if they see you in the street, they believe you owe them something; whereas in Europe, where I am better known and received than in the United States, I find that is not the case. I love being left alone in that context.

I use a quote in *The Land of Laughs* which didn't show up in the German editions. It's from Flaubert, and says, "Be bourgeois in your life so you can be crazy in your work."

In that way, I too am a very bourgeois person. I am a man who stays at home and writes his books. I don't fly gliders or parachute or take crack when the chance arises. I'm too obsessed with getting done what is important to me. I'm too involved in writing to go too far into other danger.

Most of my danger came when I was young. When I was a boy, I was — I don't know what you call it here — a juvenile delinquent. I was always in trouble with the police. And I had a friend who was the most magical bad boy I ever knew. He was in fact later killed in a gunfight with the police.

I had to write about this guy at some point in my career, because he was so fascinating. He was very evil and very wonderful, and that combination is so dangerous. I was a bad boy too, but he was a crazy bad boy.

I'm sounding insane, but at that time in my young life, especially around him, there was often something inside me which all of a sudden said to me, "Let's go down to Main Street and shoot people." There was a little, teeny, weenie flash of *wow* . . . but then it would close off, and I'd go, "You're crazy. We can't do that."

But my friend didn't just say, "Let's go down and shoot people." He'd say, "Let's go down and only shoot beautiful girls and look at their expressions to see what their faces look like after we shoot them." I'd start to go, *"Wow, that's really something,"* but luckily my sane mind would click in. But he would present it in such a way that was fascinating. That was his genius. And I was drawn and fascinated.

He's dead. Shot by the police. So he didn't get far with his genius.

So in certain ways, I am extremely close to the characters in my books. Very often when I'm writing I'm putting my own experiences through a strainer. So, for example, in *A Child Across the Sky*, the narrator tells a story about when he was a boy finding a dead body. When I was a boy I did find a body. I simply recounted what happened, then distorted it, a little bit. I turned it just *this much* for the story.

The same thing can happen in the everyday. Often when I'm living my life, I play the game of *what would so-and-so do here?*, meaning the characters that I've created. What would Lennox do? What would Thomas Abbey do? What would Walker Easterling do?

Very often it's what I would do too, or what I do do, but sometimes they have more courage, or less, or more humor, or less. It depends on the situation.

I had a very, very loud argument with an American recently, who said something I'll never forget. He said, "Vienna is safe and it's comfortable and it's beautiful, all those great things, but it's not *real life*. Real life is New York or Los Angeles, where there's danger and there's imagination and fear, and greed. . . ."

I turned to him and said, "You've become a victim of the 20th century. That's not real. *This is.* This is real life as it should be. My son can walk to school if he wants. My wife can go out at night and not be attacked. Once in a while I forget to lock my car and things are not stolen. I believe that is how life should be led. Not with fear and greed. And my imagination is doing fine here, thanks."

The mail that I get is very strange. There is a lot of it. I keep the more interesting letters. About one third of it is totally, utterly crazy.

I got a letter after *Bones of the Moon* came out that began "You dirty motherfucker, you son-of-a-bitch male chauvinist pig . ." And then it got worse. She was accusing me of being anti-abortion and a horrible monster. It was really . . . madhouse level and frightening.

The last time I gave a public reading was years ago at Shakespeare and Company in Vienna, but I haven't given a public reading since, because I got into a fist fight afterwards, because I read the abortion section from *Bones of the Moon*, and this guy physically attacked me, after screaming about abortion. . . . That's the dark side of all this stuff.   Ω

Books by Jonathan Carroll:

The Land of Laughs
The Voice of Our Shadow
Bones of the Moon
Sleeping in Flame
A Child Across the Sky

Black Cocktail
Die Panische Hand (short story collection, only in German translation)
Outside the Dog Museum (to be published in Spring 1981)

MY ZOONDEL

by Jonathan Carroll

My friend Sarah is one smart cookie. When everyone else was still parachuting in and out of each other's beds, she was already buying stock in genetic engineering and the Daimler-Benz companies.

"Sex is finished, Frank. Fear and prestige are next. Sooner or later one of those gene-splitters will find the cure for AIDS and herpes, so we buy into research now. But as long as going to bed *is* still dangerous, driving a Mercedes will be next best. You watch." I followed her advice and have never regretted it.

She was right about that, as with so many other things. When she said she had a line on a warehouse full of ugly fifties Naugahyde furniture, I shut my eyes and handed her a check. A few months later, we sold it all for a bundle to a new discotheque in town, EDSEL.

We had a fling a few years ago but found out fast that we got along better over the phone or a good dinner than nose to nose in the dark of night. Smart enough to stop while we still liked each other, we've been close ever since. There's an unspoken agreement that we can call or visit any time to complain or crow or cry and the other will be there to give what they can.

A few months ago, Sarah called and told me she was going to buy a dog. I was surprised because she'd never mentioned liking animals, besides having the kind of apartment that was always so clean you could have done brain surgery on the living room carpet.

"How come?"

"I read a book about stress. It says if you don't want a heart attack, you should get interested in the three P's: People, Pets, and Plants."

"Then why not just buy a cactus? You don't even have to water them."

"I'd feel stupid talking to a plant. No, I saw a picture of this dog in a magazine the other day and fell immediately in love. They're the greatest looking thing you ever saw."

"What kind of dog?"

"A Zoondel."

"A what?"

"They're a rare breed from Austria. They look exactly like the caboose on a train."

"How much do they cost?"

"A thousand dollars."

"*What?*"

"Will you come and help me pick it out?"

"I'll come and talk you out of it."

We met and took a train out to the tip of Long Island. At Montauk station, a round bald man named Otto Kak picked us up and drove us to his house. He talked about Zoondels the whole trip. How smart they were, how they house-trained themselves, never barked . . . I shook my head and looked out the window the whole time. I had no patience with animals, even other people's. They always seemed to be shedding, or under your feet, or sick. I could understand why old people liked them. Maybe one day when I was eighty and lonely I'd go to the pound and take one home so I could have company and something to boss around. But until then, I'd see their shit under my shoe or hear them out on the street barking me awake at three in the morning and I'd be glad they lived somewhere else.

Kak's house looked like something on

a model electric train board: small, perfectly kept, sunny. As soon as we pulled into the driveway, the front door opened and his wife came out. She was followed by three dogs that ran over to the car.

They didn't look like cabooses, but were peculiarly square and *tight* all around. Tight was the word for them. Imagine an old-time mailbox covered with short reddish fur and you get an idea of a Zoondel. About as large as a beagle, they had floppy ears and soft dark eyes that looked friendly and intelligent. Nice dogs, but a thousand dollars?

We got out and bent down to pet them. Kneeling next to Sarah, I was able to say without being overheard, "They're cute, but why are they so expensive?"

"Because there are only like a thousand of them in the world."

"Is it an investment?"

She looked at me and rolled her eyes. "No, Frank. I *like* them. Is that allowed?"

Stung, I kept quiet and petted the dog closest. It licked my hand. Its tongue was lemon yellow.

"Hey, look at that!"

Mr. Kak spoke. "That tongue is what got them into trouble! That's why there are so few of them now."

"How's that?"

"The Zoondel was originally bred in Austria by a Graf Martin von Niegel to hunt werewolves."

"Werewolves?" It was time for me to roll *my* eyes.

"Yes. The story is that von Niegel was both a wealthy landowner and a serious student of alchemy. He must have been quite a guy because rumor has it that Goethe based his play *Faust* on him. Anyway, he must have gotten himself in deep with something, dark powers or whatever, because he spent a big part of his fortune breeding a dog that could detect werewolves before they struck. That's a fact — it's in his biography."

"Maybe he was just a nut."

Sarah gave me a dirty look — she wanted to hear the story if she was going to buy one of the dogs.

"Maybe, but he did end up with a Hell of a special dog, as you can see."

"What happens when the dog sees a werewolf?"

Kak smiled. "The eyes turn the same color as the tongue once there's any kind of bodily contact between the dog and the werewolf. But that happens only after it turns six months. Before that, it's only a doggie-dog."

"What happens after it detects the, uh, enemy?"

"Nothing. It only tells you it's there. The rest is up to you."

"Have you ever had any experience with that, Mr. Kak?"

"No, I can't say as I have. Maybe there just aren't many werewolves in Montauk, eh?" He smiled a moment, then stopped. "But I'll tell you something interesting and this story *is* true. At the end of World War Two, Hitler sent an elite group of soldiers out in a last ditch effort to stop the Allies. Called them the 'Werewolves' and they were reputed to be the most vicious fighters anyone ever saw. Sort of like the L.U.R.P.'s in Vietnam, you know? Anyway, these guys did a lot of work in Austria and one of the first things they did was go to what was left of von Niegel's estate and kill every Zoondel they could find. That's documented. That's why there are so few now. Luckily, a number of them had been brought over here before the war, so the breed survived, but not by much. The question is, why would those guys go to the trouble of killing a bunch of dogs if the story wasn't at least a little bit true?"

Naturally Sarah bought one. She was so delighted with the "Werewolfbusters" aspect that I think she would have spent two thousand dollars if it had been necessary.

I must say, though, "Mailbox" (she liked my image and gave him that name) turned out to be as nice a dog as you were going to find. He slept late, almost never peed in the house (even though he was only a few months old), and liked to be with you but not on you. After some time, I sheepishly told her I liked him too.

"That's good, Frank, because I think you're going to have to do me a big favor. It looks like I'm going to have to go to Hong Kong soon for two months. That building for the Wakoski Institute is going to go up after all and they want me to be in on the planning. Which means I either put Mailbox in a kennel, or give him to you."

"Give him to me. I think I can stand him for a couple of weeks."

"That's the point, Frank. It won't be a couple of weeks. It's more like a couple of months."

"That's okay. I owe you a lot of favors anyway. I like him, it'll be fine."

"You're sure?"

"Absolutely."

So Sarah went off to her building in Hong Kong and her Zoondel came to live with me a while. It took some getting used to, but within a week I liked knowing he was around. When I came in from work at night, he was always at the door to greet me with a lot of jumping and running around the room. When I took him out for a walk he stayed close by and never pulled on the line like I'd seen so many other dogs do. An added benefit of walking a rare dog was meeting good-looking women on the street who also happened to be dog lovers.

All in all, having Mailbox as a houseguest worked out fine except for one strange occurrence. One very nice summer day weeks later, I took him to Central Park for a long walk. As we were standing next to the Dakota, about to cross 72nd Street, I heard a loud crash nearby. Jumping back, I saw that a large

piece of slate had fallen nearby and come very close to hitting us. Without thinking, I looked up and saw someone hanging half out of a high window in the building, shouting down at . . . us? It certainly appeared that way. New York is packed to the gills with loonies, but I couldn't imagine someone would be *so* crazy as to throw something like that down . . . No, it was very possible that might happen in this city. All you had to do was look at the nightly news to be reassured of that.

And speaking of the nightly news, it was right there that everything bad began. A few days after the stone fell, I was watching the news and shaking my head at a particularly awful story about a mass murder in Westchester County. A man had entered a pizza parlor in White Plains and, taking out a submachine gun, opened fire on everyone. He killed ten people before the police arrived and shot him. The newscaster gave the report with the same serious but bland tone of voice he used for every item. These explosions of horror have become so much a part of our lives that no one seems surprised anymore; even newspapers run them only on page ten, next to the weather report. People's indifference and acceptance of this growing madness scares me. We grow astonished and indignant when we hear about what happened to the Jews in Nazi Germany, but the same is happening in our everyday and our only response is to shrug and turn either the page or the channel.

"Why are there so many of these things happening now? Why does it all get worse and worse?"

The dog's only response was to wag his tail and look hopefully at me: Were we going out?

I sighed and got up to get his leash. By the time I'd reached the door, he was already next to me, bumping up against my leg. I looked at him and realized how big he'd gotten in the time we'd been together. I forgot exactly when Sarah would be back, but for many reasons, most of them trivial and sweet, I'd be kind of sorry to give him back to her. I still didn't want to own a dog, but I could now understand why so many people loved them.

"Come on, boy, let's go." I clipped him onto the line and went out the door. Sarah's return started me thinking. Exactly how long had I had him? I finally figured out almost two months.

Outside it was raining in a gentle, summery way: Nice walking weather if you didn't mind getting a little wet.

As we were going out of the building, a man and a woman walked by, heads close under an umbrella, rich sexy voices closing them off from any world other than their own lucky one. We were close enough to them for the woman to accidentally bump into Mailbox, who let out a surprised little yelp. The woman immediately stopped and bent down.

"Oh, honey, I'm sorry! Did I hurt you?" Even in the rain I could see she was one of those great New York women full of chic and warm perfume smells and enough allure to drive you crazy. What was nicest though was she appeared genuinely worried that she'd hurt the dog. While her friend waited, she stayed down petting and tickling Mailbox, trying to make up for what she'd done. He forgot what had happened and started jumping around, playing and nipping at her friendly hand.

His eyes began to grow yellower and yellower. Even in that rainy dark, they were bright fire. I looked quickly at the woman. Remembering the dog must be six months old now: Remembering what Kak had said about the origins of the breed. For one second I reeled dizzily thinking what it all meant. That is, if it were true.

"Come on, Jennifer, let's go."

"One second. Isn't he adorable? Look at those funny yellow eyes. They're like little flashlights!"

"Honey, we've got to go. The show starts in ten minutes."

From her squatting position, the woman looked up at him with such astonishing evil and hatred in her eyes, in her expression, that it felt like pure radiation. That anger could do anything, that was sure.

My God, who was she?

She got up, her face still a mushroom cloud of viciousness. Without a second's pause, she strode off down the street, leaving her embarrassed man behind. He looked at me, shrugged helplessly, and moved off after her.

Stunned by what happened, I stood there not knowing what to do. A werewolf? *That* beautiful woman? It was impossible. I heard the skittering sound of wheels and saw a young black boy coming down the street on a skateboard. When he got to us, he braked skillfully and bent down to pet the dog.

"Hey, I know this dog. It's a Zoondel, right?"

"Yeah, uh, right."

"Can I pet him?"

"Sure." I kept watching the couple walk down the street. The man caught up with her and waved his hands around.

When I looked down at the boy playing with my dog, the first thing I saw were the eyes. They were yellow.

"These dogs cost a fortune, huh?"

Bright yellow.

"Come on, Mailbox! Let's go!" I yanked him hard and pulled him behind me down the street.

"Hey, Mister, what're you doin'?"

I bent down and scooped the dog into my arms. I started running.

"Hey, you white chump!"

I ran and ran until I got home. Without thinking, I skipped the elevator and ran up five flights of stairs to my floor. If it were true, if they really were werewolves as Kak had said, why hadn't they tried to kill the dog, like the person who'd thrown the stone at us? I closed the door behind me and locked it fast. Putting Mailbox down, I looked into his eyes. They were dark again.

I watched the news again that night and found the answer to my questions. I think. I found them when I saw the latest report of the mass murder in White Plains. The killer was reported to be a quiet man who'd never done anything strange in his life. Just one day loaded a submachine gun and started killing people. It happens all the time, doesn't it?

That's the answer. It happens all the time because these people don't know who they are until *it* happens. Then they know. The woman and the boy on the street don't know yet, but they will. They will after they have done something horrible and evil and inhuman, like the quiet man with the machine gun. If they'd seen Mailbox after that then, like the person in the window, they would have tried to kill him. But until that time, they think he's only a sweet little dog, just six months old. And that was the answer to my earlier question. Why are so many of these terrible things happening these days? Because if it's true and Mailbox can "tell," then the world is once again full of these . . . things. God help us.

How do I know this? Or rather, how can I *say* this? Because I went out one more time that night to see if I was right. I let anyone touch the dog who wanted to. Twenty-three. I counted twenty-three people alone in this small part of this large city who touched my dog and made him glow.   Ω

THE PANIC HAND

by Jonathan Carroll

I'd just finished going through a time in life when one day bled into the next. Nothing worked, nothing smelled good, nothing smiled, nothing fit. Even my feet grew a little, for some mysterious reason, and I had to buy three pair of new shoes. Figure that. Maybe my body was trying to burst out of its old, failed skin like a snake and form a new one.

In the middle of this black mess I met Celine Davenant. She lived in Munich, five easy hours away from Vienna on the train. With her beautifully smooth and reassuring voice, she worked reading the news on an English-language radio station up there.

After work Friday evenings I'd hurry over to the *Westbahnhof* and catch the *Rosenkavalier* to Munich. That was really the name of the train.

Sometimes Celine came to Vienna, but made no bones about the fact she didn't like the city one bit. I told her the train trip was a pleasure for me and I looked forward to it. So we silently agreed for the time being to leave things as they were: She'd meet the train at the Munich *Hauptbahnhof* at 11:30 and our weekend would begin there amidst startled pigeons, travelers, the jerk and hoots of trains.

My first excited trip west, I made the mistake of buying a first-class ticket. But even there, the compartment was crowded with weekend people and their many bags. What I subsequently learned was to buy a second-class seat, arrive early, and go directly to the dining car. If I sat there until the town of Attnang-Puchheim, the train would have emptied by then, and strolling back to second class, I could have my pick of empty places.

The arrangement worked out well, particularly because the railroad served good food and it was delightful to sit eating by those large windows and watch the Austrian countryside slide by. Perchtoldsdorf, St. Pölten, Linz. Station masters in red caps waved. Farmers in old pickup trucks, blank-faced. Unmoving people stood frozen at small stations, rural crossings, in the middle of who cares watching us click by. Dogs barked silently. I often saw deer grazing. Rabbits darted zigzags across open fields.

It took me away from my life, it took me closer to Celine.

What is the name of that pink and white lily that smells so strongly of pepper and spice? I can't remember, but it's one of my favorites. When they entered the dining car that evening it was the first thing I noticed. Both of them were wearing that marvelous flower in their hair. Maybe it was the second thing I noticed: It was hard not to be wide-eyed about their uniquely different beauty.

The woman was tall and splendid. She looked like she'd been an actress earlier, or at least held perfect champagne glasses and looked out high windows at the Manhattan or Paris skyline. Now in her late thirties or early innings of forty, she'd come through the game strong and unimpeded. If there were lines on her face they made her look sexier, more knowing. The flower behind her ear said she had a sense of humor, give the world a smile. The flower behind her daughter's ear said here was an attentive, pleased mother. A rare

31

combination.

The girl had the same russet-colored hair and wide round eyes as her mother. At least I assumed it was the mother. They looked too much alike — senior and junior versions of the same great face. The face the girl would grow into in twenty-five years if she had luck.

I spent a good portion of every day thinking about Celine and how things would work out between us. I wanted them to work out and was hoping she did too. We hadn't talked about long range plans because that sort of discussion comes after you have surveyed the new lands of your relationship and given long thought to where you want to drive in the first permanent posts. We liked many of the same things, couldn't get enough of each other in bed, but best of all, knew there was almost always something to talk about. Very few quiet spaces in our time together, and if they came, it was only because we were savouring the silent hum of contentment that is the real electricity of love.

When I started thinking about Celine, almost nothing could distract me. And I *was* thinking about her when the mother and daughter came into the dining car. So it shocked me to realize all thoughts of my friend had disappeared while I watched these two stunners cross . . . to my table.

"Do you mind if we sit here?"

The car was about a third full and there were a number of empty tables. Why did they want to sit here? I am a good-looking man and women generally like me, but they don't cross rooms for me. Particularly when they looked like this one.

"Please." I half-stood and gestured to the empty chairs. I could smell the flowers in their hair. The little girl was blushing and smiling and wouldn't look at me. Snatching the chair out so hard that it almost tipped over, she had to grab it with two hands at the last moment.

The mother grinned and put her hands to her cheeks. "Poor Heidi. She wanted to make such a good impression on you. She saw you walk down the platform at the station and actually jumped *out* of the train to see which car you went into. She made us wait till now so we wouldn't look too eager."

The girl looked daggers at mother; her secrets were being told, laughed at. I didn't think that was funny and tried to tell her with a smile and a small friendly shrug. She was sunburn-red and wouldn't look at me after one fast, furtive glance.

Mama shook her head, still smiling and put out her slim hand. "I'm Francesca Pold. This is my daughter, Heidi. And you are?"

I said my name and shook the woman's warm hand. She held on a few seconds too long. I looked into her eyes to see if she was telling me something with that, but saw only "Wouldn't *you* like to know!" there. Her smile spread and she sat down.

Hmmmm.

"What are you reading? *Albanian Wonder Tales*? That sounds interesting." Without asking, she picked it up, opened it and started reading aloud. " 'Whether you believe it or doubt it, no matter. May all good things come to you who listen!' "

Both mother and daughter burst out laughing. The laughter was exactly the same except one was high and young, the other deep and more experienced. It was charming.

"What a funny way to start a story! Are they fairy tales?" She put the book down on the table and the girl picked it right up.

"Yes. I like to read them. It's a hobby."

The woman nodded. Her expression said she fully approved. I'd scored points.

"What do you do for a living?"

"I sell computers to the East Bloc."

"You sell computers and read fairy tales? A well-rounded man."

"That's nice to say, but it's probably only a bad case of arrested development."

That got me another approving smile.

She raised a hand for a waiter and one swept down on the table like a hawk. The world can be divided between people who can get a waiter's attention and those who can't.

Those who *can* have only to raise a tired or lazy finger and waiters lift their heads as if some secret radio signal has suddenly been beamed out on their private frequency. They arrive seconds later.

Those who can't, resort to finger snapping and other embarrassing things but it does no good. They are unheard, invisible. They might as well rot. Francesca Pold got waiters. It wasn't surprising.

The two of them ordered and our chat continued. The girl pretended to be deeply involved in my fairy-tale book, but I often saw it slip down and her eyes — all attention and interest — watch carefully. Beautiful eyes. Large and smart, they had a kind of liquidness to them that made you think she was on the verge of crying. Yet that very quality made them more singular and attractive.

The mother was a gabber and although what she said was mostly interesting, it was easy to tune in and out on her monologue. More and more I found myself looking at the daughter. When their food came, I saw my chance.

"What's your favorite subject in school, Heidi?"

"Ma-ma-math-e-ma-ma-matics." Her jaw trembled up and down.

"Is that what you want to do when you get older?"

She shook her head and pointing at me, smiled. "C-C-C-Computers."

She had a torturous, machine gun stutter that grew worse as she got more excited. But it was also very plain she wanted to talk to me. Her mother made no attempt to interrupt or explain what Heidi said, even when some word or phrase was largely unintelligible. I liked that. They'd obviously worked it out between them and, handicapped as she was, the girl would grow up in a world where she was used to fighting her own battles.

I'd already had dinner but joined them for dessert when I saw how big and fresh were the strawberries they ordered. The three of us sat there and spooned them up while the sky lost the rest of its day. It was completely dark outside when we got up from the table.

"Where are you sitting?"

I smiled. "You mean what class am I in? Second, I'm afraid."

"Good, so are we! Do you mind if we sit with you?"

I liked to look at the woman, but was growing tired of her motor mouth. More and more looks passed between Heidi and me. I would have happily sat alone with the girl and her stutter for the rest of the trip to Munich (they were going there too), if that had been possible.

Despite being able to call waiters, Francesca appeared to have the mistaken idea that beauty also means license to go on about anything, ad infinitum. I pitied her daughter having to put up with it every day of her life.

But what could I say, no I don't want to sit with you? I could have, but it would've been rude and essentially wrong. We would sit together and Francesca would talk and I'd try to make Heidi's ride a little more pleasant.

As usual, most of the compartments were empty. Once settled, Francesca reached into her purse and took out a pack of cigarettes. That was surprising because she hadn't smoked at all till then. The brand was unfiltered Camels and she drew smoke way down into her lungs. While she puffed, Heidi and I talked about computers and the things she was doing with them at school. The girl knew a lot and I wondered what she would do with the skill when she grew older. That's one of the nice things about working with computers — you don't have to *say* a word to them and they'll still do your bidding. Even if Heidi retained her stutter in later life, computers would be a good profession for her to pursue because she could do wonderful, productive things without uttering a word.

To be young and suffering from the kind of affliction she carried on her tongue must have been as bad, in its way, as having a case of the worst acne. Only pimples usually go away when we get older. Stuttering stays around and doesn't pay much heed to a person's birth date or self-esteem.

She tried so damned hard to speak. No matter what subject we were discussing, there was something she wanted to say, but her words came out so slowly and painfully that at times I literally forgot what we'd been discussing after watching Heidi strain her way through sentences.

Once when we were talking about computer games she got completely hung up on the title of her favorite and her mother had to come in and help.

"The game she likes so much is called 'Panic Hand.' Have you ever played?"

"No, I've never even heard of it."

The girl tried explaining how it worked, but when none of it came out the right way, gave up and slumped in her seat. I knew she was about to cry. She'd tried but lost another game to her inner enemy: In living contrast to a gorgeous mother who had only to sit there and carry on her own boring, unending monologue.

But even Francesca was silent a while. The girl looked out the window, flushed and tight-lipped, while her mother smiled at me and smoked one cigarette after the other.

Suddenly Heidi looked at me and said "Don't you th-th-think cigarette s-s-s-smo–king is c-c-c-c-ool? I d-d-d-do."

I shrugged. "Tried it when I was younger but never got the hang of it. I think it looks good in the movies."

Hearing this mild rebuff, the girl cringed down into her seat like I'd hit her. Was she *that* sensitive?

I was looking at her, trying to catch her eye and wink when her mother said "I'd like to sleep with you. I'd like to sleep with you right now. Right here."

"What?" I looked at Francesca. She had her hand on her blouse and was unbuttoning it.

"I said I want to sleep with you. Here."

"And what about Heidi?"

"She'll go out in the corridor. We can pull the curtain." Her hand continued to climb down the buttons.

"No."

The blouse was open and a nice lilac frilly bra showed through against the stark white of her secret skin in there.

"Look, Francesca. Just wait, huh? Christ. Think about your daughter!"

The woman looked at the girl, then back at me. "You can sleep with her too. Would you rather? I can leave!" She laughed high and fully, winked at Heidi, then began to button herself back up. "See, honey, sometimes you don't need me. You just have to find a computer man."

"Just stop." I finally had the presence of mind to stand up and start for the door.

"D-d-d-don't go, please!" The girl grabbed my arm and held on hard. Her face was fear and shame. She got up out of her seat and put her arms around my neck. "Please don't go, please! I'll m-m-m-m-make her g-g-g-g-go aw-wa-wa-wa-wa-way!"

I hugged her back, and slowly easing her arms from around my neck, pushed her into her seat at the same time. When I had her there, I turned to Francesca. Who wasn't there. Who wasn't anywhere. I was standing with my back to the door, so there was no way she could have gotten around me to get out.

Torn between a strong urge to get the Hell out of there and big curiosity to know what was going on, I more or less froze where I was and waited for something to decide the next move.

The train began to slow. The loudspeaker announced we'd arrived at Rosenheim, the last stop before Munich. I sat down. Heidi slid over next to me. Then she did something so erotic and wrong that I shiver to think of it, even now. Very gently, she took my hand and slid it under her skirt, between her child's legs. It was there a millisecond before I tried to pull it away. But couldn't because she held it there and she was much, *much* stronger than me. That power, more than where my hand rested, was what scared me. What was she, ten? Eleven? No eleven-year-old had that much strength.

When she spoke it was in a very normal, un-stuttering girl's voice. "Didn't you like her? Tell me what you like and I'll make it for you, I promise. Whatever you want!"

"What are you doing, Heidi? What are you doing?"

Her hand tightened on my own. It was so, so strong. "Didn't you think she was cool? The color of her hair and the way she smoked those Camels? That's how I'll do it. That's what I want to be like when I'm old. That's how I'm going to make myself." Her eyes narrowed. "You don't believe me? You don't think she was cool? That's what I'll be like and every man will want me. They'll all want to touch me and listen to me talk. I'll have lots of stories and things. I'll be able to say whatever I want."

"Why can't you say it now?"

She squeezed my hand till I cried out. "Because I stutter! You heard! You think I was *kidding around?* I can't help it."

Trying to pry her hand off mine, I gave up. "Why can you talk normally now?"

"Because your hand's there. Men are going to want me all the time because I'll

talk like her. I'll be beautiful and I'll talk beautifully."

"You made her?"

Her hand loosened a little. She looked at me, wanting a reaction. "Yes. You don't like her? All men like her. They always want her. Whenever she asks, they say yes. And if they want her then they'll want me too. 'Cause that's what I'll be like."

I had two choices — to play along and pretend, or tell the truth and hope . . . "She talks too much."

Heidi stopped squeezing my hand but kept it where it was. "What do you mean?"

"She talks too much. She's boring."

"B-b-b-oring?"

"Yes. She talks about herself too much and a lot of it isn't interesting. I stopped listening to her. I was paying more attention to you."

"Why? You didn't think she was pretty?"

"Pretty but dull."

"The other men didn't think that! They always wanted her! They always took her!"

"Not all men are the same. I like a woman to be interesting."

"More than pretty?" It was as if she were asking me things from a questionnaire. I had little choice but to answer.

In fact, the rest of the way to Munich she questioned me about "Francesca." Did I like her voice? What about her body? What was wrong with her stories? Would I have wanted to sleep with her if she'd been alone?

I never found out who the woman . . . "was." I did not want to make the girl angrier or more upset than she was for obvious reasons. I answered her questions as best I could and, believe me, there were a great many. I answered her right into the Munich train station where she stood up as the train was slowing and told me she had to go. Nothing more, nothing else. Sliding the glass door open, she gave me one last small smile and was gone.

What do I think happened? I think too many things. That Heidi had an idea for the perfect woman she wanted to be and created one out of her unhappiness to take her place until she could grow into her own adult skin. But she was young and made mistakes. What the young think is cool or sexy we grown-ups often smile at. That's one thought. Or she was a witch playing her own version of "Panic Hand," a game I naturally looked for but never found. Or . . . I don't know. It sounds completely dumb and helpless, but I *don't* know. I'm sorry if you're unsatisfied.

I saw her one last time. When I got off the train I saw her running down the platform and into the arms of a nice-looking couple who were delighted to see her. The man wouldn't put her down and the woman kept giving her kisses. She never turned around once.

But I walked far behind them anyway and was glad she didn't see me. Then there was Celine. And look who came with her so late at night! Fiona. The wonderful Fiona — Celine's daughter.

Ω

WITCHY WOOD

Beware the witchy wood, my child —
Avoid the shadowy things.
For there gather horrible creatures
Beyond imaginings.

Beware the witchy wood, my love —
Avoid the bloody ghost!
Let not your young eyes look upon
The thousand horrible hosts.

Beware the witchy wood, my sweet —
Heed your father dear,
For devil witches with hair of fire
Are always waiting there!

Beware the witchy wood, my dear —
And the powers which hide within!
Let not the sorcery take you:
Oh, let it not begin!

You ask how it is I know this —
What makes me speak so bold.
I met your mother there, my dear:
Now, let no more be told!

— **Lynne Armstrong-Jones**

GOBBLE, GOBBLE!

by William F. Nolan

Right now I'm a young, healthy female human being. I haven't always been human (didn't start that way) and I probably won't stay human for too much longer, but I'm having fun these days so I'll stick with it for awhile. Not that I'm from outer space or anything, but in human terms I'm an alien organism.

What I am is a feeder.

I don't feed very often — maybe once every six months or so — but when I do get hungry it takes a lot to satisfy me. But that's cool. I can always find things to eat.

And each time I feed, I change. But I'll get to that. Guess my changing can seem kind of icky, kind of a grossout, but it's really cool. Hey, I *know* I use the word cool too much, okay? But so do all of my friends.

If I sound like a dippy high school chick writing in her school notebook or something, well, that's what I am right now. That's the latest me. Sixteen and pretty. I mean, not an absolute knockout, not like some cheerleaders I know with super boobs and real cute butts, but pretty enough to make the guys go for me. Sharp looking. And I dress sharp. Plenty of boys ask me out. To dances and parties and stuff. (And to a lot of dumb movies!)

Of course, I don't eat what my friends do: gooky burgers with fries (heavy on the ketchup), jelly doughnuts and candy and junk like that. Most of my girlfriends scarf down Big Macs and pizza like mad, and a lot of them drink beer. That's sicko stuff as far as I'm concerned. Sure, I can *fake* eating junk like that (and I have to) but there's no real food value in any of it. I go for basics. I seem to get extra hungry around the holidays, especially Thanksgiving (gobble, gobble!).

My pattern as a feeder has been pretty consistent. I select a town, and a species, move in, live with them for six months or so, do my feeding (yum, yum) and then move on to another place. (I really dig France. Had me some good eating in Paris, you bet!)

I've been a bird and an insect (beetle) and a dog and an ant (African) and once I was a male housecat named Ari. Since I was "fixed" (you know, like no balls!) I didn't go around chasing females. I was real skinny, with all the little knobs on my backbone sticking out. Vet said I was hyper-thyroid and I had to swallow pills with my catfood. Real drag.

You're mixed up, right? About my feeding. Look, I didn't say I never ate "normal" food when I go between feedings; it's just that I don't *like* it and have to fake liking it.

After a few months I start to get bored, no matter what change I've made. But by the time the boredom really sets in I'm usually like *starved*. So I feed, change, and move on. (Usually eat more than once, when I begin a feeding, but I'll get to that later.)

I guess you figure I'm a creep, huh? Just because I'm different. I'm with my girlfriends at a movie and this guy in a ski mask chops off a nice lady's head with an axe and we go, ugh, that's *gross*. So I guess, to you, I'm in the same bag. A gross old feeder.

Old. That's an interesting word. How old am I? Jeez, who the freak knows? I've been around a long time, that's for sure. Feeders just keep going. We don't age like you do because we keep adapting and we're never the same long enough to get old. So I don't really have any idea of how old I am. Or care, for that matter.

Right now (existential time), as Judy Ann Singer, I'm sixteen. And I live in Lawton City, Illinois. In a green, quiet little town of three thousand. And I go to Lawton High where I'm president of the Drama Club (I'm good at acting roles, been doing it all my life).

Being female again is a blast (as my pals say). Last three times I fed I was a male and I like being female better. Everything is *softer,* somehow. It's a silky feeling, being female. Males have hard edges; they live in a rougher world. But I'd freak out, having to stay one or the other. We feeders have a choice.

Well, I guess I've done enough rambling. Since this is what I call an alien record then I'd better start recording, eh? Instead of just blah, blah, blah on paper. Get down to the important stuff. The nitty-gritty.

Okay, then. I'll start by telling you about Rick. He's my latest boyfriend. Been going steady with him for just over three months. Do we *do* it? Sure. He's cool. Safe sex, right? Anyhow . . .

Rick's on the football team. Not captain yet, but he could be next year. And he also plays basketball and baseball. All-round jock. I go to a *lot* of games, take my word!

Football is cool, with all the guys bashing away at each other. Blood sport. Basketball's okay, too, but baseball's a drag. The pits. Bore-ing.

One of our fun things to do is go to the drive-in on Fridays in Rick's yellow Mustang convertible. We put the top up (for privacy) and just make out like crazy for most of the dumb movie. Unless it's a Clint Eastwood. When he's Dirty Harry. I always have Rick cool down when big Clint's doing his thing. And he doesn't mind, really. He digs

Clint. That's when we actually *watch* the movie.

So it's Friday night and Rick asks me to go to the drive-in with him to a horror flick called *The Bloodsuckers* about a bunch of vampires on Fifth Avenue in New York who suck blood out of rich people who live in million-dollar townhouses or condos or whatever.

I dig horror flicks because I can do a lot of screaming and Rick thinks it's neat, my screaming and grabbing at him. Actually, vampires don't scare me. First of all, they don't exist and if they did they'd be real easy to fight off with garlic and crosses (two crossed tablespoons will do) and holy water and all like that. But I *do* like to watch the stakes get hammered into their chests (spurt, spurt!). That's neat.

So off we go to the Big Clock Drive-In to see this new bloodsucker movie, and right away Rick gets real attentive. You know, he's hot to trot. We haven't made it in about two weeks and he's all steamed up about the idea of being with me in my tight black-leather outfit. Boots and the whole bit. Rick's a freak for black leather. Wears it himself when he rides his Honda. (Yeah, he's a biker, too. Macho man!)

They know us at the Big Clock. We go there a lot (no other drive-ins in Lawton) and the ticket guys know us and when they see me in some of my sexy outfits they kind of drool, you know. ("Way to go, Ricko! Way to go.")

Rick keeps the Mustang real cherry. Wax job every other Sunday. It's a classic, and he treats it like one. Like he treats me. (Thinks he knows me. Oh, wow, does he ever *not* know me!)

It's dark now and we've got the top up and the black metal speaker's inside so we can hear the soundtrack, and we're eating popcorn. (Well, *he* is; I'm faking.)

Then Rick goes, "Today my parents told me they want me to go to UCLA in California for college. Wha'dya think?"

And I go, "It's a neat school. And I

hear that L.A. is neat, too."

"My ole man went to UCLA so he wants me to go there." Rick leans in close. "Will you go with me?"

"In a year? You kidding? I never plan ahead that far."

"Hey, I don't want to go unless you do."

"I'll think about it. Yeah. Maybe I'll go to California. Who knows?" I giggle. "Quit being so serious. We're here to see some vampires, right?"

And he goes, "Right," and gives me a squeeze as the screen noise starts and the previews come on.

It's really dark now, the kind of deep dark you get in an Illinois summer, and pretty soon the chief bloodsucker is sinking his fangs into the throat of some blonde rich bitch who owns a lot of Texas oil and wears a ton of diamonds around the house.

That's when I realize I haven't fed in over six months, when this ham actor is scarfing away at the blonde's neck.

Hungry. It always hits me sudden like this. I never plan a feeding, it just happens. Like pow! One second I'm doing my act, as a human or whatever, and the next I'm like into my feeding mode.

When the time comes to feed, look out world! The hunger just *consumes* me, like a wave washing over a shore. And right then, watching the rich blonde getting fanged by this chief vampire . . . I . . . am . . . suddenly . . . *starved!*

Rick goes, "You look funny, Jude."

And I go, "Yeah? Funny how?"

"Your eyes. The way you're staring at me. Kind of super intense. What's with you?"

"It's time to eat is all. I'm hungry. Gobble, gobble!"

"Eat? We ate before we came here, remember? At the break I'll get some chili dogs an' cokes, like always. How come all of a sudden you're hungry?"

"It's been almost six and a half months," I tell him.

He goes, "Huh?" Real surprised at what I just said.

Which is when I went for him. Like that shark went for the swimmer at the beginning of *Jaws*.

I've got a lot of interior strength. All feeders do. We can summon it up when we need it. Like now. And my teeth are sharp.

But this is for the record, so I don't want to mix you up about what happened to Rick.

I'm Rick now. I mean, after we left the drive-in I was behind the wheel of the Mustang and Judy Ann Singer was inside me, all part of the change, okay?

Let me try and explain. I don't feed like you'd think I would. I don't just go around gobbling up people and things the way girls at the school do Big Macs. That's not how a feeder operates.

We absorb.

We go inside and eat out the whole center of our victims (if you want to call them that), kind of leaving them hollow but still looking and acting ordinary on the outside.

And we usually go for two or three at once. At least I do. You know, I told you how it takes a lot to satisfy me once I really settle down to feed after maybe half a year. I'm starved, for sure.

So Rick wasn't enough. He was like the first course of the meal. I was still real hungry.

His parents were home, watching TV, when I parked the Mustang outside their house and used Rick's key to get in.

They're in the living room, watching a Late Night movie about some lady doctor who was saving babies in Calcutta.

I go, "Hi!" giving them a smile.

They make me wait for the next commercial before they'll talk to me.

"You're home early, son," goes Rick's father.

And his mother goes, "Yes, where's Judy?"

I shrug. "She's dead."

They go all pale.

"My God!" says Rick's old man, standing up from the couch. "Did you have an accident?"

"Nope." I walk over and switch off the TV. "No accident. She just isn't around anymore."

"You're not making sense," says Rick's mother.

I smile at her. I walk toward her. I'm strong and I'm fast and I'm *still* very hungry.

"Gobble, gobble!" I say.   Ω

THE LEGEND

The forest's paths are covered
     by the tangled boughs
     (It is called a witchwood, so the Legend says).

Travelers of ancient days
     wander with the night
     (It is a haunted greenwood, so the Legend says).

Carried on the mist of time
     they listen and they hear
     (It is a grove of magic, so the Legend says).

Hither comes a man full weary
     heavy is his step
     (Now the woodland calls to him — so the Legend says).

Be ye Warrior, Be ye Prince
     sleep upon the moss —
     (Nothing shall disturb thy slumber, so the Legend says).

Magic mingles, dawn grows nigh
     the traveler does not rise
     (Another tree has joined the wood — the Legend does not lie).

— **Meg Mac Donald**

The next issue of *Weird Tales*®, our special Robert Bloch issue, will be the magazine's 300th, with:
a never-before-published story by **Robert Bloch** and **Henry Kuttner**, "The Grab Bag"; Bloch's screenplay and original story, "Beetles," and an excerpt from his "unauthorized autobiography."
New stories by **Ramsey Campbell, Brian Lumley, Thomas Ligotti, Chet Williamson, Michael Rutherford**, and **Darrell Schweitzer**.
Gahan Wilson will do all the artwork for this special issue.

THE BARBARIAN QUEEN

Raving with brilliance and boredom
in a black lacquer chair in a white room
listening to crickets,
                I want a fight,
knee deep in fractured jade or broken syntax
of Latin suddenly turned into Spanish by hard riding Arabs
(or another tongue run over by Mongols).
I want brutal gold jewels on my neck
and a man in salt-cured ermine
to drag in sacks of delicate porcelains carried by camels
"Follow those camels," I'd demand.
                        The whole Golden Horde
would track Bactrian camels
straight back to China —
                history skewed into barbaric times.
Scythian gold, spectrums torn out
of Indian cut diamonds and emeralds and star sapphires
crash light together.
              Beautiful (oh-wreck-this-politeness)
brutality. I don't want these French doors
and delicate Southern dusk with toy jet crickets —
I want kettle drums,
             either side of a dun stallion's withers,
and a tiny Hun pounding them. The cavalry bounces
to the whole swirling concert of yells —
wild arms flying.
           I want the glint of sun
on Mandarin blood under blazing blue sky.
I want a man to crush
          in one fist
Ming cups too understated to survive.
In a black felt tent, I'll roll in all the stolen silverware
and throw out all that didn't draw blood.
                I'm really tired
of being polite. I am really tired of being bored.
I demand barbaric hobbies —
          hawks
on gaudy carved bull leather gauntlets —
cheetahs stolen in India
to kill gazelles. A sullen Confucian in chains
to explain star rotation and eclipse dragons.
Clever Europeans to invent giant clocks.
And the architects, captured in Byzantium,
force-marched to where I'd say, "Put it there, architects."

Why not wish?
I've been a student of subtle things — wiggles of ink

pressed on papers — for many years — sword arm atrophied,
even the trigger finger.
                              So harmless.
I think any cricket I see
in the next five minutes is doomed.
I'll yell at someone within the month,
but I don't talk rough enough
or country enough for cock fight invites.

Crawl back in the mind and watch flaming arrows lash the sky.
In me I have the urge
to wrench things out of socket, to impress
the physical mechanical direct way —
not through slight thin signs, but
like an engineer throwing a dam at a river —
all gravity and brute calculation.
                              Yet,
I'd sit on that dam in a small
glass walled pagoda.

                                        — Rebecca Brown Ore

SPHINX' GAME

Sphinx, monster's daughter
Lies in wait still
For the riddle-seekers.
How do civilizations die? she wonders
Sliding walnut shells
Across the surface of her column
With her paws
And dinos?
Wisdom hidden for the choosing
How many flavors to a quark?
Snaketail coils out and in
Like a collapsible universe.
What's a human?
What's a monster?
Who are you?
Juggling walnut shells
Riddles for the choosing

                                        — Ruth Berman

A TAP-TAP AT SUNDOWN

by William Beechcroft

The scent of some indistinguishable spice drifted upslope from the City of Port-au-Prince. With it came an underlying pungency of open sewers and garbage too long in the sun. Then I smelled sweat not my own. That sat me up, and I swung around in the creaky wicker chair.

Chrétien, said the plastic badge on his rumpled tan waiter's coat. Christian. At breakfast, I had bribed this man amply by local standards. He had enfolded my American ten-spot in supple fingers, stared through my request, then evaporated back into the kitchen, leaving me frustrated under the dining room's squeaky overhead fan.

"M'sieur," he said now, "the drink you ordered."

"I didn't order —"

He bent low over the table at my elbow, the planes of his face carved in oiled ironwood. "At sundown, M'sieur. The west end of the hotel. A tap-tap, mostly blue."

He handed me the check for the rum concoction in its rippled glass. I fished out the required number of gourdes, plus another oversized tip. Blank-faced, he left me without a sign he had spoken.

I'll be damned, I thought. Cast enough bread on these waters, and you get a taker. Tap-taps, I'd been told by the driver of the mufflerless taxi I had taken from the airport, were free-lance station wagons, gaudily decorated by their owners, cheap to rent — "Only one gourde, M'sieur" — which was cheap, all right. About fifteen cents. "But you may find yourself riding with chickens or a pig."

From the verandah, I squinted into the white sunlight that pressed down on Port-au-Prince. The softening pavement, the scruffy public monuments, the buildings from the rococo dazzle of the presidential palace to the dun-colored tumble of waterfront shanties — all seemed to vibrate in the heat. Down there, though, I'd seen faces shining with pride, inexplicable unless it was pride in survival despite a government in perpetual unrest.

The Gulf of Gonâve stretched from the two-mile-distant waterfront to the sea of the Windward Passage, an expanse of molten iron that held the narrow Île de la Gonâve in its grip out there through ten miles of shimmer. Only the mountains that soared behind the hotel offered a respite from the scorching breath of mid-afternoon. The air-conditioning unit in my room had clattered itself to death an hour ago, and I slumped out here on the second-floor verandah, at least in the open air, and pondered what had brought me to Haiti.

What had done it, of course, was money. Specifically, the money for a proposed book. I had already been paid the standard fifty per cent of the advance. The balance would be mine on delivery of an "acceptable manuscript." Not just any hack manuscript; an acceptable one. That was why I was here on the scabrous porch of the Hotel Bien Venue, financed by my rapidly shrinking advance money, wondering how in the world I was going to gain access into certain arcane practices of this tiny, turbulent nation.

The proposed title of my forthcoming work was *The Dark Side of Justice*. I had planned on a strong dose of voodoo, leavened by kangaroo court tactics in certain notorious locales, seasoned with a dash of Klan, and possibly bolstered with a stiff shot of Third Reich Sturm und Drang. It would be the kind of text that appeals to progressive professors and just might make a public ripple, as well as — All right, so it was an exploitation book. No worse than some cable TV offerings any night of the week.

Haiti was steeped in just the kinds of primitive goings-on I needed. And the air fare from my home base in Savannah was helpfully low. I had spent my first day here dropping hints to taxi drivers, hotel staff, and a couple of likely-looking not-quite-gentlemen at the Bien Venue's gritty bar, that I was not looking for tourist voodoo but the real thing.

For all that, I'd gotten blank looks, distant stares, and a couple of hard glances that made me wonder whether the *tonton macoute* was truly a thing of the past. I had returned to my room, discovered the collapse of the A/C unit, and taken refuge on the verandah. There I began to realize that a writer of suspense fiction is not necessarily also a writer of esoteric fact. I was face-to-face with the debilitating suspicion that I might not know what I was doing here. And at that moment, Chrétien had appeared with his whispered indication that my sowing of seed money had produced something after all.

I tried an early supper in the hotel's stifling dining room, opting for the tassot: tough, sun-dried turkey marinated in lime juice. The boiled potato with it looked innocent enough, but I found I could manage only the coffee and the bread, spread with "mamba," a kind of supercharged peanut putter. I finished too early, then killed some increasingly tense time in the lobby.

As the sun hissed itself out in the gulf, I descended the hotel's broad wooden entrance steps and walked, a little hesitantly now, toward the building's west end. Sounds of the city reached here, a distant gabble of uninhibited people threaded through with snatches of pounding merengue beat.

A stranger in a tap-tap at sundown . . . That would have been comfortably catchy in one of my novels, but living it had begun to tighten an icy cable across my chest.

I rounded the Bien Venue's hedge of ragged crimson bougainvillea and entered the narrow side street, unhappily named Rue du Repentir. Repentance Street, if my high-school French was holding up. I hardly had time to mull that over before a rattling blue Chevy station wagon, at least ten years old, pulled to the curb. Apparently its driver had been parked back along the street, watching my uncertain approach to the west end of the hotel. The multi-colored graffiti that sprawled along its near side seemed to depict a ragged marching band.

The driver, a hulk of a man black as licorice, leaned across the passenger seat. The engine snorted and coughed so loudly I had to stick my head in the window to hear him. Then I realized how chancy that little action was in a nation as turmoiled as this one.

In a Creole accent that sounded flowery for such a huge man, he said, "You are the Américain to write the book?"

I was the American desperately trying to write the book. I nodded. With a huge hand, he shoved open the door, and I climbed into his gaudy wagon. If he had indeed transported pigs or chickens on these threadbare seats, their lingering savor was drowned in the reek of exhaust fumes.

The air freshened inside and out as we bounced beyond the city's outskirts. I smelled something close to the delicate scent of frangipani, then the faint odor of decaying leaves crept through the open windows.

My giant driver was wordless through this climb into the foothills, a great, gray block in dark trousers and a white, short-sleeved shirt. Soon the shirt was all I could make out in the growing darkness. The tap-tap's sickly yellow headlights barely illuminated the tunnel of jungle growth through which we labored upward.

The driver's silence, I realized, was no help to my research. To break it, I thanked him for bringing me, but I wondered where we are going.

"It is not voodoo," he said over the engine's clatter, though I hadn't mentioned that buzz word to anyone. "The tourists, they all ask for voodoo."

A tour guide. Had I simply fallen victim to the scam of Third World freelance tour guiding? I said nothing for another mile. A succession of dangling poinciana fronds overhanging the road slapped the windshield like angry wraiths reaching out of the darkness.

"We are Efik," he said as we abruptly slowed to swing off the ragged macadam into a dirt lane that climbed even more steeply. He clashed the manual shift into second. The old station wagon growled upward into yet deeper darkness. "Efik, long ago from the River Niger. You know l'Afrique?"

I did not; not that well.

"We save some of the old customs, those worth saving. Customs that are taboo here. Comprendez?"

I wasn't sure what he was talking about, but I certainly understood taboo. Now we were more than an hour out of civilization, high in the mountains that rise nearly 9,000 feet southeast of Port-au-Prince. I began to wonder about my sanity in jumping into this battered circus wagon of a car with this immense stranger, all on the say-so of a bony waiter whom I'd bribed to gain entree into God-knew-what.

Then the driver stopped the car. My panicky conclusion was that I had let myself in for a Haitian-style mugging. New sweat began to prickle my chest.

"Before I take you further, mon ami, we must make the agreement. You may write what you will see, but you cannot say where in Haiti you saw it. And you cannot print the writing in Haiti."

Those were easy enough terms. I had little idea where we were, and Haitian book sales were perhaps the last consideration of my U.S. publisher-to-be.

"And you must be only an observer, comprendez? No matter what you see, you will remember that you are there only to see."

That sounded ominous but at the same time reassuring. Robbery of a tourist in the wilds of these mountains did not appear to be his aim after all.

"There is the small matter of cost, M'sieur. Let us say, for the gasoline."

Appropriately, the engine stalled. In the damp silence, I was willing to pay for gasoline, oil, depreciation, anything this ancient crock might require. "Would forty dollars American —"

"Bon. That will be suffisant." Twin Andrew Jacksons evaporated into his immense hand.

"It is not far distant," he said as he turned the ignition key. The starter ground over and over. A rank smell oozed out of the roadside tangle, a stench of sweet rot. I heard rustlings in that black hedgerow. Then I realized fat raindrops had begun to fall.

The engine caught. The driver flipped on spastic windshield wipers, and we grumbled higher. Through an unexpected break in the roadside trees, I caught a glimpse of the city's lights, far below and tiny in the darkness. Then we were swallowed again. Minutes later, the wagon bumped over rocks in the narrow lane, then we pulled into a small clearing and stopped. A scatter of dilapidated vehicles flanked the bulk of a windowless hut with a corrugated metal roof.

My driver hurried me inside where a dozen black men, all dressed identically to his black slacks and rumpled white shirt, milled about in lantern light. As we entered, they fell silent. The place seemed airless and smelled of nervous bodies and dirt. The floor was hard-packed earth.

The only furniture was a battered wooden table, on which glowed a seemingly out-of-place Coleman gas lantern. Three wooden chairs had been set behind the table. At the base of the crude cement wall opposite the single door was a row of straw mats.

My driver, for whom they had obviously been waiting, nodded toward the mats. All but one of the men sat. He walked to the table to stand before the giant. The big man looked at me and again indicated the mats. A space had been left in the middle of the row of squatting men. I took it, feeling that I had completely lost control of my situation — then realizing I had lost it the instant I had stepped into the tap-tap.

"Bring in the accused," ordered the huge man who had brought me here, which confirmed my assumption that he was in charge. I suspected he used English in my behalf, which was considerate since Creole was a mile beyond me.

The man who had remained standing left the hut, then returned silent moments later with a compact, scar-faced man dressed in ragged khakis. He was as close to pasty gray with fear as any black man I had ever seen. Behind him and his escort trailed a white-haired elder with a quart bottle of some yellowish fluid and a small wooden bowl. Following him was a third escort, this one spidery small, with a large wooden bowl half filled with some milky substance.

They stood the terrified man in front of the table, facing the giant. I realized now that he was serving as judge in some kind of secret and no doubt wildly illegal trial.

As rain rattled on the metal roof close overhead, my giant escort said, in a voice as ominous as muted thunder, "Philippe Prisé, you are accused of the rape of Angelique, the wife of our kinsman, Emil Thibaud."

"Non! Non! Innocent! Je suis innocent!"

"That is to be decided." He paused. "By Efik custom." The giant nodded at the two men who had remained behind the terrified accused. The old man set the quart bottle on the table. Then he handed Philippe Prisé the small bowl. The other "court attendant" walked off five paces from the table, then carefully placed the large bowl of milky fluid on the dirt floor.

"Philipe Prisé," the judge said, glaring down at the much smaller man who faced him, "you know the custom of the Efik. Eight Calabar beans have been ground to powder and placed in this bottle. In the bowl is the antidote to Calabar. You will drink. You will wait ten heartbeats. Then you will turn and take five slow steps toward it. If God lets you live long enough to drink the antidote, you are innocent in His eyes. If not, then custom has spoken."

Calabar beans! I had come across that particular poison in my random preliminary research. The beans are rich in the active component physostigmine, which almost instantly sedates the spinal cord. The resulting paralysis climbs rapidly from legs to chest. Death comes from asphyxiation.

My God! I had paid to be brought here to witness a poisoning! I came close to leaping to my feet in protest, but the huge judge threw me a glance surely meant to remind me of my promise to be "only an observer." Lord knew what these people would do to me if I tried to interfere.

The white-haired man carefully poured a stiff dose from the bottle into the doomed man's trembling bowl. Then he stood back.

Philippe Prisé's face twisted in anguish. I wished they hadn't used his name; that he had remained to me only an anonymous man brought in from the night. He shot a look of despair at the judge, who now seated himself impassively in the center chair. The two men who had brought in poison and antidote walked around the ends of the table and took chairs flanking his. They settled back, comfortably anticipating what promised to be an appalling spectacle.

I thought there should now arise the guttural throb of drums, but all I heard was the tinny patter of rain above and harsh breathing all around me. It was the kind of gape-mouthed anticipation I would have expected from the witnesses at a sanctioned electrocution. But this was a dirt-floored hut in the Haitian mountains with surely illegal barbarism about to take place.

The accused man, his body quaking with terror, slowly raised the shallow bowl. And drank.

My stomach revolted. I forced back bile that bubbled into my throat.

Philippe Prisé stood immobile for what I presumed was his required count of ten heartbeats. My own heart thundered loudly enough in my ears for a precise count.

Then he turned away from the table and fixed his eyes on the bowl of salvation that lay on the floor a dozen feet distant. He took one step. Two. He seemed unaffected, except by the fear that had stiffened his limbs since he had first entered the hut.

Maybe — Then his left leg gave way. He lurched erect. His mouth fell open. The eyes bulged. He clutched his chest, and his legs collapsed. He fell to his knees. Then he pitched forward, both arms stretched out, reaching futilely for the milky antidote only a yard from his grasp.

I was horrified. I had sat here in silence and watched . . . murder.

The judge shoved back his chair and stood. He stared down at the fallen man. Then he looked at me. I scrambled to my feet with the rest of the witnesses. The thing was over.

The big man read my expression as I strode angrily to the table. He held up a mighty palm to cut off my words before they tumbled out in violation of my agreement. I noticed that he appeared curiously perplexed.

"I would have sworn the man was innocent, M'sieur," he said softly, and to me alone.

Then he did something that stunned me anew. He picked up the nearly full quart bottle from the table and offered it to *me!*

"No need to waste good grapefruit juice, M'sieur. Because that is all this is."

Ω

THE HEART OF FAIREN DE'ATH

by Storm Constantine

The tall, black house can be reached from three directions:

From the north, through the scrubs, knots and withy-paths of Coolcandle Forest.

From the south, by way of the wide dusty road, up from lakeside towns of Celestia and Grote. Merchant chains travelling northwest around mountains, towards Speaking Tree and the Scrubplains, sometimes nudge the outer, low-tangled courts of the forest itself, and from there a person might brave the willowing paths between the trees.

From the west, it may be sought by clambering down the eastern flanks of the Knucklebones; a journey best attempted in the Summerlight or early Falltime. In the Springseed, the treacherous rocky throats are impassable, owing to the torrents of meltwater crashing down from the higher terraces. And "Wintermoan travel" are words of death in the mountains.

Nobody enters the forest from the east. Eastwards, the lush, carnivorous, bustling verdure of the wood eventually declines into a poisoned, barren land, named Only Emptiness by everyone in the south. But even though there are all these roads leading to the tall, black house, not everyone who follows them will find it.

Yolassika had dwelt in the heart of the forest in the house of black stone for two years. Other people lived among the trees, in dark and hidden glades, but Yolassika rarely saw them. It was a lonely life she led, and one quite different from that she had left behind in the lakeside town of Celestia. Yolassika was not upset by this; her seclusion was wholly voluntary.

One night, what now seemed such a long time ago, she had sat outside an inn along the Avenue of Red Eyes (there are many inns along that road) and, over her sweet but vicious cordial of direthorn and spice, faced the sadness and disappointment she felt with the way her life was heading. Her mother had recently died — there was no father she could remember — and had left her worse than penniless. More creditors than friends had attended the funeral and Yolassika had been obliged to sell the lease to her mother's spacious rooms and millinery workshops in order to satisfy them, moving all the possessions she could not sell into smaller and meaner accommodation. And even that was not enough.

There had been a series of jobs, each more poorly paid than the last; most of what she earned passing straight to the purses of the merchants and storemen to whom her mother had owed money. Yolassika wished she'd paid more attention to family finances, and considered bleakly that luck must have fled along with her mother's spirit. If luck was currency, perhaps the dead woman had owed more than earthly debts.

Barely more than a child, Yolassika's only recourse to survive had been to open her cloak along the dark alleys of The Footways of Perfect Desire, and receive coin for the brief pleasure her flesh could bring to others more financially fortunate. The reality of this trade revealed itself less dreadful than the

49

intention of it, Celestia being a town where courtezans were respected rather than reviled. They could earn themselves legendary status if they were clever. Furtive, masked gentlemen, whose breath smelled of cloves, enticed Yolassika into their carriages, where they fumbled through her flounces in absurd couplings. Sometimes, pairs of pampered, spoiled boys would come giggling to the Footways and she would take them to her lodgings to join in their laughter and offer them the delicious, dark pleasures they yearned for. Also, sleek young daughters of wealthy houses sought her services, all claiming, in bored voices, they were there because it was necessary to sample all of life's spices; it was merely curiosity. Yolassika did not care about their reasons. She took the money and walked away. It was not important.

She never experienced shame or self-hatred, having the ability to detune her conscience at will from distasteful events, but knew that her youth, however fresh for now, would not last forever, and when it left her, these activities could only sink from quasi-romantic excitement into something pathetic and dirty. Affairs of the heart, though plentiful, for many of her patrons were intrigued enough by her mystery to become regular, had always ended in sorrow. It was a game to them, an act of rebellion and daring. Should wives, lovers or parents ever begin to suspect, they fled, never to return. Yolassika was tired of trying to convince herself she did not care. Resolve hardened within her. She must seek a new life, elsewhere.

Perhaps crazed by the moon, for it was full and powerful that night, she gathered up her belongings, left a brief, vague note in her lodgings, and walked northwards, through the shuttered merchant quarter, past the low, sprawling temples, whose chimneys gouted the smoke of burnt offerings and incense,

out of the town. She wondered how long it would take for her to be missed. Tonight's regular patron would undoubtedly already be fractious at her absence from her usual corner, beneath the magnolia trees. She wondered whether she'd miss the generosity of her customers. No. All they'd given her was coin and material things. Yolassika suspected there might be more to happiness than that.

Without planned destination, if not directionless, she eventually found herself upon the road that wound along the edges of Coolcandle. The dark between the trees, rather than scaring her, seemed beckoning and soothing. Coming upon a track that led inwards, next to an old barrel whose lid proclaimed it was for lake-bound mail, Yolassika scrambled through the undergrowth, leaving the road completely. The strong scent of the foliage enveloped her like the water of a scented bath. She felt comfortably drowsy. Now, she would rest. Tomorrow, she could plan her future.

A pleasant night ensued, sleep sought among the ferns; she was shaded and fanned by fragrance. Yolassika woke with the dawn. She stared up through the shivering fronds arching over her protectively and decided she could not bear to set foot once more upon the hard, open road. She sat up, ate some food from her pack, drank some water and ventured farther into the forest.

She travelled this way for three days. To complement her meagre food supply, she ate the berries and nuts she recognized as poison-free. Later on, she unpacked her slender knife and confidently, if inexpertly, killed and skinned a small animal. She changed direction many times, doubling back, leaving the paths, investigating each intriguing sound. At no time did she feel in any danger. At first, it seemed she was the only human creature in the forest, but

as time went on she scented smoke, and once passed a camp of charcoal-burners, who paid her no attention. At night, resting in open glades, she patiently persisted in the art of building fire. During the day, as she wandered, she was wooed by the low, enchanting song of hidden life, and entranced by the stranger places, vibrating with sentience, where there was no sound at all.

On the morning of the fourth day she discovered a brown, dusty pathway between avenues of older trees. Short, fierce, dark green grass grew between the massive, moss-carbuncled trunks. In the distance, she could hear the sound of water running. She deduced the path must lead somewhere, and her heart began to beat faster. The track appeared to have been beaten down by human feet. Perhaps it would lead her to some kind of settlement. What kind of people would live there? Would they be friendly or hostile?

At length, the trees thinned and a large glade was revealed, overlooked by a soaring, craggy cliff that reared above the trees. Yolassika immediately recognised the marks of cultivation in the glade. Against the dark rock at the farther end of the glade stood a tall, black house. Yolassika froze, staring. The house exuded a powerful air of great age, its eccentric design suggesting someone quite apart from conventional thinking had built it. There was no sign of life, however, no curl of smoke, no sound, no open window or door. Brooding eaves overlooked the dark bricks. Grass and moss mantled the sagging roof. A weather-vane poised motionless among the tall, narrow chimneys. Everywhere showed signs of neglect and decay.

After maybe half an hour of cautious scrutiny, Yolassika convinced herself, if anyone lived there, they must be old or dead, and bravely walked right up to the front door. It was unlocked and swung open when she knocked on it. After a pause to muster further courage, a search within revealed the place deserted.

Dusty furniture stood disintegrating beneath shawls of spider-web. Leaves filled the large, cracked sink Yolassika found in a spacious, low-ceilinged kitchen at the back of the house. There were corridors and passages to explore, scurrying things darting from her sight as she crept through the silence. There were stairs to climb: stairs that wound, stairs that swept purposefully straight, stairs behind doors, stairs down to darkness. And there was a multitude of rooms: big rooms, small rooms, empty rooms, rooms with books, rooms with torn, heavy curtains, rooms with bare, high window-frames, rooms with beds. The place was enormous. Enormous and unused.

Yolassika found herself once more in the kitchen, after having carefully made her way down a narrow, dark stairway with a door at the bottom. She dropped her bags upon the large central table, tested the pump above the sink and was eventually rewarded by a trickle of clear water. It was obvious no one had lived in the tall, black house for considerable time. Yolassika took a drink of the water, found it good, and straightened up to assess her find. She breathed deeply. Yes, as she thought, the house had a good feel. Solemnly, she spoke aloud, introducing herself, bowing, asking if she might be allowed to stay for a while. Silence. But not a menacing silence. "Well, that's settled, then," Yolassika declared.

She only planned to stay there for a couple of days until some plan presented itself for the future. In the meantime, she thought, she could tidy the place up a little. She took off her thick cloak, bound up her long, black, glossy hair and rolled up her linen shirt-sleeves.

Brooms were found in a cupboard and she tore down some of the ragged curtains to use as cleaning cloths. By mid-afternoon, the kitchen was almost habitable. Pausing to refresh herself, Yolassika heard an eerie scratching at the back door. Suppressing a tremour of fear, she purposefully wrenched open the protesting door and looked out. At first nothing. Then: "meow." Yolassika looked down. A small grey cat sat upon the doorstep, smiling. "Meow, pe-urr, yeowrrr!" it said and for all the world it sounded as if the cat was saying, "At last, you've finally arrived."

The couple of days extended into a couple of weeks. Treasure after treasure revealed themselves in the tall, black house as Yolassika advanced daily, broom and water bucket and mop and duster in hand. Not jewels or gold or rare paintings, or any such riches, but useable crockery, knives, packets of seeds, a keg of salt, bales of twine, bottles, some still full of wine, a chest crammed with blankets packed in lavender and sage — still sweet; mirrors, bolts of cloth, jars of beeswax, dried herbs hanging like mummified limbs in a closet, and oh, so many books. The cat, whom she named Segila, followed her from room to room, jumping onto the windowsills, whispering cruelties at the birds outside, jumping down again to wash herself and generally keep the girl company. Time sped by; a holiday of exploration and renovation. Gradually, Yolassika accepted some part of her had decided to stay indefinitely, and she gave in to that desire with little fight. The house seduced her, constantly leading her to find things of use, to bring comfort to her life. There were caves in the cliffs behind the garden, some filled with sweet, clear water. At one time, someone had constructed a plumbing system, using as supply a natural reservoir found within the caves, and had connected it to the house. Yolassika inspected the pipework and found it sound. A survey of the garden and orchard revealed overgrown vegetable plots, masses of riotous, giant herbs and fertile fruit trees. There were hives for bees, sadly empty; but, Yolassika reasoned, if she could restore the garden, she could grow things to sell in the villages that punctuated the road to Celestia and Grote. Maybe she could buy some bees one day.

Buy bees she did. And a goat, some hens, grain, meat, and white, glistening sugar in a sack. The garden responded eagerly to her attentions and even the first harvest, only months after she'd begun work, rendered a pleasing income. Sometimes, Yolassika wondered who had lived in the house before her, why they had left it, and whether they'd been as contented as she was now. Surely, countless lives before her own had whiled away the dark, green hours beneath this roof? Many of the books she'd found had been written by hand, in graceful, curling script. The subject matter was often esoteric and strange, as well as being practical and eminently useful. Since studying them, Yolassika had learned how to heal her body, whether of disease, wounds or spiritual ennui. She could treat her animals with impunity. All of the plants required were on hand in the garden, waiting to be discovered and nurtured once more as Yolassika cleared the ground of weeds. The strength of will to empower the remedies she drew from the trees themselves.

There was only a single stain on her happiness. One afternoon, in Summerlight's full heat, Yolassika took her mop and brooms to the uppermost floor of the house. It consisted of a single passage-way, with three doors leading off it, and had the feeling and smell of a place that had not been disturbed for years. There was almost an air of resentment at Yolassika's intrusion. Summerlight was shut out there. Yolassika did not like it. She turned to say to Segila, "Perhaps this part can wait . . ." and then noticed Segila was not behind her. A shiver of unease slipped up her spine. Usually, the cat followed her everywhere. She stepped backwards, not through feeling threatened, but through wanting to avoid something she thought would be unpleasant, sickening. The house would not allow that. It was quite emphatic. As if dazed, Yolassika let it show her a small, dismal room at the end of the corridor. Afterwards, she could not remember clearly what she had seen; only a feeling of depression had remained, but words whispered through her head for the rest of the day, faint yet persistent: "This is why, this is why, this is why . . ." Yolassika avoided that area of the house thereafter.

Two years passed and during that time, Yolassika devoted herself to repairing the tall, black house and its gardens. Her old life seemed a hideous, tawdry, contemptible existence in comparison to what she had now. It was very rarely she missed the town, although one damp, Wintermoan evening, when her spirits were low, she found herself thinking about old friends and, perhaps unwisely, wrote a couple of letters to people she knew. She remembered the place at the edge of Coolcandle, where the woodcutters, charcoal-burners and local villagers left items they wished to be taken to the towns. A man on a grey pony came regularly to collect them, leaving behind any mail or packages he'd picked up.

Yolassika went out into the drizzly night, swishing through the trees. She began the journey to the edge of the forest, unable in her sudden anguish to wait till morning. By that time, she'd learned a quicker route to the road and had reached the collection bin by the following afternoon. She left two dozen

eggs with the letters and hoped that would be enough payment to cover their delivery.

The morning after her return dawned bright and optimistic and Yolassika's brief depression passed. The flight through the wood, the burning desire to communicate seemed a silly, feverish thing to have done. She did not need anybody. The advantages of her new life far outweighed the ephemeral loneliness she experienced. After all, here, in the forest, the only twittering was that of the birds, not of gossips and quick-tongues. The only harshness that of the elements, never of a human temperament. Not long after she had taken up occupancy of the house, Yolassika had drawn herself a likeness of Celestia to serve as a reminder and perhaps a warning. It hung on the wall in the kitchen, in an old, wooden frame she had found. That evening, as she sat in the kitchen after her meal, relaxing, sipping herb wine and smoking one of her green cigarettes, she gazed at the picture thoughtfully. It seemed she'd poured all the filth and subtle cruelty of the past right into it. A purge. She was truly rid of it. The letters would reach the town and people would laugh at her strangeness, and think her mad. No one would come to find her and that was for the best. The pangs of lust and hopeless love would never touch her here. All she needed now was that which the tall, black house had given her. All the company she needed was that of Segila, her hens, her rather sour-tempered but amusing goat and the spirits of the forest itself, never seen but often felt. In time, she forgot she'd sent the letters completely.

One day, as a Summerlight evening bloomed around her like a late flower, Yolassika was seated outside her house and taking a glass of wine, fermented from honey and elder flower, when she heard the unmistakeable sound of human movement through the trees. Very occasionally, other wood-dwellers crossed Yolassika's glade, but they travelled with the silky, silent ease of the wilderness-footed. An understanding existed among all forest natives; contact was minimal unless invited, and respect for privacy observed. This movement was accompanied by the warble of voices, the sound of iron-shod hoofs, the swish of outraged branches, pushed to the side. The noises came from the south. Whoever travelled towards her must have come upon the wide, dusty road from the direction of Celestia and Grote.

Yolassika watched with a mixture of fascination and fury as horses burst from the trees. She stood up and put down her glass of wine. The horses trotted nearer, two of them; one spotted grey, one dark dun. Yolassika wasn't sure whether to be pleased or annoyed when she realised she recognised the person riding the dun. A hand was raised in a splash of yellow silk. A voice cried "Yo! Yolassika, you imp!" and an old friend urged his horse into a canter, spewing up clods of turf behind him. Yolassika felt weak. She remembered the letters; more than twelve months sent. Finally, it seemed, someone had decided to sniff her out.

Yolassika had known Ricardo Neathtree since they'd been children. Their careers had diverged somewhat over the years — Ricardo had nestled comfortably into his father's merchant business — but their friendship had remained constant, if rather shallow. Ricardo, after all, had never considered their relationship close enough to offer Yolassika the funds she'd desperately needed after her mother died. And Yolassika had had more pride than to ask for it, although she'd fought resentment at the time. Ricardo liked having a courtezan as a friend, rather like he enjoyed owning exotic, foreign pets. In all the years she'd known him, he had never suggested their friendship change its platonic state. She, herself, had never desired him either, and was secretly glad he was not her real brother, even though the pair of them behaved as if he was. She supposed, as she watched the expensively-clad Ricardo spring down from his horse, that she still harboured a vestige of feeling for him, but it was faint.

Ricardo's companion — a young man — silent and unremarkable in shadow, was overlooked during the first flurry of greeting, the inevitable shower of city gifts, the exclamations, comments, mandatory viewing of the tall, black house and the gardens beyond, the quickly offered refreshment, quickly prepared. Ricardo's companion kept his head hung low, shuffling behind the others, quite invisible a satellite in orbit around Ricardo's sunshine. "You have yourself a palace here!" Ricardo declared, nodding round the rooms. It would cost a fortune to own such a place as the tall, black house in Celestia or Grote, even more to build one. Yolassika thought waspishly how Ricardo would probably go and commission himself a copy of it immediately when he got home, using his father's money, without a second thought.

"I would have come before if I'd known you lived in such a place!"

Yolassika flinched.

"I prefer to live alone," she said, and then added hastily, "but it is good to see you, Rico, after all this time."

Yolassika laid out a table with white linen in the porch. She set a bowl of smouldering resin by the door, which exuded a delicious smoke into the heavy, sensual evening air. She carried out bowls of salad chopped freshly from her garden and arranged one of the cooked fowl which Ricardo had brought her on a plate. The little group sat down to eat. Ricardo smiled at Yolassika's exquisite, delicate wines and then shook his head.

"Delightful! So clever! But tonight, a treat!" He had brought expensive liquor with him from Celestia, fiery with spice, smoky as the town itself on Falltime nights. It did not taste of the green forest at all.

As they sat down, Ricardo indicated his companion and said, almost as an afterthought, "Ah, this is Fairen De'ath. He had a whim to accompany me here. Needed a rest too, I expect." He laughed heartily, offering no more explanation or introduction than that.

Fairen De'ath ducked his head and shrank into a seat. Yolassika thought it looked as if the young man was shrouded in smoke, as if he was somehow fuzzy at the edges. How strange. She blinked quickly and the smokiness vanished. Perhaps a trick of the light, something in her eye . . .

Ricardo didn't stop talking, throwing his arms about, indicating further gifts he'd forgotten to mention. Yolassika wondered if Ricardo was faintly embarrassed coming to a place like this where the silence of the forest was so huge and its strength so pure and near. "So how is your life going now?" Ricardo enquired boisterously. "Quiet, eh?"

Yolassika smiled sweetly and replied that all was going very well, thank you and yes, it was quiet, but she liked it that way, having got used to it.

Fairen De'ath sat silently, his head bowed as if in timidity. Yolassika was reminded of the boys and girls she had known in the town, too young to solicit alone, too desperate not to, who had fallen under the protection of older men and women, who undertook to manage their business. They, too, used to sit bowed and humble, deaf to the haggling that occurred over their heads. Was Ricardo Fairen's patron in some way?

The moon rose over the chimneys of the black house, which stood nearly as tall as the tallest tree. Nimble bats flitted in and out of the eaves, peeping out their high, navigational squeaks. Below, sitting comfortably in the glow of a lighted globe of glass, the three talked long and deeply. The presence of the forest stole over them, seeming to bring the mysteries of life very close to hand. It was inevitable the conversation should turn towards the mysterious, the baffling, the arcane. Ricardo Neathtree squinted nervously at the black, rustling forest and said,

"It must unnerve you often, Yolly, living here."

"No," Yolassika answered, "I am never afraid." It was true. She feared what she had left behind in the town more.

"No ghosts then? Not even in this dark old house?" Ricardo's smile held an edge, as if he had only just realised he too would be spending the night inside it.

Yolassika grinned. "No ghosts," she said, sipping her glass of liquor. Had it tasted this harsh back in Celestia or had her palate become refined these past two years?

"You don't get lonely?"

"Only once." Yolassika remembered, with mixed feelings, that sad, cold night she'd sat and written the letters telling people where she was. Thank All That Breathed, Ricardo had been the only one to respond.

Ricardo shrugged petulantly, perhaps affronted that his old friend didn't seem more relieved to see him. Yolassika hoped this presaged no further surprise visits and then silently reprimanded herself for being so antisocial. She smiled at her friend. "I'm glad you came," she said. "Really."

Ricardo grinned roguishly. "I half-expected to find you'd already know I was coming!" He indicated their surroundings. "You were always mystically inclined. I was not surprised when you left so abruptly, or at your letter telling where you'd decided to root. No, not at all. You are a proper witch now of course. Did you sense me coming? A scrying ball wouldn't be out of place here. Do you have one hidden away perhaps?"

Yolassika shook her head and laughed. "I cannot read the future," she said.

Fairen De'ath, nudged from his silence by alcohol, said suddenly, "Upon the table in my house there stands a sphere of perfect crystal. I look into it often."

"And does it tell your future?" Ricardo asked, winking at Yolassika. The brow of Fairen De'ath, which was pale and high, wrinkled in thought.

"Sometimes. I have seen hints, presentiments perhaps."

Ricardo laughed. Though he would not dismiss the existence of sorcery, he clearly doubted whether his young companion had any knowledge of it. Yolassika merely looked on warily.

"So tell us, tell us," Ricardo chided. "What hints present themselves to you? Daughters of rich houses clad in jewels I should hope!"

Fairen De'ath shook his head seriously. "No, nothing like that. Other things." He looked up. Yolassika was shocked from a lazy comfort by the glance. Dark eyes in a pale face, wistful as a slave, perhaps lovely. What had Ricardo brought here, and why? Discomfort pooled itself in Yolassika's breast. She felt as if a rushing, rushing wind, foul with destruction, had come gusting up the south road, and not two travellers on iron-shod horses. She sensed turmoil.

After a moment, Yolassika excused herself, rose, and went into the shadows of the house. She let its cool, sinuous presence invade her troubled mind and closed her eyes. Balm. Security. Sighing, she padded into the kitchen and poured herself a long, cold glass of clearest water to rid her palate of the sting of Ricardo's liquor. Her brain seemed full of the echoes of past noise: voices, laughter, hot, smoky taverns, yellow light and stale air. She did not want that here, in this house. She would be glad when Ricardo and his strange companion left her alone, to bask in the luxury of solitude once more. *Fairen De'ath: even the name inspires fear. Loveliness he disguises with smoke. A trickster. No. A boy; shy and faltering. Pretty boy. Dangerous.* Like all those pretty boys who'd come to the Footways, their brief attraction to her light. *And yet. . . . A look? Desire? Was it there? No. No. Too long alone here. A mistake. He is Rico's plaything. Must be. A mistake . . .*

Then, in the darkness behind her, there was a movement: so slight Yolassika wondered whether she had really perceived it.

A voice came out of the darkness, a furtive whisper.

"In the crystal . . . It was you, Yolassika. Just a moon ago, the crystal showed me, told me. You, you, you."

Yolassika turned and saw the pale shape of Fairen De'ath, standing in the doorway.

"I beg your pardon?" False confidence. False cool. It was an angel gliding towards her.

Fairen De'ath advanced into the room, his hands wrestling with each other in discomfort. "The letter you sent. I read it. Months ago. And then, in the crystal, I saw you. I saw all of this!"

"You must have been mistaken," Yolassika said coldly, filled with dread. "I do not know you at all."

Fairen still crept forwards into the moonlit room, still wringing his slim, pale hands.

"No, but I know you," he said, babbling, almost incoherent. "I've seen you. Before. Many times. If only I'd spoken, but you seemed so distant, so aloof . . . I watched. I saw. Others came, others touched you. But not me. Not me. And then you were gone, vanished. It was like the light went out of the town. When Ricardo showed me the letter, months after you'd sent it, I wanted to come then, but I was nervous, shy. Ricardo kept mentioning he would visit you one day, but that day never came. I waited and waited, and then . . . the crystal. I had to act. I was out of my mind. I persuaded Ricardo to come here. He was tired. Needed a rest. The forest, I said, would do him good. I asked him to bring me with him, introduce me to you. Two years. I have not forgotten you. I had to see you. I had to tell you this. You are my life!"

Yolassika made a dismissive gesture. "This is . . . a shock. What you are saying sounds like madness."

"It is!" Fairen agreed. "I had no alternative but to obey the call of this insanity."

"You don't understand," Yolassika said. "I have chosen this life, this privacy. I have no desire to share it with anyone, no desires at all, in fact. I am touched by your feelings, it's very flattering, but . . ."

Fairen came and put his hands on Yolassika's arm, and oh, how cool that touch was, so cool yet vibrant with promise. How dark were the eyes that implored to be recognized, how winsome the face. She could smell the maleness of him, young and vibrant. Yolassika looked away, pierced by a swift, insidious spear of lust. She'd forgotten the bittersweet poignancy of such attacks. "I have no wish to share my life with anyone," she repeated and paused before adding, "not even someone as lovely as you." The words hung like crystal in the air between them. Then, Fairen De'ath made a bitter sound.

"I will not leave here," he declared fervently. "Do not underestimate my feelings. I will stay until I make you want me to stay."

"Does Ricardo know of this obsession?"

Fairen shook his head. Yolassika sighed deeply. She felt as if she was being offered a flaming torch and, although the torch could give her light, it might also burn her fearfully. In the past, such offers had been made to her; accepting, she had only brought herself pain.

"You are not of my world," Yolassika said gently. "I am here in the forest to escape civilisation. Do you really want to cast off the luxuries of your life and live here, in this quiet place, for the sake of desire?"

"If it means I will be with you, yes!" Fairen replied without a pause. Yolassika sighed again, prompting Fairen to say, "It is more than desire, I swear it."

"You may find, if your desires are satisfied, your feelings are not as enduring as you presently believe," Yolassika said drily.

Fairen made an angry sound. "I should hate you for that," he said, "insulting my love for you, because it is love. Can't you imagine the risk I have taken approaching you like this? Would I do such a thing lightly?"

Yolassika looked at the glowing, pale form of Fairen De'ath. Had the house brought her this final, complete miracle? She had everything now but human love. Was it possible she was now being offered that too, in the shape of this pretty, effeminate boy? Impulsively, she held out her arms.

"It may be you are simply mad, or misguided, or even lying to me, but for tonight at least, then I am here for you," she said, and in the moonlight, they embraced.

When they went back to Ricardo, it was to carry an air of celebration with them. No more talk of dark mystery. Now Ricardo regaled them with ribald tales of his experiences and the glade rang with the sound of laughter, the clink of glasses being refilled. The air was redolent of the smoky thrill of anticipation. When at last they all retired for the night, Fairen De'ath crept to Yolassika's room, his voice hot with the passion of his desire: his hands, his eyes, his lips. Yolassika swam in a sweet delirium of ecstasy. So long since she'd touched warm skin, so long. Fairen De'ath told her a hundred times with what impatience he'd waited for this moment, with what dread it might never be fulfilled. Yolassika's happiness was so exquisite, it almost made her afraid.

So followed a blissful week. Ricardo was content to drink his liquor in the porch of the house and in the gardens all day, reading some of Yolassika's books, so that Yolassika herself was free to initiate the fey Fairen De'ath into the mysteries of the forest. Yolassika showed him the icy pool where she bathed in the light of the sickle moon, obeying a suggestion one of her books had mentioned. Have I ever wished for love on those nights? Yolassika wondered silently, thinking about all the wishes she had made, while sluicing herself with the water. Hadn't they all been for good harvests, for health, for more rain, for less rain and such like? Never this, surely? And yet . . . This feels like heaven. If I didn't wish for it, I should have done.

She and Fairen made love in the pool and Yolassika marvelled at the svelte contours of Fairen's body, the cleanness of limb, the sweep of hair, the deep, sulky eyes. Perfection. Fairen kissed her, saying, "Never have I seen such beauty as you. You are a gypsy raven! Say that you love me!"

"You are a silver wildcat," Yolassika answered. "Yes, I love you."

Whether Ricardo Neathtree guessed what happened, Yolassika did not know. He certainly never professed a desire to accompany their forest walks, but his eyes and smile were free of innuendo. "I

have had such a holiday here!" he cried. 'I feel renewed. Thank you, Yolassika."

"Thank *you*," Yolassika said, with a smile.

She and Fairen had not spoken of the future, but Yolassika had no doubt that when Ricardo returned to Celestia, he would return alone.

At the end of the week, Ricardo said, "Tomorrow, I'll have to get back to town. But I'll return one day, for another refreshment, never fear!"

Yolassika smiled and squeezed Ricardo's hand. "You cannot guess what pleasure your visit has given me," she said.

When morning came to the black walls and the black chimneys of Yolassika's house, Fairen De'ath rose alone from the shared warmth of Yolassika's bed and went to the open window. He could not see the wide road leading south through the trees from there. And the air was cool, too fresh for him. He shivered.

Yolassika awoke, smiling into the dawn sunlight, savoring the crisp, perfumed air.

"And now I must go," Fairen De'ath said, without looking backwards. He closed the window.

"Go?" Yolassika felt the shining cocoon of happiness around her crack. She felt blood must surely pour from this wound. "What do you mean?" she asked. "Only a week ago, you were begging me to let you stay here!"

Fairen shrugged awkwardly. "I know, but . . ." He looked around the room.

Yolassika's shock expressed itself in anger. "You virtually forced me to love you!" she cried. "What is this talk of leaving so soon?"

Fairen still stared southwards through the window. "It is not right," he said. "One day I shall have to return to Celestia and, when I do, I do not want to have to hide from knowing eyes. If I stay here when Ricardo leaves, he will know why. I realise now I do not want that."

"Because of what I was?" Yolassika asked bitterly. "Is that it? You don't want people to know you lived with a whore?"

Fairen De'ath did not answer. He put his fingers on the window glass, long, slender fingers. Yolassika's heart turned over. "Haven't I pleased you?" she asked softly. "You said you loved me. You made me feel that too."

Fairen shook his head. "I know. You have pleased me, you have been wonderful and I do . . . feel for you, but . . . We achieved the miracle, didn't we? We fulfilled my prophecy, and it was good. But now it is done. Such affairs as this can only be brief."

Yolassika was stunned. Fairen De'ath had broken her defences, every one. She felt naked and wretched and helpless.

"I'm sorry," said Fairen De'ath.

By mid-day, Ricardo Neathtree, still blissfully unaware of what had transpired, oblivious to any dark atmosphere, set his horse once more upon the path that led to the wide, dusty road, taking Fairen De'ath with him. Yolassika steeled herself and mouthed goodbyes, smiling; stood on her porch and watched them go. Only once the leaves had hidden them completely did she allow herself to fall down upon the grass outside the tall, black house and surrender to bitter grief. She wept aloud for several hours. "What have I done to deserve this?" she raged, bewildered. "Why did he do this to me? Why did I let him?" Fairen De'ath had destroyed her contentment. Yolassika had not needed company, but now Fairen had gone, after bestowing that brief, vicious gift of lust and heat, Yolassika felt she could not live with the weight of solitude any longer. All the things that she most enjoyed seemed blighted. Where was the delight in bathing in the forest streams if she had to bathe alone? Where the delight in discovering the dens of the wild creatures, spilling tumbling mounds of cubs and kittens in the sunlight, if there was no one but the grey cat to show them to? Was the sense of satisfaction in a job well done valid if it was not shared? Could she live knowing she would not touch Fairen's skin again, nor hear his voice and bask in his radiant smile? A torment! Unbearable! Yolassika's heart felt broken. She was sure it could never heal. Not now. Not this time. Never. Everything was gone: light, hope, happiness. She could not escape the past. She was a whore. Used for sex. Simple as that. Even here. She did not want to be this thing.

As the afternoon sloped towards sunset, Yolassika picked herself up off the grass and went back into the tall, black house. With bowed posture, she slowly mounted the steepest flight of stairs and ventured deep into the shadowed corridor beyond them. This was the house's most secret place, and never visited, but for that one afternoon, long ago. Yolassika went to the door at the end of the passage and turned the handle. Inside, a small room, brown with age, lit by a single, dusty skylight. The room reeked of sadness, of betrayal, and had been used before. It was completely empty, but for a slim, silver dart hanging from a nail upon the wall. Yolassika had only been here once before, and that just to acknowledge what lay within and why. The house had granted her permission then to see. It had said to her heart, without words, "Remember this, but be wise." It had intimated the power of what lay within the room, its varied uses. It explained something of why the house had been unoccupied, but not everything. Yolassika felt she had no choice now but for a certain course of action. She knew what use to make of the slim, silver dart, kissed with poison. Numb, she lifted it down from the wall, turning it in her hands. A beautiful thing, smooth as satin. It felt good to the touch. And so sharp! She raised her face to the evening sunlight coming in through the roof and held the point of the dart against her throat. It was as cool as a sliver of ice. She knew it would take very little effort on her part to ease it right into her flesh. Such is the way of deadly things, she thought. So little effort. A piercing. Then darkness. She took a deep breath, prepared to push the dart and then . . .

Then, through the dusty window, she saw the moon sailing high into a dark blue, lustrous sky. She smelled the perfume of warm earth drifting in from outside and heard the echoing calls of the night creatures, stirred from rest, slithering forth into the pale light. Coming in through the door behind her, the grey cat mewed for supper and wound her long tail around Yolassika's legs. If Segila sensed her mistress' distress, her own comfort was obviously more important.

The moment cracked: cracked like ice. The dart felt cold and wicked in Yolassika's hands. She dropped it, uttering a cry of distaste. "Meow?" said Segila. Yolassika rubbed her face, smiled and bent down to caress the furry head.

"You are right," she said, and then to the room, "I misunderstood."

She bent down and picked up the dart. Holding it loosely, carelessly, she spoke six precise words of power over it and carried it downstairs. Laying it carefully on the kitchen table, she gave meat to her cat, went outside, threw corn to her hens and cabbage leaves to her goat. Then she fetched the dart and held it up to the moonlight. The silver glinted icily. A purposeful, condensed thing it was.

Yolassika closed her eyes and threw the dart high, high into the air.

Twisting, turning, glittering, it seemed the dart would fall back to earth, but then, with a strange shiver of a song, it paused and flew, point first, southwards, above the trees. Yolassika wiped her hands, smiled into the moonlight and went back inside. She made herself a fine supper of the food that Ricardo had brought her and then sat down to read, smoking one of her favourite blends of herbal cigarettes, Segila purring happily in her lap. After a while, she shuddered, got up, removed the picture of Celestia from the wall and put it outside. Tomorrow she would bathe in the clearest, coldest stream she could find and it would all be gone from her. Forever.

Outside, the silver dart flew southwards, towards the city. It reverberated to one, single, burning, inexorable sentiment. Yolassika had breathed six words into it. Six to make it live, to instill its one true purpose. The room in the secret place of the tall, black house was completely empty now. Nothing would ever come to fill it but the silence of peace. Six words. All the hurt condensed. Six words.

"Pierce the heart of Fairen De'ath!"

Oblivious of the fiery, white progress above it, the forest continued as always, a surge of silence, and the tall, black house, as always, looked after its own. It may be reached from three directions, that house, but few who follow the paths will find it.   Ω

POSTGRADUATE

by Jonathan Carroll

Why do hearts beat, cigarettes burn, or some dogs smell good? There are answers. There are answers for everything if we look hard enough, but this time Louis Kent wasn't given the opportunity to look. It just happened and then there wasn't anything he could do about it.

He woke up to the sound of a bell, a piercing, vicious clanging that even through the snow of sleep he recognized. "Christ!"

He turned in bed and saw a face he hadn't thought much about, much less seen, for fifteen years. Mark Schuster groaned in his bed across the room and pulled the pillow over his face.

Mark Schuster, eighteen years old and early acceptance at Brown. Mark Schuster, who kept six bottles of Italian cologne in his dresser. Mark Schuster with a girlfriend in town and another in New York City.

"Isn't it Saturday? Why the Hell isn't it Saturday?"

It had taken a long time, but at the age of thirty-two Louis Kent could finally call himself a happy man. He had an interesting job, a wife who thought he was sexy, a small child who wouldn't go to sleep at night unless Daddy tucked her in.

Kent came into his own in college after an unhappy period as a teenager at a snobby boys' school in New Hampshire, where teachers played favorites and it snowed twenty times a year. Soon after he graduated from the school, however, he began having dreams about the place and the people there. They weren't bad dreams, but he often woke from them wide-eyed and a bit short of breath. In these dreams, algebra tests, lacrosse practice, and the smell of dormitory food were as real as they'd once been years ago.

In these dreams he was sixteen or seventeen again, running to class and tying his tie at the same time or else feeling his bowels melt as he entered history class on the day of a test.

But Kent wanted to put that time as far behind him as he could. His wife often remarked on the fact that he rarely talked about his days as a teenager. He replied in his calm and kind way that it wasn't much fun to reminisce about a time that hadn't been much fun to live.

Things we're sure we'll forget in time aren't as easy to jettison as we think. A face pained by something we've done, a love that came and went when we were fourteen . . . We are intelligent and rational, but we aren't in control. Kent dreamed of high school the way one touches the scar of an old, deep cut: tenderly, with remembered fear and possessiveness. Childhood memories are our scars, and we often protect and caress them as much as we hate them.

"Jesus, Kent, it's after eight!" Schuster leapt out of bed in his white underpants and ran out of the room for the bathroom. Kent continued to look at the other's empty bed. Outside he heard boys' voices yelling, cursing, laughing. He looked groggily out the window and saw a steel-gray sky. Over a gap of fifteen years, he still knew he had only seven minutes to get up and dress and be down in the cafeteria for check-in. Check-in! In fifteen years he'd graduated cum laude from college, served in Vietnam, and married a girl he once thought impossibly beautiful and even more impossible to get. Yes, he had accomplished all these

63

things, but now, once again, he was afraid of breakfast check-in.

He sighed and slowly pushed the covers away. All right, he would play this dream's game as he'd done all the other times before. He *knew* he was dreaming, and that was reassuring. He knew that in the middle of the morning assembly or a candy bar between classes, he would suddenly be returned to a world years in the future where his skin was clear of acne, the foreign car in his garage was only a year and a half old, and Ronald Reagan was president.

The first of many shocks came when he walked to the mirror and saw his reflection. His face *was* clear. His hair had receded to its thirty-two-year-old horizon, and lines that would have looked like progeria on a teenage face told him and everyone else he was the world's oldest postgraduate.

Always, *always* in his previous school dreams, he was a teenager again. The adult Louis Kent face was a frightening new development.

"Come on, Kent, get your ass in gear." Schuster zoomed through the door of the room and went straight to his closet. "If the man-eater's on duty this morning, we are royally screwed."

Louis stood there wearing the flannel pajamas he remembered throwing out freshman year in college.

"Schuster, look at me."

The other looked over his shoulder and rolled his eyes. "What're you, queer? You're beautiful. Come *on,* man! You wanna get another detention?" He turned back to the closet and pulled a rumpled shirt off a hanger. "If *I* get another detention I ain't getting out of here this weekend, and that is a no-no."

"Mark, I'm thirty-two years old! Look at me!"

"Kent, my man, you can be as old as you want. Right now I am in transit and can't worry about your mental illness."

Schuster was dressed a few moments later and, with a sad shake of his head at his doomed-to-lateness roommate, ran out of the room.

Kent sat down on the side of his bed and put his head in his hands. "My daughter's name is Giuliana Patricia. I have twenty thousand dollars in the bank. My account number is 35203560. There are thirty-one thousand miles on my car. . . ."

Head in hands, he spent minutes reciting what he knew were the real facts of his life: clients' names, expensive restaurants, the way his wife liked to kiss. While he went through this sacred litany, he heard bells ringing and knew, again by memory, that breakfast was over and chapel was over and the first class of the day had begun.

Some time later (by then he'd fallen back on the bed but kept his eyes closed), the housemaster came in and quietly spoke his name.

"Mr. Kent? Are you all right, son?"

Louis looked at the man and smiled savagely. "Mr. Halston, I'm thirty-two years old. I *graduated* in 1968!"

"Are you feeling all right, Kent? Would you like to go to the infirmary?"

"Halston, I'm Louis Kent. I give to the alumni fund. I'm older than you, for God's sake!"

It was true. The younger teacher sat down on Schuster's messy bed and put his hands on his tweedy knees.

"Louis, you know I'm one of your biggest supporters around here. You've got a brain in your head when you feel like using it. But this, kiddo, this is *not* using your head. You've skipped chapel without an excuse six times this quarter and that is not playing it cool."

"But, Mr. Halston, can't you see? I'm a *man!* I'm thirty-two years old. I don't *have* to go to chapel anymore. I'm married! I've got a gold American Express card!"

"All right, Louis, we'll play it your way. Just lie back and be the fool. I've got a class now. I've said exactly what I came to say."

Halston closed the door quietly behind him and Louis was left, alone and afraid.

Blasingame leaned over and sneaked a glance at Kent's almost empty test paper. Kent knew nothing. All he could remember was the Pythagorean theorem and this was calculus. The other boy snorted in disgust and looked back at his own paper. "I thought *I* was stupid, Kent," he whispered meanly.

All Kent could think of to say in return was a weak "But I'm thirty-two!"

The teacher whipped around from the board and threw an eraser at him.

"Kent, you're not intelligent enough to cheat, so please don't embarrass us all by trying."

Nothing he did could stop it. At football practice, someone hit him so hard he fell down and broke an expensive cap he'd had made in New York by Leonard Bernstein's dentist. When they had to run wind sprints at the end of the day, years of smoking unfiltered cigarettes drove hot, cruel spikes through his chest and he didn't care if all the others were twenty and thirty yards in front of him every time. All he wanted in the world was to blink awake and find himself in bed beside Sandra, under the marvelous *Daunendecke* they'd bought in Zürich a few years ago while on a business trip.

What was worse, the team he practiced with wasn't even varsity or JV; it was intramural football — the team made up of every peewee, zonk, bookworm, and weirdo in the school. He'd recognized the faces from his past immediately. Dave Miller, who kept a rat in his room, never took a bath or shower and scored an 800 on the High-Level Physics Achievement test as a junior. Tom Connolly, who thought the greatest human being who ever lived was Thomas Aquinas. Jonathan Minifee, who did nothing but read magazines about guns and had a membership in the American Nazi party.

This was his competition, the ones who raced ahead of him in everything now, hit the tackling dummies like war arrows, and smirked together when he collapsed on the field after getting a monstrous stitch in his side.

Luckily the coach was Winston, the Latin-and-Greek teacher who coached only because he had to and who brought his miniature collie, Orestes, to every practice. When he saw Louis lagging, he kept saying things like "Oh, *run*, Kent! Don't be a big bore."

In the locker room afterward, the few teammates who actually took showers looked at him with a mixture of pity and disgust. They knew how low *they* were on the school's status pole, and for someone to be worse than them was hard to believe. Only Patoprsty, famous in the school simply because he was five feet tall, came over and asked Kent if he wanted to go up to his room after and look at old copies of *Model Railroader.*

While he was slowly dressing, the varsity team came in, laughing and beautiful and exhausted. Again, he knew the faces instantly, but particularly that of Grey Harris.

At eighteen, Harris was almost frighteningly perfect. He had so much going for him people stood in stupefied awe. He was friendly, brilliant, handsome, and athletic. Everything he did turned to gold, and what's more, he did it so effortlessly. You had to stand back and shield your eyes from the glare of his everything.

Harris came down the row of lockers and placed his scarred helmet on the wooden bench. Louis looked at him out of the corners of his eyes and remembered how jealous he'd been of the boy years ago. Surprisingly, Harris turned to him and began to talk in a low voice.

"Look, Kent, the word is out about you these days, you know what I mean?" He reached down to undo one of his shoelaces. "Halston came up to me after class and told me to talk to you. What a doofus he is! Look, as far as I'm concerned you can do whatever the Hell you want. The only thing is, if you get another detention you're suspended, right? That means the debate team is out of luck. Both of us know this stuff is a big crock of bull, and if I had your guts or nuttiness I'd be out skipping more classes than you, but that's not the point. You're the best debater we've got, and there's no way on earth we're going to make it as a team in the finals if you're not there with us. Okay?"

Louis looked at Harris and nodded. He was so touched. They needed him. Grey Harris actually said he and the others on the team *needed* him.

"Yeah? You'll be a good boy for a little while? Fabulous! Thanks a lot, man. That's great." Harris smiled warmly and went back to unlacing his cleats.

A moment later the magic of Harris's face and words wore off and Louis realized he'd been feeling guilty about letting down the guys on the debate team!

"This is *crazy!*"

Harris looked over and smiled angelically. "What is?"

"You! This! What do I care about the goddamned debate team? I'm thirty-two years old." He bounded up and ran for the door.

It had gone much too far. The dream had pulled him too close and was smothering reality out of him. A dream was all right so long as it remained finite, but this one gave no indication of ending soon and in the meantime had increased its mental bear hug on him. He had to do something, and fast.

"Hel-lo?" His daughter's voice was there, recognizable and real. He stood in the phone booth in Adelaide Hall and looked at the million years of student graffiti written on the walls.

"Giuli? Giuli, baby, it's *Daddy!* It's Daddy, baby!"

"Hi, Dah-dy. Mommy, it's Dah-dy." A loud **thump** gave him another foothold back in the real world: He knew his daughter had dropped the telephone receiver on the table, an act he'd scolded her for again and again. But now the painfully amplified sound made his heart and hopes sprout wings.

"Louie? Hello, darling. How's school?"

"Sandra! Sandra, it's me!"

"I know, sweet. Don't you think I know your voice, silly?" She laughed for a moment, until he realized what she'd said. How was *school?*

"Sandra, you know?"

"Know? Know what? How did you do on your calculus test?"

Little bombs of fear and ice began exploding all over the insides of his body. "Sandra, I'm *back in school!* They think I'm eighteen years old!"

"Louie, honey, I'm really tired. Giuli's been a big pain today and I just don't have it in me. Are you coming home this weekend or not? Did you get a weekend pass?"

He said nothing.

"Louie, are you not telling me something?" Her voice grew hard and cold as a rock in winter. "Did you flunk your calculus test?"

He heard her voice repeating the question, very loudly and abrasively, as he gently put the receiver back on its cradle. He leaned back against the booth and looked again at the words gouged and carved in brutal permanence on the wall facing him. He knew some of their names. Schmalz. Olding. Smith. Names in the back of the alumni magazine. Bank vice-presidents. Researchers. Failures. Successes. Bigshot and small fry.

The bell that had plagued him every day of his new life here broke his reverie and warned him it was time for evening study hall. He would go to the library. Seniors had that privilege. Even seniors on detention. He would go to the library and look at the magazines and be scared. Finally, when the world was within an inch of closing in on him completely, he would go back in the stacks and start looking for books on the debate team's topic for the competition: "Capital Punishment: A Step Forward or a Step Back?" Ω

STALIN'S TEARDROPS

by Ian Watson

Part One: *The Lie of the Land*

"This is the era of *clarity* now, Valentin," Mirov reproved me. "I don't necessarily like it, but I am no traitor. I have problems, you have problems. We must adapt."

I chuckled. "In this office we have always adapted, haven't we?"

By "office" I referred to the whole cluster of studios which composed the department of cartography. Ten in all, these were interconnected by archways rather than doors so that my staff and I could pass freely from one to the next across a continuous sweep of parquet flooring. In recent years I had resisted the general tendency to subdivide spacious rooms which, prior to the Revolution, had been the province of a giant insurance company. For our drawing tables and extra-wide filing cabinets we needed elbow-room. We needed as much daylight as possible from our windows overlooking the courtyard deep below. Hence our location here on the eighth floor; hence the absence of steel bars at our windows, and ours alone. Grids of shadow must not fall across our work.

On hot summer days when breezes blew in and out we needed to be specially vigilant. (And of course we used much sealing wax every evening when we locked up.) In winter, the standard lighting — those big white globes topped by shades — was perfectly adequate. Still, their illumination could not rival pure daylight. We often left the finalization of important maps until the summer months.

Mirov's comments about clarity seemed spurious in the circumstances; though with a sinking heart I knew all too well what he meant.

"We have lost touch with our own country," he said forlornly, echoing a decision which had been handed down from on high.

"Of course we have," I agreed. "That was the whole idea, wasn't it?"

"This must change." He permitted himself a wry joke. "The lie of the land must be corrected."

Mirov was a stout sixty-five-year-old with short grizzled hair resembling the hachuring on a map of a steep round hillock. His nose and cheeks were broken-veined from over-indulgence in the now-forbidden spirit. I think he resented never having been attached to one of the more glamorous branches of our secret police. Maybe he had always been bored by his job, unlike me.

Some people might view the task of censorship as a cushy sinecure. Not so! It demanded a logical meticulousness which in essence was more creative than pedantic. Yet it was, well, dusty. Mirov lacked the inner forcefulness which might have seen him assigned to foreign espionage or even to the border guards. I could tell that he did not intend to resist the changes which were now in the air, like some mischievous whirlwind intent on tossing us all aloft. He hadn't come here to conspire with me, to any great extent.

As head of censorship Mirov was inspector of the department of cartography. Yet under my guidance of the past twenty years cartography basically ran itself. Mirov routinely gave his imprimatur to our products: the regional and city maps, the charts, the Great Atlas. Two years his junior, I was trusted. The occasional spy whom he planted on me as a trainee invariably must deliver a glowing report. (Which of my staff of seventy persons, busily drafting away or practising, was the current "eye of Mirov"? I didn't give a hoot.) As to the *quality* of our work, who was more qualified than myself to check it?

"What you're suggesting isn't easy," I grumbled. "Such an enterprise could take years, even decades. I was hoping to retire by the age of seventy. Are you implying that I stay on and on forever?" I knew well where I would retire to. . . .

He rubbed his nose. Did those broken capillaries itch so much?

"Actually, Valentin, there's a time limit. Within two years — consisting of twenty-four months, not of twenty-nine months or thirty-two; and *this* is regarded as generous — we must publish a true Great Atlas. Otherwise the new economic plan . . . well, they're thinking of new railway lines, new dams, new towns, opening up wasteland for oil and mineral exploitation."

"Two years?" I had to laugh. "It's impossible, quite impossible."

"It's an order. Any procrastination will be punished. You'll be dismissed. Your pension rights will diminish: no cabin in the countryside, no more access to hard-currency shops. A younger officer will replace you — one of the new breed. Don't imagine, Valentin, that you will have a companion in misfortune! Don't assume that I too shall be dismissed at the summit of my career. My other bureaux are rushing to publish and promote all sorts of forbidden rubbish. So-called experimental poetry, fiction, art criticism. Plays will be staged to shock us, new music will jar the ears, new art will offend the eye. Happenings will happen. Manuscripts are filed away

under lock and key, after all — every last item. We only need to unlock those cupboards, to let the contents spill out and lead society astray into mental anarchy."

I sympathised. "Ah, what we have come to!"

He inclined his cross-hatched hill-top head.

"*You*, Valentin, *you*. What you have come to." He sighed deeply. "Still, I know what you mean . . . Colonel."

He mentioned my rank to remind me. We might wear sober dark suits, he and I, but we were both ranking officers.

"With respect, General, these — ah — orders are practically impossible to carry out."

"Which is why a new deputy-chief cartographer has been assigned to you."

"So here is the younger officer you mentioned — already!"

He gripped my elbow in the manner of an accomplice, though he wasn't really such.

"It shows willing," he whispered, "and it's one way out. Let the blame fall on her if possible. Let her seem a saboteur." Aloud, he continued, "Come along with me to the restaurant, to meet Grusha. You can bring her back here yourself."

I should meet my nemesis on neutral territory, as it were. Thus Mirov avoided direct, visible responsibility for introducing her.

Up here on the eighth floor we in cartography had the advantage of being close to one of the two giant restaurants which fed the thousands of men and women employed in the various branches of secret police work. The other restaurant was down in the basement. Many staff routinely turned up at eight o'clock of a morning — a full hour earlier than the working day commenced — to take advantage of hearty breakfasts unavailable outside: fresh milk, bacon and eggs, sausages, fresh fruit.

As I walked in silence with Mirov for a few hundred metres along the lime-green corridor beneath the omnipresent light-globes, I reflected that proximity to the restaurant was less advantageous today.

At this middle hour of the morning the food hall was almost deserted but for cooks and skivvies. Mirov drank the excellent coffee and cream with almost indecent haste so as to leave me alone with the woman. Grusha was nudging forty but hadn't lost her figure. She was willowy, with short curly fair hair, a large equine nose, and piercing sapphire eyes. A nose for sniffing out delays, eyes for seeing through excuses. An impatient thoroughbred! An intellectual. The privileged daughter of someone inclined to foreign and new ways. Daddy was one of the new breed who had caused so much upset. Daddy had used influence to place her here. This was her great opportunity; and his.

"So you were originally a graduate of the Geographical Academy," I mused.

She smiled lavishly. "Do I take it that I shall find your ways a little different, Colonel?"

"Valentin, please."

"We must mend those ways. I believe there is much to rectify."

"Are you married, Grusha?"

"To our land, to the future, to my specialty."

"Which was, precisely?"

"The placing of names on maps. I assume you know Imhof's paper, *Die Anordnung der Namen in der Karte*?"

"You read German?"

She nodded. "French and English too."

"My word!"

"I used my language skills on six years' duty in the DDR." Doing what? Ah, not for me to enquire.

Her shoulders were narrow. How much weight could they bear? Every so often she would hitch those shoulders carelessly with the air of an energetic filly frustrated, till now, at not being given free rein to dash forth — along a prescribed, exactly measured track. There lay the rub. Let her try to race into the ambiguous areas I had introduced!

I covered a yawn with my palm. "Yes, I know the Kraut's work. He gave me some good ideas. Oh, there are so many means for making a map hard to read. Nay, not merely misleading but incomprehensible! Names play a vital role. Switch them all around, till only the contour lines are the same as before. Interlace them, so that new place names seem to emerge spontaneously. Set them all askew, so that the user needs to turn the map around constantly till his head is in a spin. Space the names out widely so that the map seems dotted with unrelated letters like some code or acrostic. Include too many names, so that the map chokes with surplus data."

Grusha stared at me, wide-eyed.

"And that," I said, "is only the icing on the cake."

Back in cartography I gave her a tour of the whole cake. In line with the policy of clarity I intended to be transparently clear.

"Meet Andrey!" I announced in the first studio. "Andrey is our expert with flexible curves and quills."

Red-headed, pock-marked Andrey glanced up from his glass drawing table, floodlit from below. Lead weights covered in baize held sheets of tracing paper in position. A trainee, Goldman, sat nearby carving quills for Andrey's later inspection. At Goldman's feet a basket was stuffed with an assortment of wing feathers from geese, turkeys, ducks, and crows.

"Goose quills are supplest and wear longest," I informed Grusha, though she probably knew. "Turkeys' are stiffer. Duck and crow is for very fine work. The choice of a wrong quill easily exagger-ates a pathway into a major road or shrinks a river into a stream. Observe how fluidly Andrey alters the contours of this lake on each new tracing."

Andrey smiled in a preoccupied way. "This new brand of tracing paper cockles nicely when you block in lakes of ink."

"Of course, being rag-based," I added, "it expands on damp days by, oh, a good two percent. A trivial distortion, but it all helps."

The second studio was the scale room, where Zorov and assistants worked with camera lucida and other tricks at warping the scales of maps.

"En route to a final map we enlarge and reduce quite a lot," I explained. "Reduction causes blurring. Enlargement exaggerates inaccuracies. This prism we're using today both distorts and enlarges. Now *here*," I went on, leading her to Frenzel's table, "we're reducing and enlarging successively by the similar-triangles method."

"I do recognize the technique," answered Grusha, a shade frostily.

"Ah, but we do something else with it. Here is a road. We shrink a ten-kilometre stretch to the size of one kilometre. We stretch the next one kilometre to the length of ten. Then we link strand after strand back together. So the final length is identical, but all the bends are in different places. See how Antipin over here is inking rivers red and railway tracks blue, contrary to expectation."

Antipin's trainee was filling little bottles of ink from a large bottle; the stuff dries up quickly.

Onward to the blue studio, the photographic room where Papyrin was shading sections of a map in light blue.

"Naturally, Grusha, light blue doesn't photograph, so on the final printed map these parts will be blank. The map, in this case, is correct yet cannot be reproduced —"

Onward to the dot and stipple studio

. . . Remarkable what spurious patterns the human eye can read into a well-placed array of dots.

All of this, even so, was only really the icing. . . .

Grusha flicked her shoulders again. "It's quite appalling, Colonel Valentin. Well, I suppose we must simply go back to the original maps and use those for the Atlas."

"What original maps?" I enquired.

"Who knows any longer which are the originals? Who has known for years?"

"Surely they are on file!"

"All of our maps are in a constant state of revolutionary transformation, don't you see?"

"You're mocking."

"It wouldn't be very pure to keep those so-called originals from a time of exploitation and inequality, would it?" I allowed myself a fleeting smile. "Nowadays all of our maps are originals. A mere two percent change in each successive edition amounts to a substantial shift over the course of a few decades. Certain constants remain, to be sure. A lake is still a lake, but of what size and shape? A road still stretches from the top of a map to its bottom; yet by what route, and through what terrain? Security is important, Grusha. I suppose by the law of averages we might have returned to our original starting point in a few cases, though frankly I doubt it."

"Let us base our work on the first published Atlas, then! The least altered one."

"Ah, but Atlases are withdrawn and pulped. As to archive copies, have you never noticed that the published products are not *dated*? Intentionally so!"

"I must sit down and think."

"Please do, please do! I'm anxious that we co-operate. Only tell me how."

My studios hummed with cartographic activity.

Finding one's way to our gray stone edifice in Dzerzhinsky Square only posed a serious problem to anyone who paid exact heed to the city map; and which old city hand would be so naive? We all knew on the gut level how to interpret such maps, how to transpose districts around, and permutate street names, how to unkink what was kinked and enlarge what was dwarfed. We had developed a genius for interpretation possessed by no other nation, an instinct which must apply anywhere throughout the land. Thus long-distance truck drivers reached their destinations eventually. The army manoeuvred without getting seriously lost. New factories found reasonable sites, obtained their raw materials, and despatched boots or shovels or whatever with tolerable efficiency.

No foreigner could match our capacity; and we joked that diplomats in our capital were restricted to line of sight or else were like Theseus in the labyrinth, relying on a long thread whereby to retrace their footsteps. No invader would ever broach our heartland. As to spies, they were *here,* yes; but where was here in relation to anywhere else?

Heading home of an evening from Dzerzhinsky Square was another matter however. For me, it was! I could take either of two entirely separate routes. One led to the flat where tubby old Olga, my wife of these last thirty years, awaited me. The other way led to my sleek mistress, Koshka.

Troubled by the events of the day, I took that second route. I hadn't gone far before I realized that my new assistant was following me. She slipped along the street from doorway to doorway.

Should I hide and accost her, demanding to know what the devil she thought she was doing? Ah no, not yet. Plainly she had her reasons — and other people's reasons too. I dismissed the speculation that she was another "eye of Mirov." Mirov had practically dissociated himself from Grusha. She had been set upon me by the new breed, the reformers, so-called. Evidently I spelled a special danger to them. How could they create a new country while I held the key to the old one in my keeping?

I had not intended a confrontation quite so soon; but she was provoking it. So let her find out! I hurried up this prospekt, down that boulevard, through the alley, over the square. Workers hurried by wearing stiff caps. Fat old ladies bustled with bundles. I ducked down a narrow street, through a lane, to another street. Did Grusha realize that her gait was springier? Perhaps not. She had not lost her youthful figure.

At last, rounding a certain corner, I sprinted ahead and darted behind a shuttered kiosk. Waiting, I heard her break into a canter because she feared she had lost me. By now no one else was about. Leaping out, I caught her wrist. She shrieked, afraid of rape or a mugging by a hooligan.

"Who are you?" she gasped. "What do you want?"

"Look at me, Grusha. I'm Valentin. Don't you recognize me?"

"You must be . . . his son!"

"Oh no."

The distortions wrought by age, the wrinkles, liver spots, crow's feet and pot belly: all these had dropped away from me, just as they always did whenever I took my special route. I had cast off decades. How else could I enjoy and satisfy a mistress such as Koshka?

Grusha had also shed years, becoming a gawky, callow girl — who clutched my arm now in awkward terror, for I had released her wrist.

"What has happened, Colonel?"

"I can't still be a Colonel, can I? Maybe a simple Captain or Lieutenant."

"You're *young!*"

"You're very young indeed, a mere fledgling."

"Was it all done by make-up — I mean, your appearance, back at the Centre? In that case how can the career records . . . ?"

"Ah, so you saw mine?" Despite the failing light I could have sworn that she blushed. "Make-up, you say? Yes, *made up!* My country is made up, invented by us map makers. We are the makers of false maps, dear girl; and our national consciousness is honed by this as a pencil is brought to a needle-point against a sand-paper block, as the blade of a mapping pen is sharpened on an oilstone. Dead ground occurs."

"I know what 'dead ground' means. That merely refers to areas you can't see on a relief map from a particular viewpoint."

"Such as the viewpoint of the State . . . ? Listen to me: if we inflate certain areas, then we shrink others away to a vanishing point. These places can still be found by the map-maker who knows the relation between the false and the real; one who knows the routes. From here to there; from now to then. Do you recognize this street, Grusha? Do you know its name?"

"I can't see a signpost . . ."

"You still don't understand." I drew her towards a shop window, under a street lamp which had now illuminated. "Look at yourself!"

She regarded her late-adolescent self. She pressed her face to the plate glass as though a ghostly shop assistant might be lurking inside, imitating her stance. Then she sprang back, not because she had discovered somebody within but because she had found no one.

"These dead zones," she murmured. "You mean the gulags, the places of internal exile . . ."

"No! I mean places such as this. I'm sure other people than me must have found similar dead zones; and never breathed a word. These places have their own inhabitants, who are recorded on no census."

"So you're a secret dissident, are you, Valentin?"

I shook my head. "Without the firm

foundation of the State-as-it-is — without the lie of the land, as Mirov innocently put it — how could such places continue to exist? That is why we must not destroy the work of decades. This is magical — magical, Grusha! I am young again. My mistress lives here."

She froze. "So your motives are entirely selfish."

"I am old, back at the Centre. I've given my life to the State. I deserve . . . No, you're too ambitious, too eager for stupid troublesome changes. It is *you* who are selfish at heart. The very best of everything resides in the past. Why read modern mumbo-jumbo when we can read immortal Turgenev or Gogol? I've suffered . . . terror. My Koshka and I are both honed in the fires of fear." How could I explain that, despite all, those were the best days? The pure days.

"Fear is finished," she declared. "Clarity is dawning."

I could have laughed till I cried.

"What we will lose because of it! How our consciousness will be diminished, diluted, bastardised by foreign poisons. I'm a patriot, Grusha."

"A red fascist," she sneered, and started to walk away.

"Where are you going?" I called.

"Back."

"Can't do that, girl. Not so easily. Don't know the way. You'll traipse round and round."

"We'll see!" Hitching herself, she marched off.

I headed to Koshka's flat, where pickles and black caviar sandwiches, cold cuts and mushroom and spirit were waiting; and Koshka herself, and her warm sheets.

Towards midnight, in the stillness I heard faint footsteps outside so I rose and looked down from her window. A slim shadowy form paced wearily along the pavement below, moving out of sight. After a while the figure returned along the opposite pavement, helplessly retracing the same route.

"What is it, Valentin?" came my mistress's voice. "Why don't you come back to bed?"

"It's nothing important, my love," I said. "Just a street walker, all alone."

Part Two: *Into the Other Country*

When Peterkin was a lad, the possibilities for joy seemed limitless. He would become a famous artist. He dreamed of sensual canvases shamelessly ablush with pink flesh, peaches, orchid blooms. Voluptuous models would disrobe for him and sprawl upon a velvet divan. Each would be an appetizing banquet, a feast for the eyes, as teasing to his palate as stimulating to his palette.

Why did he associate naked ladies with platters of gourmet cuisine? Was it because those ladies were spread for consumption? How he had lusted for decent food when he was young. And how he had hungered for the flesh. Here, no doubt, was the origin of the equation between feasting and love.

Peterkin felt no desire to *eat* human flesh. He never even nibbled his own fingers. The prospect of tooth marks indenting a human body nauseated him. Love-bites were abhorrent. No, he yearned — as it were — to *absorb* a woman's body. Libido, appetite, and art were one.

Alas for his ambitions, the requirements of the Party had cemented him into a career niche in the secret police building in Dzerzhinsky Square; on the eighth floor, to be precise, in the cartography department.

Not for him a paint brush but all those damnable map projections. Cylindrical, conical, azimuthal. Orthographic, gnomonic. Sinusoidal, polyconic.

Not Matisse, but Mercator.

Not Gauguin but Gall's Stereographic. Not Modigliani but Interrupted Mollweide.

The would-be artist had mutated into an assistant in this subdivided suite of rooms where false maps were concocted.

"My dreams have decayed," he confided to friend Goldman in the restaurant one lunchtime.

Around them, officers from the directorates of cryptography, surveillance, or the border guards ate lustily under rows of fat white light-globes. Each globe wore a hat-like shade. Fifty featureless white heads hung from the ceiling, brooking no shadows below, keeping watch blindly. A couple of baggy babushkas wheeled trolleys stacked with dirty dishes around the hall. Those old women seemed bent on achieving some quota of soiled crockery rather than on delivering the same speedily to the nearest sink.

Goldman speared a slice of roast tongue. "Oh I don't know. Where else, um, can we eat, um, as finely as this?"

Dark, curly-haired, pretty-faced Goldman was developing a hint of a pot-belly. Only a proto-pot as yet, though definitely a protuberance in the making. Peterkin eyed his neighbour's midriff.

Goldman sighed. "Ah, it's the sedentary life! I freely admit it. All day long spent sharpening quills for pens, pens, pens . . . No sooner do I empty one basket of wing feathers than that wretched hunchback porter delivers another. Small wonder he's a hunchback! I really ought to be out in the woods or the marshes shooting geese and teal and woodcock. That's what I wanted to be, you know? A hunter out in the open air."

"So you've told me." Peterkin was lunching on broiled hazel-hen with jam. However, each evening — rain, snow, or shine — he made sure to take a five-kilometre constitutional walk, armed

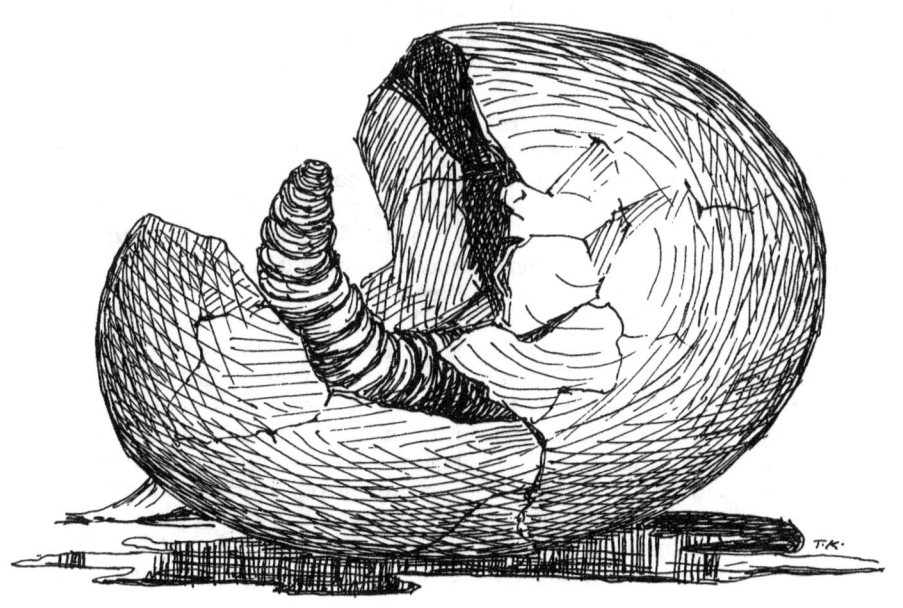

with a sketchbook as witness to his former hopes; rather as a mother chimp might tote her dead baby around until it started to stink.

Peterkin was handsome where his friend was pretty. Slim, blond, steely-eyed, and with noble features. Yet all for what? Here in the secret police building he mostly met frumps or frigid functionaries. The foxy females were bait for foreign diplomats and businessmen. Out on the streets, whores were garishly painted — do-it-yourself style. Slash lips, cheeks rouged like stop-lights, bruised eyes. Under the evening street lamps those ladies of the night looked so lurid to Peterkin.

Excellent food a-plenty was on offer to the secret servants of the State such as he. Goose with apples, breaded mutton chops, shashlik on skewers, steamed sturgeon. Yet whereabouts in his life were the soubrettes and odalisques and gorgeous inamoratas? Without whom, how could he really sate himself?

"So how are the, um, projections?" Goldman asked idly.

"Usual thing, old son. I'm busy using Cassini's method. Distances along the central meridian are true to scale. But all other meridian lines stretch the distances. That makes Cassini's projection fine for big countries that spread from north to south. Of course ours sprawls from east to west. Ha! Across a few thousand kilometres that's quite enough distortion for an enemy missile to miss a silo by kilometres."

"Those geese and turkeys gave their wings to shelter us! Gratifying to know that I'm carving patriotic pens."

"I wonder," Peterkin murmured, "whether amongst our enemies I have some exact counterpart whose job is to deduce which projections I'm using to distort different areas of land . . ."

Goldman leaned closer. "I heard a rumour. My boss Andrey was talking to Antipin. Andrey was projecting *the future*. Seems that things are going to change. Seems, for the sake of openness, that we'll be publishing true maps sooner or later."

Peterkin chuckled. This outlook seemed as absurd as that he himself might ever become a member of the Academy of Arts.

Yet that very same evening Peterkin saw the woman of his desires.

He had stepped out along Krasny Avenue and turned down Zimoy Prospekt to enter the park. It was only early September, so the ice-skating rink was still a lake dotted with ducks: fat quacking boats laden with potential pens, pens, pens. The air was warm, and a lone kiosk sold chocolate ice cream to strollers; one of whom was her.

She was small and pert, with eyes that were brimming china inkwells, irises of darkest brown. Her curly, coal-black hair — not unlike friend Goldman's, in fact — formed a corona of sheer, glossy darkness, a photographic negative of the sun in eclipse; the sun itself being her round, tanned, softly-contoured face. From the moment Peterkin saw her, that woman suggested a sensuality bottled up and distilled within her — the possibility of love, lust, inspiration, nourishment. She was a liqueur of a lady. She was caviar, licking a chocolate cornet.

Her clothes were routine: cheaply styled bootees and an open raincoat revealing a blotchy floral dress. Yet Peterkin felt such a suction towards her, such a powerful current flowing in her direction.

She glanced at him and shrugged with what seemed a mixture of resignation and bitter amusement. So he followed her out of the park, across the Prospekt, into a maze of minor streets which became increasingly unfamiliar.

Some empty stalls stood deserted in a square which must serve as a market place, so he realized that he was beginning to tread "dead ground," that unacknowledged portion of the city which did not figure on any plans. If inspectors approached by car they would be hard put to find these selfsame streets. One-way and no-entry signs would redirect them away. Such was the essence of this district; impenetrability was the key that locked it up safely out of sight.

Of course, if those same inspectors came on foot with illicit purposes in mind — hoping to buy a kilo of bananas, a rare spare part for a washing machine, or a foreign pornography magazine — they could be in luck. Subsequently they wouldn't be able to report where they had been with any clarity.

The moan of a saxophone assailed Peterkin's ears; a jazz club was nearby. Rowdy laughter issued from a restaurant where the drapes were drawn; he judged that a heavy drinking bout was in progress.

A sign announced *Polnoch Place*. He had never heard of it. How the sky had darkened, as if in passing from street to street he had been forging hour by hour deeper towards midnight. At last the woman halted under a bright street lamp, her ice cream quite consumed, and waited for him, so unlike the ill-painted floozies of more public thoroughfares.

He cleared his throat. "I must apologize for following you in this fashion, but, well —" Should he mention voluptuous canvases? He flourished his sketchbook lamely.

"What else could you do?" she asked. "You're attracted to me magnetically. Our auras resonate. I was aware of it."

"Our auras — ?"

"Our vibrations." She stated this as a fact.

"Are you psychic? Are you a medium?"

"A medium? Oh yes, you might say so. Definitely! A conduit, a channel, a guide. How else could you have strayed so far into this territory except in my footsteps?"

Peterkin glanced around him at strange facades.

"I've heard it said . . . Are there really two countries side by side — one where the secret police hold sway, and a whole other land which is simply *secret?* Not just a few little dead zones — but whole swathes of hidden terrain projecting from those zones?"

"Why, of course! When human beings yearn long enough to be some place else, then that somewhere can come into being. Imagine an hourglass; that's the sort of shape the world has. People can drift through like grains of sand — though only so far. There's a kind of population pressure that rebuffs intruders. For the second world gives rise to its own geography, but also to its own inhabitants."

"Has anyone mapped this other terrain?"

"Is that what you do, draw maps?" Her hair, under the streetlamp! Her face, like a lamp itself unto him!

His job was a state secret. Yet this woman couldn't possibly be an "eye" of the police, trying to trap him.

"Oh yes, I draw maps," he told her.

"Ah, that makes it more difficult for you to come here."

"Of course not. Don't you realize? Our maps are all lies! Deliberate lies, distortions. In the department of cartography our main brief is to warp the true shape of our country in all sorts of subtle ways."

"Ah?" She sounded unsurprised. "Where I come from, artists map the country with kaleidoscopes of colour. Musicians map it in a symphony. Poets, in a sonnet."

It came to Peterkin that in this other land he could at last be the painter of his desires. He had never believed in psychic phenomena or in a spirit world (unless, perhaps, it was the world of ninety-proof spirit). Yet this circumstance was different. The woman spoke of a *material* other world — extending far beyond the dead ground of the city.

Peterkin knew that he must possess this woman as the key to all his hopes, the portal to a different existence.

"So do you despise your work?" she asked him.

"Yes! Yes!"

She smiled invitingly — and wryly, as though he had already disappointed her.

"My name's Masha."

Her room was richly furnished with rugs from Central Asia, silverware, onyx statuettes, ivory carvings. Was she some black marketeer in art treasures or the mistress of one? Had he stumbled upon a cache hidden since the Revolution? Curtains were woven through with threads of gold. Matching brocade cloaked the bed in a filigree till she drew back the cover, disclosing silk sheets as blue as the clearest summer sky. Her cheap dress, which she shed without further ado, uncovered sleek creamy satin camiknickers . . . which she also peeled off carelessly.

"Take fright and run away, Peterkin," she teased. "Take fright now!"

"Run away from *you*?"

"That might be best."

"What should frighten me?"

"You'll see."

"I'm seeing!" Oh her body. Oh his, a-quiver, arrow notched and tense to fly into her. He laughed. "I hardly think I'm impotent."

"Even so." She lay back upon the blue silk sheets.

Yet as soon as he started to stroke her limbs . . .

At first he thought absurdly that Masha had concealed an inflatable device within her person: a dildo-doll made of toughest gossamer so as to fold up as small as a thumb yet expand into a balloon with the dimensions of a man. This, she had liberated and inflated suddenly as a barrier, thrusting Peterkin aside . . .

What, powered by a cartridge of com-pressed air? How risky! What if the cartridge sprang a leak or exploded? What if the compressed air blew the wrong way?

The intruder had flowed from Masha in a flood — from her open and inviting legs. It had gushed out cloudily, spilling from her like pints and pints of leaking semen congealing into a body of firm white jelly.

He gagged, in shock.

"Wh — what — ?"

"It's ectoplasm," she said.

"Ectoplasm —"

Yes, he had heard of ectoplasm: the strange fluidic emanation that suppos-edly pours out of a psychic's nostrils or ears or mouth, an amorphous milk that takes on bodily form and a kind of solidity. It came from her vagina.

Pah! Flimflammery! Puffs of smoke and muslin suspended on strings. Soft lighting, a touch of hypnosis and auto-suggestion. Of course, of course. Went without saying.

Except . . .

What now lay between them could be none other than an ectoplasmic body. A guard dog lurked in Masha's kennel. A eunuch slept at her door. She wore a chastity belt in the shape of a blanched, clinging phantom. Peterkin studied the thing that separated them. He poked it, and it quivered. It adhered to Masha, connected by . . .

"Don't try to pull it away," she warned. "You can't. It will only go back inside when my excitement ebbs."

And still he desired her, perhaps even more so. He ached.

"You're still excited?" he asked her.

"Oh yes."

"Does this . . . creature . . . give you any satisfaction?"

"None at all."

"Did a witch curse you, Masha? Or a magician? Do such persons live in your country?" Perhaps Masha belonged to somebody powerful who had cast a spell upon her as an insurance policy for those times when she crossed the in-between zone to such places as the park. If composers could map that other land with their concerti, or painters with their palettes, why not other varieties of magic too?

She peered around the white shoulder of the manifestation. "Don't you see, Peterkin? It's you. It's the template for you, the mould."

What did she mean? He too peered at the smooth suggestion of noble features. His ghost was enjoying — no, certainly not even enjoying! — Masha. His ghost simply intervened, another wretched obstacle to joy. A twitching lump, a body equipped with a nervous system but lacking any mind or thoughts.

"And yet," she hinted, "there's a way to enter my country. A medium is a bridge, a doorway. Not to any spirit-world, oh no. But to: that other existence."

"Show me the way."

"Are you quite sure?"

How he ached. "Yes, Masha. Yes. I must enter."

As his thoughts and memories flowed freely — of old desires, of canvases never painted and bodies never seen, of stuffed dumplings and skewered lamb and interminable cartographic projections — so he sensed a shift in his personal centre of gravity, in his prime meridian. He felt at once much closer to Masha, and anaesthetized, robbed of sensation.

His body was moving; it was rolling over on the bed, flexing its arms and legs — no longer his own body to command. Equipped with the map of his memories, the ghost had taken charge.

Now the ghost was making Peterkin's body stand up and put on his clothes; while he — his kernel, his soul — clung against Masha silently.

That body which had been his was opening and shutting its mouth, uttering noises. Words.

"You go along Polnoch Place —" Masha gave directions and instructions; Peterkin couldn't follow them.

He himself was shrinking. Already he was the size of a child. Soon, of a baby. As an Arabian genie dwindles, tapering down in a stream of smoke into a little bottle, so now he was entering Masha.

"I shall be born again, shan't I?" he cried out. "Once you've smuggled me over the border deep into the other country, inside of you?" Unfortunately he couldn't hear so much as a mewling whimper from what little of him remained outside of her. All he heard, distantly, was a door bang shut as the phantom left Masha's room.

Warm darkness embraced his dissolved, suspended existence.

Only at the last moment did he appreciate the worries of the persons in that other, free domain — who had been forced into existence by the frustrations of reality and who depended for their vitality upon a lie, which might soon be erased. They, the free, were fighting for the perpetuation of falsehood. Peterkin had been abducted so that a wholly obedient servant might be substituted in his place in the cartography department of the secret police.

Only at the last moment, as he fell asleep — in order that his phantom could become more conscious — did he understand why Masha had trapped him.

Part Three: *The Cult of the Egg*

Church bells were ringing out across the city in celebration, **clong-dong-clangle.** The great edifice on Dzerzhinsky Square was almost deserted with the exception of bored guards patrolling corridors. In the mahogany-panelled office of the head of the directorate of censorship, General Mirov rubbed his rubicund boozer's nose as if an itch was aflame.

"How soon can we hope to have an accurate Great Atlas?" he demanded sourly. "That's what *I'm* being asked."

Not right at the moment, however. The six black telephones on his vast oak desk all stood silently.

Valentin blinked. "As you know, Comrade General, Grusha's disappearance hasn't exactly speeded the task. All the damned questioning, the interruptions. Myself and my staff being bothered at our work as though we are murderers."

The ceiling was high and ornately plastered, the windows taller than a man. A gilt-framed portrait of Felix Dzerzhinsky, architect of terror, watched rapaciously.

"If," said Mirov, "a newly appointed deputy-chief cartographer — of reformist ambitions, and heartily resented because of those, mark my words! — if she vanishes so inexplicably, are you surprised that there's a certain odour of rats in your offices? Are you astonished that her well-connected parents press for the most thorough investigation?"

Valentin nodded towards the nobly handsome young man who stood expressionlessly in front of one of the embroidered sofas.

"I'll swear that Peterkin here has undergone a personality fluctuation because of all the turmoil."

Clangle, dong, clong. Like some mechanical figure heeding the peal of a carillon, Peterkin took three paces forward across the oriental carpet.

"Ah," said Mirov, "so are we attempting to clear up the matter of Grusha's possible murder hygienically in private? Between the three of us? How maternal of you, Colonel! You shelter the members of your staff just like a mother hen." The General's gaze drifted to the intruding object on his desk, and he frowned irritably "Things have changed. Can't you understand? I cannot suppress the investigation."

"No, no, no," broke in Valentin. "Peterkin used to be a bit of a dreamer. Now he's a demon for work. That's all I meant. Well, a demon for the old sort of work, not for cartographic revisionism . . ." As if realizing that under present circumstances this might hardly be construed as an endorsement, Valentin shrugged.

"Is that *thing* supposed to be a sample of his most recent work?" The General's finger stabbed accusingly towards the decorated egg which rested on his blotting paper, geometrically embellished in black and ochre and yellow. "Reminds me of some tourist souvenir on sale in a foetid East African street. Some barbaric painted gourd."

"Sir," said Peterkin, "it is executed in Carpathian *pysanka* style."

"You don't say?" The General brought his fist down upon the painted egg, crushing the shell, splitting the boiled white flesh within. "Thus I execute it. In any case, Easter is months away."

"You're unhappy about all these new reforms, aren't you, Comrade General?" Valentin asked cautiously. "I mean, *deeply* unhappy. You hope to retire honourably, yet what sort of world will you retire into?"

"One where I can hope to gather mushrooms in the woods to my heart's content, if you really wish to know."

"Ah, but will you be allowed such tranquility? Won't all manner of dark cupboards be opened?"

"I'm busy opening those cupboards," snapped Mirov. "As quickly as can be. Absurdist plays, concrete poems, abstract art, economic critiques . . . We scurry to grease their publication, do we not? Grow faster, trees, grow faster! We need your pulp. Bah! I'm somewhat impeded by the sloth of your department of cartography. I demand true maps, as soon as can be." With a cupped hand he swept the mess of broken boiled egg into a trash basket.

"Those dark cupboards also contain corpses," hinted Valentin.

"For which, you imply, I may one day be brought to book?"

"Well, you certainly oughtn't ever to write your memoirs."

"You're being impertinent, Valentin. Insubordinate in front of a subordinate." The General laughed barkingly. "Though I suppose you're right. The world's shifting more swiftly than I imagined possible."

"We aren't safe here, in this world that's a-coming."

The bells continued to ring out cacophonously and triumphantly as if attempting to crack a somewhat leaden sky, to let through rifts of clear blue.

Peterkin spoke dreamily. "The egg celebrates the mysteries of birth and death and reawakening. Simon of Cyrene, the egg merchant, helped Jesus to carry his cross. Upon Simon's return he found to his astonishment that all the eggs in his basket had been coloured with many hues."

"I'll bet he was astonished!" said Mirov sarcastically. "There goes any hope of selling my nice white eggs! Must I really listen to the warblings of this tinpot Dostoevsky? Has the cartography department taken leave of its senses, Colonel? Oh, I see what you mean about Comrade Peterkin's personality. But why do you bother me with such nonsense? I was hoping to catch up on some paperwork this morning and forget about the damned —"

"Ding-dong of rebirth in our land?"

"Carl Fabergé made his first imperial Easter egg for the Tsar and Tsaritsa just over a century ago," said Peterkin.

"Please excuse his circuitous approach to the meat of the matter, General," begged Valentin. "Almost as if he is circumnavigating an egg? I promise he will arrive there sooner or later."

"An egg is like a globe," Peterkin continued. "The department of cartography has never designed globes of the world."

"The world isn't shaped like an egg!" objected Mirov, his cracked veins flushing brighter.

"With respect, it is, Comrade General," murmured Valentin. "It's somewhat oblate . . . Continue, Peterkin!"

"Fabergé cast his eggs from precious metals. He inlaid them with enameling, he encrusted them with jewels. He even kept a special hammer by him to destroy any whose craftsmanship fell short of his own flawless standards."

"What is this drivel about the Tsar and Tsaritsa?" exploded Mirov. "Are you preaching counter-revolution? A return to those days of jewelled eggs for the aristocracy and poverty for the masses? Or is this a metaphor? Are you advocating a *putsch* against the reformers?"

"Traditions continue," Peterkin said vaguely.

"Yes," agreed Valentin. "We are the descendants of the secret police of the imperial empire, are we not? Of its censors; of its patriots."

"Bah!"

Peterkin cleared his throat. He seemed impervious to the General's displeasure. "The craft of decorating eggs in the imperial style continues . . . in the dead ground of this very city."

"Dead ground?"

"That's a discovery some of us have made," explained Valentin. He gestured vaguely through a window, to somewhere beyond the onion domes. "The wholesale falsification of maps produces, well, actual *false places* — which a person in the right frame of mind can genuinely reach. Peterkin here has found such places, haven't you, hmm? As have I."

Peterkin nodded jerkily like a marionette on strings.

"You're both drunk," said Mirov. "Go away."

"I can prove this, General. Comrade Grusha strayed into one of those places. She was following me, acting as an amateur sleuth. Ah, the new generation are all such amateurs compared to us! Now she haunts that place because she lacks the cast of mind that I possess — and you too, General."

"What might that be?"

"An instinct for falsification; for the masking of reality."

"I'm charmed at your compliment."

"You'd be even more charmed if you came with me to visit my darling young mistress Koshka who lives in such a place."

One ageing man regarded the other quizzically. "*You*, Valentin? A young mistress? Excuse me if I'm skeptical."

"You might say that such a visit is a rejuvenating experience."

Mirov nodded, misunderstanding. "A youthful mistress might well be as invigorating as monkey glands. Along with being heart attack territory."

"To enter the dead ground is rejuvenating; you'll see, you'll see. That's one frontier worth safeguarding — the border between the real and the ideal. Perhaps you've heard of the legend of the secret valley of Shangri-la? The place that features on no map? To enter it properly, a man must be transformed."

"That's where the egg crafters come into this," prompted Peterkin.

"*Internal exile,* General! Let me propose a whole new meaning for that phrase. Let me invite you to share this refuge."

"You insist that Comrade Grusha's still alive?"

"Oh yes. She walks by my Koshka's apartment at nights."

"So where does she go to by day?"

"I suspect that it's always night for her. Otherwise she might spy some escape route, come back here, stir up more trouble . . ."

"Are you telling me, Colonel Valentin,

that some zone of aberrant geometry exists in our city? Some other dimension to existence? I don't mean the one advertised by those wretched bells."

"Exactly. Just so."

Mirov stared at the portrait of Dzerzhinsky, who would have answered such an eccentric proposition with a bullet, and sucked in his breath.

"I shall indulge you, Colonel — for old time's sake, I'm tempted to say — if only to study a unique form of psychosis which seems to be affecting our department of cartography."

"It's best to go in the evening, as the shadows draw in."

"It would be."

"On foot."

"Of course."

"With no bodyguard."

"Be warned, I shall be armed."

"Why not, General? Why ever not?"

But Peterkin smirked.

So that same evening the three men went by way of certain half-frequented routes, via this side street and that alley and that square until the hollow raving of the bells was muffled, till distant traffic only purred like several sleepy kittens, and a lone owl hooted from an old-fashioned cemetery amidst century-old apartment blocks.

As if playing the role of some discreet pimp, Peterkin indicated a door. "Gentlemen, we will now visit a lady."

Mirov guffawed. "This mistress of yours, Colonel: is she by any chance a mistress to many?"

"My Koshka lives farther away," said Valentin, "not here. Absolutely not here. Yet don't you already feel a new spring in your gait? Don't you sense the weight of years lifting from your shoulders?"

"I admit I do feel somewhat sprightly," agreed the General. "Hot-blooded. Ripe for adventure. Ah, it's years since . . . Valentin, you look like a younger man." He rubbed his hands. "Ah, the spice of anticipation! How it converts tired old mutton into lamb."

Peterkin admitted them into a large foyer lit by a single low-powered light bulb and decorated by several large vases of dried, dusty roses in bud. A faint memory of musky aroma lingered, due perhaps to a sprinkle of essential oils. A creaky elevator lifted them slowly to the third floor, its cables twanging dolorously once or twice like the strings of a double bass. Valentin found himself whistling a lively theme from an opera by Prokofiev — so softly he sounded as though he was actually labouring up marble stairs, puffing.

The dark petite young woman who admitted these three visitors to her apartment was not alone. Mirov slapped the reassuring bulge of his gun, as if to stun a fly, before relaxing. The other two occupants were also women, who wore similar cheap dresses patterned with roses, orchids, their lips and cheeks rouged.

"May I present Masha?" Having performed this introduction, Peterkin slackened; he stood limply like a neglected doll.

"This is my older sister Tanya," Masha explained. Masha's elder image smiled. If the younger sister was enticingly lovely, Tanya was the matured vintage, an intoxicating queen.

"And my aunt Anastasia." A plumper, far from frumpish version, in her middle forties, a twinkle in her eye, her neck strung with large phoney pearls. Absurdly, the aunt curtsied, plucking up the hem of her dress quite high enough to display a dimpled thigh for a moment.

"We are chief Eggers," said Anastasia. "Tanya and I represent the Guild of Imperial Eggs."

The large room, replete with rugs from Tashkent and Bokhara hanging on the walls, with curtains woven with thread of gold, housed a substantial carved bed spread with brocade, almost large enough for two couples entwined together, though hardly for three. All approaches to it were, however, blocked by at least a score of tall narrow round-topped tables, each of which served as a dais to display a decorated egg, or two, or three. Some ostrich, some goose, others pullet and even smaller, perhaps even the eggs of canaries.

On gilt or silver stands, shaped as swans, as chariots, as goblets, these eggs were intricately cut and hinged, in trefoil style, gothic style, scallop style. Some lids were lattices. Filigree windows held only spider's webs of connective shell. Petals of shell hung down on the thinnest of silver chains. Pearl-studded drawers jutted. Doors opened upon grottos where tiny porcelain cherubs perched pertly. Seed pearls, lace, gold braid, jewels trimmed the doorways. Interior linings were of velvet . . .

To blunder towards that bed in the heat of passion would be to wreak devastation more shattering than Carl Fabergé could ever have inflicted on a faulty golden egg with a hammer! What a fragile cordon defended that bedspread and the hint of blue silk sheets; yet to trespass would be to assassinate art — if those eggs were properly speaking the products of art, rather than of an obsessional delirium which had transfigured commonplace ovoids of calcium, former homes of bird embryos and yolk and albumen.

Aunt Anastasia waved at a bureau loaded with egging equipment: pots of seed pearls, jewels, ribbons, diamond dust, cords of silk gimp, corsage pins, clasps, toothpicks, emery boards, a sharp little knife, a tiny saw, manicure scissors, glue, nail varnish, and sharp pencils. The General rubbed his eyes. For a moment did he think he had seen jars of beetles, strings of poisonous toadstools, handcuffs made of cord, the accoutrements of a witch in some fable?

"Aren't we just birds of a feather?" she asked the Colonel. "You use the quills of birds for mapping-pens, so I hear. We use the eggs of the birds."

"I've rarely seen anything quite so ridiculous," Mirov broke in. "Your eggs are gimcrack mockeries of Tsarist treasures. Petit bourgeois counterfeits!"

"Exactly," agreed queenly Tanya. "Did not some financier once say that bad money drives out good? Let's suppose that falsity is superior to reality. Did *you* not try to make it so? Did you not succeed formerly? Ah, but in the dialectical process the false gives rise in turn to a *hidden truth*. The map of lies leads to a secret domain. The egg that apes treasure shows the way towards the true treasury."

Tanya picked up a pearl-studded goose egg. Its one oval door was closed. The egg was like some alien space-pod equipped with a hatch. Inserting a fingernail, she prised this open and held the egg out for Mirov's inspection.

On the whole inner surface of that goose egg — the inside of the door included — was a map of the whole world, of all the continents in considerable detail. The difference between the shape of the egg and that of the planetary globe caused some distortion, though by no means grotesquely so. Mirov squinted within, impressed despite himself.

"How on earth did you work within such a cramped volume? By using a dentist's mirror, and miniature nibs held in tweezers? Or . . . did you draw upon the outside and somehow the pattern sank through?"

"Somehow?" Tanya chuckled. "We *dreamed* the map into the egg, General, just as you dreamed us into existence by means of your lies — though unintentionally!"

She selected another closed egg and opened its door.

"Here's the map of our country . . . Ours, mark you, not yours. If you take this egg as your guide, our country can be yours, too. You can enter and leave as you desire."

"Be careful you don't break your egg."

Aunt Anastasia wagged a warning finger.

"The same way you broke the *pysanka* egg," squeaked Peterkin, emerging briefly from his immobility and muteness. "Most of those eggs are technical exercises — not the one you hold." (For Mirov had accepted the egg.) "That was dreamed deep within the other country." Having spoken like a ventriloquist's dummy, Peterkin became inert again.

However, he left along with his two superiors — presently, by which time it was fully night.

"Maps, dreamed on the insides of eggs! Deep in some zone of absurd topography!" Mirov snorted. "Your escape hatch is preposterous," he told Valentin, pausing under a streetlamp.

"Actually, with respect, we aren't *deep* in the zone at all. Oh no, not here. But that egg can guide —"

"Do you believe in it, you dupe?"

"Why didn't I receive one for my own? I suppose because I already know the way to Koshka's place . . ."

Mirov snapped his fingers. "I know how the trick's done. They use transfers. They draw the map on several pieces of paper, wet those so they're sticky, then insert with tweezers on to the inside of the shell. When that dries, they use tiny bent brushes to apply varnish."

Mirov removed the map-egg from his overcoat pocket, knelt, and placed the egg on the pavement under the brightness of the streetlamp. Was he surprised by the limber flexibility of his joints?

"I can prove it." Producing his pistol, Mirov transferred his grip to the barrel, poising the handle above the pearl-studded shell. "I'll peel those transfers loose from the broken bits. Ha, dreams indeed!"

"Don't," said Peterkin in a lame voice only likely to encourage Mirov.

"Don't be a fool," said Valentin.

"A fool, is it, Comrade Colonel?"

"If you're told not to open a door and you insist on opening it —"

"Disaster ensues — supposing that you're a child in a fable."

Valentin knelt too, to beg the General to desist. To an onlooker the two men might have appeared to be fellow worshippers adoring a fetish object on the paving slab, cultists of the egg indeed.

When Mirov brought the butt of the gun down, cracking the egg wide open and sending tiny pearls rolling like spilled barley, a shock seemed to ripple along the street and upward to the very stars, which trembled above the city.

Although Mirov probed and pried, in no way could he discover or peel loose any stiffly varnished paper transfers.

When the two sprightly oldsters looked around again, Peterkin had slipped away without a word. The two men scrambled up. Night, and strange streets, had swallowed their escort utterly. Despite Valentin's protests — which even led the men to tussle briefly — Mirov ground the shards of egg to dust under his heel, as if thereby he might obliterate any connexion with himself.

Eventually, lost, they walked into a birchwood where mushrooms swelled through the humus in the moonlight. An owl hooted. Weasels chased mice. Was this woodland merely a park within the city? It hardly seemed so; yet by then the answer scarcely mattered, since they were having great difficulty remembering who they were, let alone where they were. Already they'd been obliged a number of times to roll up their floppy trouser legs and cinch their belts tighter. Their sleeves dangled loosely, their shoes were clumsy boats, while their overcoats dragged as long cloaks upon the ground.

"Kashka? Kishka? Was that her name? What *was* her name?" Valentin asked his friend.

"I think her name was Grusha . . . no, Masha."

"Wasn't."

"Was."

Briefly they quarrelled, till they forgot who they were talking about.

Through the trees, they spied the lights of a village which strongly suggested home. Descending a birch-clad slope awkwardly in their oversized garments — two lads dressed as men for a lark — they arrived at a yellow window and peered through.

Beautiful Tanya and Aunt Anastasia were singing to two huge eggs resting on a rug. Eggs the size of the fattest plucked turkeys, decorated with strange ochre zig-zags.

Even as Valentin and Mirov watched, the ends of the eggs opened on brass hinges. From each a bare arm emerged, followed by a head and a bare shoulder. The two women each grasped a groping hand and hauled. From out of each egg slowly squeezed the naked body of a man well past his prime, one with a beet-red face, though his trunk was white as snow.

"How did they fit inside those?" Mirov asked Valentin.

"Dunno. Came out, didn't they? Maybe there's more space than shows on the outside . . ."

The two newly-hatched men — who were no spring chickens — were now huddling together on a rug by the stove, modestly covering their loins with their hands. Their faces looked teasingly familiar, as if the men might be a pair of . . . long-lost uncles, come home at last from Siberia.

By now the two boys felt cold and hungry, so they knocked on the cottage door. Aunt Anastasia opened it.

"Ah, here come the clothes now!" Anastasia pulled them both inside into the warmth and surveyed them critically. "Oh, what a mess you've made of those suits. Creases, and mud. Never mind. They'll sponge, and iron. Off with them now, you two, off with them. They're needed. Tanya, fetch a couple of blankets for the boys. We mustn't make them blush, with a chill or with shame."

"Do we have to sleep inside those eggs?" asked Mirov, almost stammering.

"Of course not, silly goose! You'll sleep over the stove in a blanket. Those two other fellows will be gone by the morning; then you'll have a better idea who you both are."

"Koshka!" exclaimed Valentin. "I remember. *That* was her name."

"Now, now," his aunt said, "you needn't be thinking about girls for a year or two yet. Anyway, there's Natasha in the village, and Maria. I've kept my eye on them for you two. How about some thick bacon broth with a sprinkle of something special in it to help you have nice dreams?"

"Please!" piped Valentin.

When he and his brother woke in the morning a lovely aroma greeted them — of butter melting on two bowls of cooked buckwheat groats. The boys only wondered for the briefest while where they had been the evening before.

Tanya and Anastasia had already breakfasted, and were busy sawing ducks' eggs.

Ω

HOUSE HAUNTED

Where memories linger, and Now's an infringer,
You'd opt to partake of the Past for a bout.
But while you're recessing, the ghosts, coalescing,
Recite as a choir: "This is *our* place. GET OUT!"

— **Robin June Nakkula**

Weirdisms

HOMUNCULUS: The transmutation of metal wasn't the only goal of alchemy. The creation of artificial life obsessed many medieval philosophers and "miracle men." Paracelsus and Fludd were among those who concerned themselves with creating *homunculi.*

SACRED TO WOMEN

by Robert Sampson

White light slipped across cracked limestone the color of elephant hide. Back glow from the flashlight faintly illuminated the rough cave walls, more faintly touched the faces of two men and a girl. In the darkness, their faces glimmered like suspended masks.

The light beam twitched along the stone. It stopped perhaps twelve feet above the dirt floor, illuminating a figure painted on the wall.

"That is The Sorcerer," Lane said. "This is his holy place."

It was "He" by courtesy. The monster, glaring malignantly from its height, showed no human attribute. Round black eyes stared from a square white head. From the skull jutted two stiff horns. The spotted black and white body bulged thickly, a swollen horror. But it was powerful. The figure shuddered with power.

David Barron snicked on his flashlight, playing additional brilliance upon the figure. He was a solid man in his early thirties, with the shoulders and neck of a professional athlete. Sunburn reddened his nose and forehead. He stood with one hand spread against the chilly limestone, staring hard-faced at the painted figure. Finally he realized that the others waited for his reaction.

He said noncommittally: "That's sure weird."

Lane said: "The Sorcerer is represented as gravid. We're not sure why."

His daughter, Sharon, said, "It's a holdover from the rites of the Great Mother." Her eyes glittered white in the white light. "Ten thousand years later, they still used her symbols."

"The symbolization is quite different," her father said sharply.

She laughed. "Pregnant is pregnant."

The tension between them ached like a torn muscle. They had forgotten their careful politeness of an hour before. They were more angry now, less careful. Their words glinted with cutting edges.

Barron said hastily: "How old is the painting?"

Lane shrugged. "Eight thousand, ten thousand years."

For ten thousand years, it had crawled across the rock like a spotted slug. Holding down disgust, Barron said: "Long time."

"Show David the animals," Sharon cried.

The light bobbed and darted along the walls. As it steadied, Barron saw confusion. Cracks, black lines writhed among dull blurs of color. He stared, without understanding, at dim red and yellow, mottled brown, orange darkening to brown.

Smiling, he shook his head: "I can't . . ."

At that moment, his mind pulsed, as if some profound internal resistance had yielded. Lines and colors took on form. He saw that painted animals swarmed across the wall, plunged out over the ceiling into darkness beyond the light.

"Bison," Sharon said. "Thirty of them. And horses."

Her arm jabbed into the light, fragile against the enormity of the wall. "There's a deer. See the horns?"

Barron thought her voice overstressed. She glittered with excitement and her head tossed in the glow.

"Look behind it all. Can you make it out, David?"

"Mastodon," he said at last.

"Mastodon," she cried in triumph. "It was the first thing they drew. It outlines the whole wall."

He saw now that the sprawling outline of the mastodon contained dozens of animals. The drawings tangled one over the other, presenting no common size or orientation in space.

"It's a unique find," Lane said. His light jabbed and darted. "Thousands of years, they drew on that wall. And redrew. You can see the style of their art change, the attitudes of the animals. The way they used to paint inside the outlines."

The air was cold and moist in Barron's nose. By then he realized that he should not be in the cave at all. It was wrong for him. It exerted nearly a physical pressure. His body hardened itself against the dangerous air, the menace of the walls. Aware of the Sorcerer's stare, he forced himself to stand unmoving, taking slow, long breaths.

"Beautiful work," he said.

"Unique," Lane said in a low voice. "A unique addition to the history of art."

Sharon laughed again. "Some art. It's death magic. Hunters' magic. Draw the animal and you'll be sure to kill it."

Lane said in a slow voice, strongly ironic: "How nice if it were that simple."

She said: "We should seal up the whole thing and forget it."

Barron said: It's pretty overwhelming. It's hard to take it all in."

"It becomes oppressive," Lane said. He glared toward Sharon, who stood swinging the beam of her flashlight across the wall, lighting a succession of figures. "And I'm afraid it becomes late."

"Five o'clock," Barron said, not too quickly.

"It's a long way out," Lane said. "We'd better start. I'll lead."

His light ran across the dirt floor to an irregular opening at the base of the wall.

Kneeling in the dust, he bent forward, pushing the flashlight ahead of him. The opening seemed barely wide enough to admit his shoulders.

As his legs and feet vanished, Sharon said: "I hate this place. It's an anomaly, really — a holy place dedicated to death. That's what makes it strange. The Great Mother was life, you know: the flow of life, continuing creation, increase. But this room celebrates killing. In polychrome."

"I'll follow you out," he said.

As her legs disappeared, he turned, gliding his light across the wall for a final inspection. In this sanctuary, he thought, he should feel at home. Here among these symbols of death.

Later, as he inched along the crawlway from The Sorcerer's room — a narrow tube smelling intensely of damp earth and stone — it seemed to him that The Sorcerer had changed position on the wall. He could not remember; he was not sure.

Fear came down the crawlway. His legs felt cold and horribly exposed.

At last the crawlway widened. He saw their flashlight beams reaching toward him.

They stood in the mouth of the cave, packing away their gear. The huge lift of the overhang arched above them. Beyond stretched evening sky, the dark blue streaked by yellow and gray clouds and flecked by darting dots of gold.

"Sun birds," Sharon cried. She stood beside him and pointed upward. The golden dots swung in slow spirals. "The story is, you see sun birds just before great magical forces appear."

He stared down at her face with regret and pity. Hollow eyes, sunken cheeks, the bone pressing hard against the pale skin. The skeleton feel of her fingers against his wrist. The girl he had once known had starved away to this gaunt rack. Only her voice was familiar.

He said: "I never associated the Cro-

Magnon with magic."

"Their lives were saturated in magic. Hunters' magic, women's magic."

Cold breeze whipped against their faces. A mile away, beyond the silver streak of the river, he saw the lighted windows of the chateau. On the slopes slanting toward the river, it was already night.

Barron picked up his pack and Sharon's. They followed Lane down a rocky trail.

"When the Cro-Magnon were here," Sharon said, "the river was much wider. They only walked a hundred meters to the water. The valleys were all grassland then. The herds grazed along the foot of the mountains."

"Sounds like you were there."

"I've got a vivid imagination."

"Watch your footing," Lane said. "The car's right over here."

Barron took Sharon's arm. She said softly, in a private voice: "You didn't like The Sorcerer much, did you?"

"No," he said. "No. He reminded me of a slug. A spotted slug."

He hesitated, fighting back the words. But they came in spite of him. "I saw one once on a dead man's face."

"That's awful."

"Well, that was a long time ago."

They found the Land Rover and it carried them jarring down a French slope away from the cave in the Pyrenees that had known the voices of Cro-Magnon. He felt tense and soiled. In his mind was the face of a dead man in Baylor, Alabama. A spotted slug angled across his forehead.

Barron followed Sharon up a steep staircase into the hushed heights of the chateau. They entered a dim green corridor that smelled clean and hot and looked as impersonally neat as a museum exhibit.

Barron said: "I had no idea Uncle Henry had this kind of money."

"Grandfather was in oil when you made money in oil," Sharon said. "And Daddy married a rich woman — he did it twice." Her voice grated with sour gaiety. "When he retired, we wandered over to Europe and he met Eloise — and here we are. This chateau's been in Eloise's family for like two hundred years. So she says. I suppose she knows."

"I'd like to meet her before I leave."

"You probably won't. She drops in every six weeks or so. She's very famous. Full professor at Pasteur Institute. In Biology. You mention Eloise Aumont and people light up like you were talking about the Grand Canyon. They never heard of Eloise Lane."

"The Great Mother," he said lightly.

She glared up at him, her face all eyes. "My mother's dead. I wish we could go home."

"Home? You've been here, what? Ten years?"

"I hate it. Dear God, I hate it. What am I doing in France? I want to be back in Texas. I could earn a living in Texas. What can I do here? Look at the mountains and tell Daddy the food bill's too high."

They walked slowly past innumerable small polished tables brilliant with glassware.

"This place is a big old memorial to the glories of the Aumonts," she said. "Their pictures. Their chairs. Their mirrors. Their china for sixty. And an army to keep it up — sixteen servants for the three of us."

"Four, counting me," he said gently.

"You go back to the States in a couple of weeks, and that leaves two. And the famous professor of Biology."

"Next year, I'll come stay a month, how's that?"

"I'd like that. I love your southern accent."

"Lawsey me," he said. "Well, Dad's been on me for years to come visit you."

"Listen to your father." They stopped before a door of dark wood, glowing with polish. Within the shining surface, he saw the blur of their reflections, as if buried faces peered out.

"Well, here's my wonderful room," she said. "Listen, after you change, come on down to the Sun Room. I want to show you something." She hesitated. "I need a favor."

"Anything I can do," he said, moved by the harshness of her stripped face.

He walked on to his own room, which was wide and high and filled with polished wooden surfaces.

"Rich girls don't have fun," he muttered.

He stood holding his soiled shirt, eyes half closed, his features set and grave, struggling against the lift of his own private anger. The Lanes and their problems pressed him mercilessly. He felt choked by their problems, the vagueness and urgency of them, the ambiguity of their needs.

The day he had arrived, before he unpacked his bags, Uncle Henry had slipped into this room, guilt in his smile, as if he meant to speak of shameful things.

Instead, he spoke of Sharon.

"She's a troubled girl, I guess that describes it, David. Talking to her, it's like shoving your hand into a sackful of broken bottles. She's always angry."

In stress, his speech lost its pedantic quality and took on a different rhythm, a different imagery. His stubby fingers fumbled around his mouth.

"She wars with her step-mother and she bites at me. She spends her time at the cave, digging up bones in the Mother's Room — so she calls it. She says she is researching. I dread to think what a qualified archaeologist would call it. I'm afraid she's become — somewhat odd."

Twisting up his face, he turned away. "It bothers me a great deal. While you're here, if you happen to learn anything . . . Understand, I don't ask it. But if you find out anything you can decently tell me, I'd appreciate it."

Remembering his uncle's smothered voice, Barron hurled his shirt at the bed. "Appreciate it!" he snarled.

He needed no one else's trouble. He had trouble enough. His mind was rotten with trouble.

Half an hour later, he stepped from a short stairway into the immensity of the Sun Room. It was less a room than an architectural event, being as large as a basketball court. French windows lined along two sides gave it a curious insubstantiality. The vast floor contained groups of chairs and divans that huddled about floor lamps like primitive tribes about hearth fires.

Barron wound his way among furniture clusters toward a fireplace flaring in the north wall. As he approached, Sharon looked up sharply from a low-toned dispute with her father.

"There you are. I wondered if you got lost. I want to show you something marvelous."

Lane uttered an acrid syllable of amusement. "Don't let her batter you with theory, David. Dinner will be in half an hour."

Her urgent fingers tugged him through the shadows at the left of the fireplace. A switch clicked. White light streamed upon a table sheeted in plastic, its length strewn with stones and tobacco-brown fragments arranged in ranks. After a moment, he realized that he was looking at human bones. A dark odor, musty and disagreeable, hovered over the table.

Extending her hand, Sharon caressed an irregular chunk of stone, perhaps two inches thick, about fourteen inches high. The color was gray, the sides chipped and irregular, the surface split by repaired cracks.

She said: "This just might be the oldest statue in the world."

Stubby projections at the base could have represented legs. He could see no arms or head.

"It's hard to make out," she said. "Here are the breasts, the hips here. All grossly exaggerated, like all Venuses."

Her slender finger darted and pointed. He could see no more than that the stone had been worked.

"What is this?"

"I think it represents the Great Mother," she said. "That's what's so wonderful."

He said, watching her shining face: "It must be old."

"Nearly twenty-five thousand years old," she said. "The Great Mother came first, you see. They worshipped her seven or eight thousand years before the Hunters and The Sorcerer. It was a matriarchy then. Woman's magic ruled their lives. A priestess led the rites. She became the embodiment of The Great Mother during their ceremonies. They celebrated the continuity and continuation of life. They called the herds to return each year. Isn't that a lovely concept. The Great Mother stood for the constant renewal of life."

With an effort at lightness, Barron said: "Sounds like Pleistocene feminism."

Her emaciated face tightened. "Please don't patronize me."

"You're awful touchy," he said. "I'm interested. Where did you find this?"

"About a foot and a half under the floor of the Mother's Room. Mixed in with a tangle of skeletons. Female skeletons. With their skulls broken."

Her eyes flared at him, as if she made a telling point. He lifted a long, shaped stone from the table and ran his fingers across the ancient surface. "Wonder what happened back then."

"I call it murder. Mass murder. I think it happened all at once. For thousands of years, women ruled and they followed The Great Mother. Then one day, the Hunters rose up and killed the worshippers. They broke the statue and left it in the dirt. And there it's been all these centuries. Till I dug it out and cemented the pieces together."

The intensity of her conviction astonished him. He started to speak and stopped, feeling that something old and feral had risen between them, an intangible presence smelling of old bone.

His hand clenched the stone. It was as if he gripped the handle of a pistol. Disorientation shivered through his mind. He might have been standing in the humid Alabama evening, three months ago, peering across the yard toward that figure crouched dark against a gray-white sky. Seeing the hot, white wink of shots. Hearing glass smash and brick shatter to his right.

As he lifted his pistol and fired, as he had fired a thousand shots before. Brief flame startled his eyes. The figure darted right into darkness.

He became aware that he stood staring down into Sharon's eyes. Cold whispered through him.

She was saying: "They slaughtered The Great Mother. Murder's the quick answer, isn't it? Settles all debate. A typical male response, a feminist might say." Her voice lifted and shook. "You have to admit that."

He felt himself grinning fixedly. Saw her face change and horror round her eyes.

She cried: "Oh, David, I'm sorry. I didn't mean . . ."

She would, of course, know about that night in Alabama.

He stood measuring the knowledge in her eyes until Lane approached them, saying, in his quiet voice: "I think dinner's ready."

Servants came and went with easy grace, changing the dishes. Lane ate with appetite, but Barron could not taste his food. Sharon pushed at her meal like a sullen child. She seemed infatuated with the story of The Great Mother and repeated it again, less emotionally but with total belief hardening her eyes. She would not look directly at

Barron.

Finally, over dessert, Lane thrust down his spoon with an impatient gesture and said: "For what it's worth, David, our Cro-Magnon, in this region, at that period, did seem to have a matriarchal society. Unfortunately, the tale of The Great Mother cult and its eventual destruction, that Sharon has so richly embellished, is hardly substantiated by any facts I'm aware of."

Sharon balefully regarded her dessert, a glory of cherries and brandied cake. She pushed it away. "They died with violence. You've seen the skulls."

"Hundreds of years may separate those deaths." His voice said that they had argued this point before. "I suspect a trained archaeologist couldn't distinguish simultaneous deaths within that fraction of time. It may be that the Mother's Room was used for the burial of female criminals."

"Nonsense," Sharon jeered.

She watched narrow-eyed as a servant removed her dessert and substituted, with the air of performing a small miracle, a tiny cup of coffee.

She said: "All you have to do is sit in the cave and feel the atmosphere. The story comes out of the walls."

In an uninflected voice, Lane said: "Intuition is no substitute for informed judgement." Turning to Barron, he added: "In deference to the remarkable wall art, I've asked Professor de Ruelle to come make an initial survey of the site."

Sharon's hands jerked and coffee dripped from her fingers. "De Ruelle? Daddy, he's impossible."

Ignoring her, Lane said: "De Ruelle is head of the Prehistoric Studies section of the Bordeaux museum. He's quite interested in what we — and particularly Sharon — have found. He has promised to arrive tomorrow for an initial examination."

"Not tomorrow," Sharon exclaimed.

"His party will arrive about ten."

She thrust out of her chair, looking absurdly like a small hawk in attack. "He can stay out of the Mother's Room. That's my discovery."

"He'll wish to inspect that part of the cave, of course. He's particularly interested in the statue — and exactly where you found the fragments. I certainly hope you took care in marking the original positions of the pieces."

Her face glared in the warm light. She said in a brittle voice: "He can't have the Mother's Room."

Lane's slitted mouth whispered: "Your behavior is intolerable."

She cried shrilly: "Why can't I make you understand anything? The Mother's Room's not for men. It's sacred to women. That's the whole point of it. It's sacred to women."

An hour later, Barron sat shivering in his dark bedroom. His chair faced an open window through which poured a breeze smelling of cold stone. The air bristled with electricity. When he moved, hairs stiffened along his arms and sparks snapped irritably in his clothing.

He growled: "That's crazy, Sharon. Uncle Henry would skin me alive."

"It's got to be tonight."

"That's too bad."

"David, that puffed-up professor will be here tomorrow. It'll be too late then."

"If you want to take the statue back to the Mother's Room, then do it. Just don't ask me."

"She's too heavy for me to carry far, David."

Through the window he looked out across the faintly glittering river to the mountain slope heaving blackly against a clear black sky. The Cro-Magnon cave was invisible in the darkness. But he could feel it out there on the slope, gaping like an unhealed wound, the painted slug in its belly.

He muttered, "Damnit," with controlled violence. "It's way too late."

"It's not nine-thirty. Remember, you

promised to help me."

"Not to do some fool thing like this."

She had stopped crying now and sat in ceremonial rigidity at the other side of the window. He could see only the pallid smudge of her face, blurred as if her features were partially erased.

"So maybe it's crazy," she said. "It is crazy. But I'm responsible for The Great Mother. I really feel that. I found her. I patched her. Now I want to put her back in her sanctuary, the way it used to be. One last time."

"That's awful neurotic, Sharon."

"I'm responsible for her, David. That's me — responsible. That's the way I felt after Mom died. I felt responsible for that, too. Isn't that ridiculous? Doing penitence. Not sleeping or eating. Maybe I am crazy."

"Not crazy," he said. "That's grief."

"That's guilt. So what am I guilty about?"

His fist battered the soft arm of the chair. He felt sullen reluctance to think about entering the cave. His heart seemed to shrink and harden. With surprise, he realized that he was afraid, and that he was going to confront that fear.

His mouth uttered a hard little whisper of sound. Heaving to his feet, denying fear and anger, he said in a heavy voice: "Yes, I suppose I did promise. Fool me."

When he opened the bedroom door, a hard little flash of electricity jabbed from the handle into his finger.

She said: "I'll bring the Land Rover around the side. You can carry the statue through the French windows right to the car."

He nodded sullenly. She hurried away down the dim hall. Each time she took a step, the carpet seethed with greenish-white sparks. She might have been a goddess striding across a thunderstorm. He found the sight vaguely frightening.

At the table in the Sun Room, he lifted the statue of The Great Mother from the table, grunting with the effort. It seemed heavy as boilerplate. The limestone gritted under his fingers and hard edges bit into his skin.

"Well, let's go," he muttered.

He moved away from the table, placing his feet carefully, gripping the stone against his chest. Its weight pulled mercilessly at his arms and shoulders.

Before he had crossed the room, the muscles in his back convulsed in cramp. A searing pain cut into his side. For a moment, he thought the statue would fall and his heart made a sick leap. He reeled against a chair, let the statue fall to the cushion. Pain wrenched his face and exposed his teeth.

Kneeling by the chair, he rested his forehead on cold wicker. The pain advanced from red to white. His thoughts confused and he felt himself begin to slide upward into dimness. But he did not quite faint. Twisting his shoulders, flexing his arms, he resisted stubbornly. After a while the cramp eased, the dimness receded. The world cleared. He felt wicker against the cold moistness of his skin.

Finally he rose, cautiously testing the balance of his body.

"Good grief," he said to the statue. "Knock it off. I'm trying to take you home."

Moving with elaborate care, he lifted the statue from the chair. It did not seem to drag so relentlessly against his muscles. Superstitious fright flickered in some remote part of his mind, as if a window shade had trembled in the wind. Elbowing aside one of the open French windows, he crossed the stone-paved terrace toward the Land Rover. Sharon's anxious face peered toward him.

"What kept you?"

"Had a cramp."

He lowered the statue onto crushed newspaper in a cardboard box and adjusted this on the car floor. They rolled quietly from the courtyard into the outer dark.

Sharon drove rapidly along a road the width of a string, turned left over a low cement bridge. Gun-metal water winked below. Then the slope lifted them. The road shrank to a rock-studded track. The Rover jolted and pitched, headlights bobbing. Branches snatched at the windows. Far below and to the left, chateau lights glowed serenely above massed foliage.

She said: "It's so big out here on the slope. All that sky open over you and the mountain wall. You feel so small."

"We're pretty little compared to the scenery." He considered his own emotions. "Vulnerable. I don't care much for your cave."

Her eyes flickered toward him. "Because of The Sorcerer?"

"Not hardly." He hesitated, feeling the presence of the statue at his feet. "The Sorcerer's my kind, isn't he? After all, I shot a man."

Limestone masses flashed palely in the pitching headlights. She said: "I heard something about it."

"I tell you what I think. You kill a person, you lose something. Some protective skin gets stripped away. You're exposed. I think after you've shot somebody, you become completely accountable. Nothing more is excused. From then on, you're fully responsible for whatever you do."

"I know the feeling," she said.

"It wasn't anything like a television shoot-out." He felt vague surprise that he would tell her this. "It was all messy and confused. When I shot, I thought I'd missed. He ran away. See, back of our house, there's this big drainage ditch. Usually it's dry, full of Johnson grass. Well, when the police finally got there, they found him about fifty yards off, down in the ditch. He was on his back, looking up out of the grass. The bullet cut an artery. So he bled to death down in there. While he lay there, a big spotted slug crawled up on him. That's how I saw him. With the flashlights on his face and the slug across his forehead. I keep remembering that."

"He could have killed you."

"But he didn't. I killed him. He'd broken into the house and stolen mother's silver tea pot and a creamer. If she'd been alive, she'd of had a fit. And he got my VCR rewind unit. Not two hundred dollars worth of stuff. Not worth shooting a man for."

Her chilly hand briefly touched his. "I'm terribly sorry."

"In a hundred years, who'll know or care?"

But he had not told her everything. Not quite. One private thing he kept unspoken. It remained buried in his mind, hard as a flint arrowhead.

"Let's talk about something else," he said.

"Here's the cave," she said. They jarred to a stop, and he stepped out among ancient stones.

Just inside the entrance to The Mother's Room, Barron stood holding a flashlight in either hand.

As Sharon labored forward, arms clutching the statue, he lighted the rough floor ahead of her. It seemed to be hard clay coated with a greasy gray dust. Clusters of flat stones studded the surface. Among these, she shuffled slowly, head strained back, sucking in violent breaths.

Finally she knelt, lowering the statue to the floor. He saw her shoulders heave as she fought for air.

"Are you all right?" he called.

She nodded without speaking. The room smelled coldly of raw earth and dust.

He allowed one flashlight beam to stray from her hunched figure. Blackness swallowed the light. He could not see the far wall. Overhead lifted harsh stone, all knobs and angles, nearly twenty feet above her. By the left wall, a wide ditch had been dug, bordered by piles of dirt darker than the floor. He thought of the skeletons tangled there out of sight and flicked the beam away.

He had seen enough; he was ready to leave.

Her flashlight snapped on. Its white light touched a mound rising from the floor.

"Come in a little," she called. "I want you to see this."

He advanced warily into the room, conscious of the dark.

She said: "That is the mound where the Priestess sat. You can see how the floor stones are grouped around it."

He saw a squat mound of brownish clay, flattened at the top and front. It looked like something children had piled up during half an hour's play. But this had endured for twenty thousand years.

"I imagine they covered the mound with skins during their rites," she said. "Now look at these."

Her light ran across two smaller mounds positioned before the seat of the Priestess. Hollowed out like crude open shoes, they brimmed with shadow.

"I can't quite see," he said, taking an unwilling step forward. His skin felt dry in the damp chill and his heart seemed unsteady. Reacting badly to this place, he thought.

"I expected at first that they would hold the feet of the statue. But they're too wide apart."

"Holes for lights, maybe."

"No. Look here."

Seating herself on the mound, she adjusted her booted feet over the hollows, spreading her legs wide apart. Her skeletal face grinned at him. "Very immodest position."

"Very. And I suppose the statue was propped against the mound?"

She rose, startled. "Why'd you say that?"

"The mound's flat in front."

"Wait a minute." With an effort, she caught up the statue of The Great Mother and settled it heavily against the face of the mound. They stood measuring it with their eyes.

"Good fit," he said.

"I never noticed," she cried. "The Priestess straddled the statue. . . . Fertility rites, of course! It's the childbirth position."

"You have a good imagination."

He took a careful step back toward the entrance. His light jerked across bare stone and sterile clay, and he was acutely aware of the ceiling overhead, half a mile of pitiless rock concentrated above them.

She came to stand beside him. He felt her shiver.

"We'd better go," he said.

"So that's the way it was," she said. For a moment, her light touched the statue erect against the mound. "Well, I've done my part."

They moved from The Mother's Room back through the linked chambers leading to the cave entrance, sixty feet away. In the blackness behind them, The Great Mother waited patiently for the commencement of her rites.

The Land Rover crept into the courtyard behind the chateau. It had rained ten minutes earlier, and the stone pavement gleamed as if waxed.

Sharon stopped the machine by a plastered wall where a yellow-tile roof drain chuckled rainwater into the court. "You go on up," she said. "It's awful late. I'll see you in the morning."

"I'll wait for you."

"No need." She tossed her head gaily and her narrow face glowed. He was startled by her happiness. Rummaging in her purse, she said: "Take this with you. Look at it a while. I saved it to show you after you saw The Mother's Room."

She pressed a hard object into his palm and closed his fingers over it.

"This is a real Paleolithic Venus," she said. "You find lots of them at Russian sites. Not many in the Pyrenees. She's what The Great Mother is all about — a real honest-to-God woman. You can give her back tomorrow."

They said good night. He climbed out and stood, faintly scowling, as the Land Rover splashed away. Suspicion worked in him like a fermenting must. At last he moved to the light by the doorway and opened his hand.

He held a thick oval of greenish stone, smoothed and carved to the shape of an enormously obese woman. Head, shoulders, arms were barely suggested and the feet merged to a blunt point. Massive hips and buttocks bulged from the body. Over the swollen belly sagged immense breasts. It was an odious caricature of woman. It felt vaguely warm.

In his room, he placed the Venus on the dresser and crossed to the window. He stood looking out across the river toward the unrelenting black mass of the mountain. After a few minutes, he saw distant automobile lights flicker along the slope.

He watched them rise, feeling no surprise and no anger. Finally they stopped and darkness took them. He closed the window.

"Good night, Sharon," he said.

Early the following morning, Henry Lane paused in the doorway to the breakfast room, pouring out a violence of French that had the sound of water rushing downhill. Servants darted in the corridor. Wheeling, Lane marched stiff-shouldered toward Barron, sitting at the table.

"David," Lane said in the thinly over-polite voice of strain, "have you any idea where Sharon has got to?"

Guilt pulsed behind Barron's smile. Setting down his coffee cup, he said with diplomatic inaccuracy: "I haven't seen her since early morning. She was going up to the cave."

"The cave," Lane said. "Obviously the cave." His hands clenched, as if gripping a disobedient daughter. "We're leaving for Foix at once, and she's at the cave."

"She isn't back yet?" David asked sharply.

"Apparently not. And we must leave now to meet the train."

Alarm rose in Barron like suddenly uncovered flame. He said: "You go on. I'll drive up and get her."

"Please, David. If you would be so kind. You might," he added, with quiet ferocity, "remind her to change her clothing and to wash her hands, when she returns. Good Lord! Wish your enemies willful daughters."

Barron grinned. His lips felt inflexible, and apprehension, like a sickly cloud, swelled in his body.

He forced the car as fast as the road permitted.

The sun floated low in a milky sky. Clear pale light struck gray shadows from every tree and rock.

His mind pulsed and jerked. He could make no time. From the chateau, the slope appeared smoothly green. When experienced at first hand, it was creased by dips and rises, like the robes of a marble statue. The road convulsed among these, the car rocking and jittering.

His negligence horrified him. To watch her go. To do nothing. But who would think she'd spend the night in that cave?

To honor The Great Mother, he thought. Responsible. The last Priestess.

Gravel crackled as he crested a rise. The suspension shuddered. Ahead the trail angled sharply up past limestone crumbled by weather and fat little trees. He saw cliffs stern against the sky.

He fought the steering wheel with a kind of angry pleasure. It was how you felt when succeeding at a difficult job. His mind grew airy and large, capable of many things at once. He knew that sensation well. It was the satisfaction of the quarterback, seeing his pass arc exactly into the receiver's arms. The pleasure of the hunter making the hard shot, seeing the quarry stumble and drop.

The same complex joy he had felt, that Alabama night, facing another man's bullets, concentrating as his own weapon discharged its single precise round. Too dark for sights. Align by intuition, squeeze, fire — full mastery of his weapon, a technically excellent performance. A beautiful shot.

As if a paper target waited for the bullet.

He could not forgive himself that moment of pride. In exercising his skill, he had forgotten consequences. Only later, looking at the dead face, seeing the spotted slug, symbols of his achievement, did he examine his own self-satisfaction.

To feel shame rip him now, more terrible than any bullet.

His eyes burned. The arch of the cave was a black cancer against the streaked gray stone. He stared intently toward that hole where life and death co-existed in separate rooms.

Perhaps his anxiety was wasted; perhaps the Land Rover was gone and Sharon back at the chateau, looking for him, grinning faintly.

But the Land Rover, he saw, was still parked near the cliffs. And so she was still in there.

Snatching a flashlight and first-aid kit, he loped from the car toward the cave.

A deep gouge slanted back into the cliff, creating a wide-floored shelter open to the sun. Boulders studded the slanting floor. Some thirty feet back, floor and ceiling closed to a black gap, high as a small child, and split by a septum of stone. On the right, the way into the deep cave; at left, entrance to the two small chambers leading to The Mother's Room.

Into the left entrance Barron trotted, harried by anxiety.

The first chamber was narrow and tall, the raw stone smudged by lichen, gray-green and black. Tiny leaves, vivid green, scattered the rock face. In the mud along the far wall clustered minute orange flowers.

As he stooped to enter the second chamber, a dangling vine touched his face. He dodged, thinking *snake*, felt the cold constriction of his heart. He entered a shallow room where vines sprawled along the walls and ferns trailed their fronds down the rock. From boulders bordering the path thrust dozens of small leafed branches.

He could not understand why she had decorated this outer chamber.

As he jogged past, he pulled a branch free. It had not been cut and crammed into a hole, but was a growing plant. White roots fuzzed the end.

His mind shrank to a single cold point, intensely aware.

Across his face blew humid air that smelled of soil and vegetation. Branches thick with leaves bent into the trail. He eyed them sharply and ducked away. As he did so, his temple struck stone.

White light burst behind his eyes. He fell to one knee, open-mouthed. Ice ran along his back. For one terrible moment, he thought the flashlight broken. Then through distorting tears, he saw the beam white against his boot.

He pushed erect. The corridor ahead seemed filled with silver-gray light, like that of a clouded moon. He wiped his eyes, tested the strength of his legs. Stepped forward and saw that the light remained.

In the glow he saw long branches trembling from the walls, their ends sheathed in bright-green leaves. Ahead, across the entrance to The Mother's Room, hung a waterfall of vines and fern. Behind the leaves blazed light like luminous milk.

He shoved furiously, without comprehension, against the leaves and plunged through into blinding shine.

Currents of light, rich as star stuff, flowed around him, rolling and eddying like boiling milk. Within the flow glimmered scarlet and shadings of blue, hard clear green, and yellow like stabs of sunlight. Light streamed in sheets along the walls, across fern and leaf. Overhead, light rotated in frothing layers, as it seemed to drain upward through stone toward the sky.

He roared: "Sharon!" Shielding his face, he squinted toward the mound.

Sprawling on the mound, the source of the light, lolled a figure without shape. He could not see it clearly. Through a cloud of tears, he saw a form white as meringue. Rolling thick surfaces gleamed and sagged, and vast limbs seemed to sprawl apart. From between these, a dazzling core gushed light. Light rushed against him, warm and thick, harsh with erotic sweat.

Hands spread before his eyes, he waded through light toward the mound. Tripped. Fell heavily. A remote part of his mind remarked that one hand was hurt, but he felt no pain. Streaming face set, he crawled forward across a shuddering surface of leaves and tiny flowers, yellow and orange.

"Sharon!"

Masses of flesh elastic under his hands, the body like greased pulp. She mouthed rhythmically in a voice he did not recognize, with words he could not understand.

Locking both arms around her nakedness, he tugged her immense weight against him. He hauled her free of the mound. Grunting with strain, he struggled with her toward the entrance.

Concealed stones struck his feet. Her dreadful weight resisted his strength. From her poured cadenced sound, part song, part chant, wholly strange.

Into the room spilled vines, twisting as they grew. Along their length burst fat red flowers. The wall jarred against his back. Leaves rustled. He could not find the entrance. The chamber crackled with growth and wings beat behind the shining air. Terror disoriented him.

As he stumbled suddenly backward among pitching branches. As he strained the unresisting bulk of her into the next chamber, his breath white thorns. As he struggled backward through masses of leaves.

Bright moss coated the trail. From the stones, small white flowers reached toward her light.

He fell, cracking his knee. Rose and pulled, gone mindless with effort, conscious only of pulling and stepping. Fell. Tasted blood in his mouth. Struggled erect, strain stabbing his back, pain in his stomach, fingers deep in her slippery flesh.

One step back. And another.

The rasp of rock against his arms; the odor of crushed leaves.

Behind him, something snorted sharply. He smelled musk, heard a frantic rattle of hooves.

He could not think. The fierce light dimmed and she no longer cried out. He dragged.

Until pale light surrounded them, and, with lunatic strength, he lifted her, weaving toward the bar of white light, and collapsed to his knees, and tugged her into the front area of the cave.

They lay a long time, shuddering and gasping. Blood darkened on her lacerated back. At last he pushed up on a quivering arm to stare down into her puffy face. She opened opaque eyes, regarding him as if he were far away.

"Sleepy," she muttered.

"Come on. Sleep in a minute."

He weaved erect. It was Sharon, sure enough. A thick-bodied, round-faced Sharon, skin flabby at arm and throat. He wrapped her in his coat. She did not seem to understand where she was. Pain knotted his stomach and he pressed one hand against it, wondering if he had torn a muscle. The sodden shirt clung to his chest.

They blundered into the sunlight.

Before them, the slope fell away and he could see for miles across the valley.

A few hundred yards away ran a broad river, milky with sediment. The air was moist and chill. He could not see the chateau. To his right scattered dark evergreens. On the lower slopes, thick foliage, flecked with red and yellow leaves, shook in a light wind.

Beyond the trees, extending to the limits of sight across the yellow and green valley, moved the herds. Endless herds, drifting slowly in clusters and strings, grazing as they moved. Longhorned bison and horses shaggy with hair, and many light-brown animals with creamy bellies and graceful legs. From the far side of the river, a pair of deer, hugely antlered, stood rigid, watching him.

The beauty of the scene lifted him. He felt light and large, his senses brilliant. He seemed to float above a sea of life, seeing every eye, tracing every hair. Their low muttering filled the air with a tone low and continuous and so exciting that he found it hard to breathe.

He called her to look. Her head drooped against his shoulder and she spoke indistinctly. The sky was, he noted, a hard blue, the color as intense as antique glass. High up the color softened to milky blue, streaked by pallid clouds. Across that different sky, a single bright contrail slowly extended itself.

Even as he realized that the scene was an image superimposed upon the air, it trembled and began to thin. The center melted out, as if wind blew against a design in cloud. Behind showed a dimmer, harder landscape.

Part of the chateau, grotesquely small, appeared behind the bison. The deer and milky river hung suspended above the flash of the modern river, far down.

He saw valley, animals, sky pale, dissolve, vanish.

Pain brought him to his knees. Inside

his lower body, he felt a thrusting and pushing, as if something alive struggled there. He cried out, jerked loose his belt, tore at his shirt.

From his swollen nipples dripped a pale fluid, sticky to the touch.

He clutched himself without understanding. He felt that his body had somehow become glossed with female flesh. As if male and female shared the same bones.

Pain concentrated itself. He rolled over on his side, making a low feral sound. His eyes glittered with sick amazement.

At his side, Sharon slumped, arms wrapped across her eyes. She cried.

Cold wind rose behind and caught up dry leaves within the cave entrance and spun these lightly across them. As that chilled air flowed over him, dark patches gradually mottled his skin.   Ω

CALIBAN'S NAME

Cannibal is the anagram
Of the name Prosper gave me,
Caliban, a harsh thing,
A savage eater. Who knows
What crimes I might commit,
What dire dreams inherit?
But he could reshape me cleverly
Like the letters of my identity.
His music made me tame,
And overgorged on sound,
Laid low with words,
I let my bleaker appetites sleep.
But if my nature is impermeable,
My nurture impossible
(As the magus said),
Then I must wake. Why should he
Think unwisely otherwise or call me names
Worse than the one he gave
Before Prosper punished
Or Caliban betrayed?
My self is a sea where evil blows
With storms darker than any wizard owns,
And even he cannot fed this glutton
For long on songs.

— Ace G. Pilkington

EXACT CHANGE

Nina Kiriki Hoffman

I flew to the school bus stop in the old-fashioned way, by turning into a bird — a raven, to be exact. Great-Aunt Fayella had been telling the class at home in Chapel Hollow about other methods of flying, something about understanding the forces of air, but all the understanding I wanted to do yet was to understand that muscles plus feathers plus air and a little technique equaled loft. Flying fast above the land that frosty morning, delighting in the warmth of movement and feathers, I looked down at brown fields edged with green and black pine, the creek a gray ribbon under the overcast sky, pale dirt roads creeping across the ground like mole tunnels. The air tasted of cold and woodsmoke. North, the little town of Arcadia huddled in a fold between hills, on the Oregon side of the Columbia River. I could have flown all the way to Arcadia, but I liked taking the bus. All us Chapel Hollow kids did, now that we were growing into our powers and could take care of the town kids.

Dropping down to earth at the bus stop on Lost Kettle Road, I shifted back into my black-haired self, wearing a black dress, black stockings, and black ankleboots, and joined my sister Annis, who walked, most mornings; she had her magics, but shape-shifting wasn't a strong one with her; her power was more earth than sky, a slow, strong, unstoppable force once she put her mind to anything. More dangerous and less flashy than mine. She was bundled in her lavender jacket with the fur trim around the hood. She hugged herself. We both watched our breath rise. I let my skin thicken and fur a little under my clothes so I was warm enough.

"Did you see the bus, Jaimie?" she asked.

"I forgot to look. I was watching the Harrisons' sheep."

"Did you get your homework done?"

"Me?" I said, and grinned at her.

"Of course not," she said, and sighed.

"Just marking time in school," I said. I grabbed half my hair and started braiding it. Some of it was still feathers, but I worked it in, loving the raven blackness of it. I thought about school. Lots of people at school would have been happy if I stayed home, which was one of the main reasons I went.

Just then our cousins Michael and Laura dropped out from the sky, Michael dragon-shaped, Laura, Laura-shaped, hunched uncomfortably on his back. She looked almost as pale as her white winter coat. She never engineered her own changes; what little power she had would thread a needle for her, but not much more. She depended, for most of the things that went on at the Hollow, on the kindness of family, and of course we weren't really kind. Michael would carry her to the bus stop — which was two miles from the house — if she were late getting started, but he never promised to be nice about it.

Laura pulled a comb out of her backpack and ran it through her heavy blond hair, which had been disarrayed by the winds of passage. Michael changed back to his winter self, wearing a brown jacket, black jeans, and black boots, but there were still whiskers at the outer ends of his eyebrows.

"Dork," said Annis, "you shouldn't dragon so close to the road."

"Nobody was on it. I checked." They stuck out their tongues at each other.

"Not even the bus?" Annis asked when she got her tongue back in her mouth.

"No sign of it," said Michael. "What do you want to do to the driver today?"

"Maybe it was something he couldn't help, like a flat tire," said Laura.

"Maybe it was something somebody could help, like a kid being late. Barney. Maybe it was Barney." Michael glanced sideways at Annis, a wicked grin on his face. He knew Annis liked Barney even though we weren't supposed to like anybody from outside Chapel Hollow. Especially not town kids. "Now that we're learning Change, everything should be more interesting. I can't wait to experiment. I think Barney would make a great owl, with those glasses."

"Not very original," I said. "You know what would be really interesting? Turning someone into a tapeworm."

"You're horrible," said Laura.

"They'd remember it the rest of their life. I wonder if tapeworms enjoy being tapeworms. Living on leftovers. Ugh."

"Not leftovers," said Michael. "If they're leftovers, they go in the ice cave. This is stuff in somebody's stomach."

"Gross," said Laura.

"Turning somebody into a tapeworm. Hmm. Picking the stomach to put them in, that would be another tricky part," I said. I smiled at Laura. "Your stomach might be nice."

"Oh, stop it, Jaimie," said Annis. "You're disgusting."

I subsided. Annis didn't interfere very often, but when she did, she was likely to steam-roller over anybody who bothered her.

Presently the bus drove up. Just before it stopped, Laura looked at her watch. "Scotty's not late," she said. "You were early. Leave him alone."

"Bossy," said Michael, tugging on her hair. I checked my watch. Laura was lying. Scotty, the bus driver, was fifteen minutes late. I decided to let it ride; maybe this way we'd be late for school, and I wouldn't have to spend so much time arguing with Mrs. Cherry about why I hadn't done my homework, and then figuring out something nasty to do to her for bothering me. We picked up our day packs and waited for Scotty to open the door. Like everybody else connected with school besides us, Scotty was a townsperson. Some days it looked like he wasn't going to open the door; he never really wanted to at all; but in the end, he always did. He knew if he didn't open the door we'd open it for him.

Today he opened the door right away. Scotty, a young guy with long brown hair and a bushy mustache that drooped down to his collar practically, looked more upset than usual. Annis, Michael, and I climbed on first. Laura, coming up behind us, said, "What's the matter?"

"Nothing. Nothing," said Scotty. His voice sounded strained. I glanced back and saw him touch her hand, and suddenly I felt something new and different and odd. My usual reaction to seeing somebody touching Family uninvited would be to devise a punishment and mete it out without thinking about it, but there was something about this touch —

"Come back, children," said an oily voice from the back of the bus. "Come back and sit down and be good."

I looked toward the back of the bus. A man with a gun stood there. His clothes were light gray and looked a little like pajamas; there was a number stenciled across the front. The man was large and pale and his eyes looked almost clear; his forehead was covered with sweat beads. He was aiming the gun at Barney Vernell's head and smiling. Barney was the only other kid on the bus, which was wrong; there ought to be the Gallagher kids, and the Doughertys, and Wendy Harrison, and Paul Davis.

I took a step back, to be directly in front of Laura, who probably couldn't stop bullets. I was pretty sure I could. Michael and Annis paused, frozen, in the aisle. I reached behind me, and Laura took my hand. "Tapeworms," she murmured.

"What?"

"Shut up!" said the man. "Come sit down this instant, or I'll hurt your friend."

"Why should we worry about someone else?" Michael said loudly.

"Would you rather I shot you or your sister?"

"Nuts to that!"

Laura squeezed my hand. "Toads, Jaimie," she muttered.

"What?" I said again. My head felt full of cotton balls. My tongue was dry. My heart was beating like a trapped bird's wings.

"Shut up!" yelled the man. "Sit down! Be good!"

"Why change the habits of a lifetime?" Michael said. "Jaimie, do something, will you?"

I blinked, and started thinking again. Michael, not the best of magic students, always lost it when something unexpected happened, and Annis took too long to heat up, though seeing Barney at risk had probably gotten her started. "Uh," I said. Laura's thumb stroked my hand, reassuring. I thought back to Saturday's lesson, about change. "Changing yourself is natural," Great-Aunt Fayella had said. Michael and I had nodded; we loved changing into other things and were both precocious at it. "Changing others is a much more complicated task. The first element of change is understanding. Understand what change means, understand the object you are going to change, and understand the thing you will change it into." She had given us each a toad to hold. "Study these carefully. Try to understand them. I assure you that understanding will stand you in good stead the rest of your lives."

I had carried my toad around all day, watching it, touching it, letting it catch flies, noticing how unhappy it was when it got too dry, giving it moisture, listening for its voice. I touched every part of it, and used innersight to see its tiny organs and systems. Michael had left his toad in the classroom after an hour's study, and Laura put hers in a terrarium. Annis dropped hers in her pocket and forgot about it.

None of us had tried a really big change on someone else yet, just talked about it. Great-Aunt had taught us to be afraid of our powers. "If you're afraid of them, you will respect them. I had a cousin once, very strong in fire, who burnt herself up because she felt cold. Be careful, children. Power can kill you."

I thought about my toad, and I stared at the man with the gun, who was aiming it at Michael now. Annis stood sideways in the aisle, her arms crossed over her chest, her eyes wide, and I could sense the power building up in her, hot and heavy and scary. She hadn't learned much control yet. If I didn't do something soon, she'd unleash her power, and I wasn't sure anybody would survive that. I tuned to innersight and stared at the man. He was obscured by the seat and by Barney (who looked strange in all his organs and bones and things, without those glasses and that shock of tow hair and the air of diffidence), but after a moment I focused just on the man.

"Be good children!" yelled the man. His lungs moved and his throat moved and his tongue moved; his teeth moved, and even his stomach moved. "Be good children!" he yelled again. I looked at his brain, and down at the muscles stretching and curling, a plaited mosaic laid over his organs, gripped to his bones. My sight dived deeper, swam to the surface, dived again, so that he flickered: white bones, red muscle, gray, olive green, dark red organs; vertebrae strung like beads on his spinal cord; then back out to the surface, patterned hair rooted to the double-layered skin. As I studied him, other information came to me: I understood he was full of dark need, a need that was dirty and oily, a need that reminded me a little of how I had felt when I teased Annis and Laura about turning Barney into a tapeworm. I shivered. I looked at his hand as my sight shifted from muscle to bone to capillaries to skin (the gun like black smoke with his fingers curled around it) and saw along his arm and hand a flex of muscle, a ripple, traveling —

I felt a click in my head and thought, I understand. I brought my toad image forward and settled it over the man's image. I bit my lip and reached for power, asking the Presences for more than I had ever channeled before, and it came to me, flowed through me, seeped into these two images. First they flashed: man, toad, man, toad. Then they strobed, switching places more quickly. Then they blended.

A shot broke the air, and then a thud sounded as the gun hit the floor. Back in my body, having lost my concentrated detachment, I felt the tension in my shoulders, the frozen grip I had on Laura's hand. I turned quickly to see if she was all right behind me. She nodded; we both glanced at Scotty. His eyes were wide, his face utterly pale.

"Ow," said Michael.

I looked back. Annis was hugging Barney, who looked astonished. Michael had a hand to his right shoulder. Blood was seeping between his fingers and down the back of his winter jacket, losing itself under his pack straps. "Annis, when you've got a minute," he said. His voice had lost its earlier stridency.

She let go of Barney, who shakily steadied his glasses. She still had an aura of dark, churned-up power surrounding her like a cloud of bees. She went to Michael and, pulling his hand away, cupped his shoulder in her hands and channeled power through it.

Presently she let go. "Thanks," said Michael, probing the shoulder with gentle fingers. They came away red. He stared at his own blood a minute, moved his arm, nodded. He took a deep breath, exhaled, then turned around, his expression remote. He stared at Scotty, who looked back. "You picked us up," said Michael.

"Seemed like my best bet," said Scotty.

"I don't understand," Annis said.

"He had that man on board, and he picked us up. Not the other kids. Us."

"I thought you might be able to handle him. I knew the other kids couldn't."

We all stared at each other for a long moment.

"Chapel Hollow Promise," said Scotty.

I bit my lip. I had forgotten the covenant our family had made with the Arcadia townspeople, to protect them against outside threats. Most of them didn't like us; and we weren't very nice to them; but if anything went wrong, they could ask us for help, and we would give it. In return for the Chapel Hollow Promise, Arcadia kept silent about who we were and what we could do.

Michael's shoulders relaxed. He took another deep breath. "You're right. I forgot. You're right."

"I know you're too young to honor it, but I didn't know what else to do."

Michael shuddered. "I'm sorry. You're right. Okay." He sat down suddenly and leaned his head back over the edge of the seat, his eyes closed. His face was pale.

"You handled it, Miss Jaimie?" said Scotty to me.

"I think so," I said. It was the first time he'd called me Miss. The honorifics started when we had proved ourselves. We both looked back. Barney held up a large toad, gripping it with finger and thumb behind its forelegs.

"He was on the bus before I started it. I didn't know until after I'd picked up Barney. I've never seen him before, but it looked like he escaped from prison somewhere. What are we going to do with him?" said Scotty, just as if we were grown-ups and deserved to decide.

And Laura, least-powered Laura, bleeding-heart Laura, inadequate, incapable, too kind, said, "Let's just leave him on the road."

I looked at her face and realized there was someone behind it I didn't really know at all.

"Sounds about right," said Scotty. He opened the folding bus door and walked down the steps, and the rest of us followed him, Barney coming last and carrying the toad.

"It's cold," Laura said. There were frost ferns across the dirt of the ditch by the road, and the thin thread of water in the bottom had ice sheeting across it.

"Yes," said Scotty. "He might freeze. He might get run over. He might survive, who knows."

"And menace the children of toaddom," said Michael.

Barney set the toad down and we watched it. It hopped away from the ditch, toward the center of the road. It hopped again. Barney stuck out his shoe and headed the toad off, so that it hopped back toward the ditch.

"Do we tell anybody?" Annis asked Scotty.

"Probably not. Unless you want to tell your Family."

"If Jaimie wants," said Michael. We held celebrations when people passed certain milestones.

I shrugged and watched my toad hop away. It was beautiful.

"Guess I better go see if any of the kids I skipped on the way in are still waiting," said Scotty. "We're going to be real late. Anybody want to invent a reason for that?"

"Flat tire," said Laura as we filed back on the bus. Barney and Annis, together in public for the first time, sat in the very last seat on the driver's side. Michael sprawled across one in the middle, and Laura picked the one right behind Scotty as he started the bus.

I walked back and picked up the gun, gripping it by the handle between finger and thumb. "What about this?" I asked.

"Could you change that into some-

thing else?" said Scotty, watching me in the rearview mirror. "I'd just throw it out the door, but some kid might pick it up and shoot himself."

"I'll see," I said, and sat in a seat on the door side, holding the gun in both hands, trying to understand it, using innersight to study it. Curved, tempered metal, small explosive packets coiled inside, hammer, strength, power, trigger, handle. I thought, this thing is my brother. Elegant and dangerous, likely to go off without warning, hurting people. I met Scotty's eyes in the rearview mirror, wondering if that was how he thought, that Chapel Hollow kids were loose guns. I held the gun and understood it, then imagined a billiard ball, a solid chunk of something with a smooth hard coating on it. I brought the images together, with the same flicker/strobe/-blending, and found myself holding an eight-ball. I grinned and set it in the aisle. It rolled along the ridged black rubber floor mat down toward the front of the bus as Scotty stopped by the Gallagher farm, where Megan and Charlie and Sarah and Eddie were waiting.

Scotty picked up the eight-ball before he opened the door. He snorted, and smiled at me, and put the eight-ball in the glove compartment, and, as he let the children and the cold air in, I realized something else had changed: I had a strange new sense of community. For a little while it hadn't been us against them, Chapel Hollow versus townspeople, but six people working together against a menace. It reminded me of my Uncle Hal's stories of the floods of '48 and '62, when Chapel Hollow and Arcadia joined forces to keep the town safe from the waters.

A strange change, a change that brought warmth to my insides. I sat and thought of flickering change, and tried to understand what had happened. If I could understand it, maybe I could make it happen again. Ω

WEIRD TALES TALKS WITH DEAN KOONTZ

by Robert Morrish

Weird Tales: You've been very outspoken about writers' need to take care when dealing with agents and publishers. Is it safe to assume that you've had your share of bad experiences along the way?

Dean Koontz: Quite a few of them. I had two agents before my current one and my worst experience involved an agent turning down deals without telling me, rejecting a $100,000 movie sale and never informing me that an offer had been made until months later. And then sloughed it off and said "Well, you'll sell that book without any problem anyway and you'll get a better deal."

Subsequently we never sold that book for films and I never had the money. And this was back in the early 70's when I didn't have any money and that much was a fortune beyond conception.

Also, with both of my early agents I had pressure at various times to write something other than what I wanted to write, and when I would resist them I would get a response to the effect that if I didn't want to write what they thought I should write, then I wasn't going to have any sort of career that mattered. That's *death,* because you have to write what you're driven to write and what you're obsessed with. If I didn't do what I wanted, there would be no point in being a writer anyway.

And publishers — God yes, I've had lots and lots of problems with publishers. I've had every possible thing happen to me. I've had scores and scores of young writers call me up with problems, and they all begin by saying "You've never heard one like this. You won't believe what my publisher did to me." And I've never had one of these young writers start out this way without the problem turning out to be something that had actually happened to me. So the experiences are the same, year after year.

WT: Could you summarize the reasons behind your use of so many pen names earlier in your career?

Koontz: It used to be the wisdom of the business that if you wrote more than one book a year, you had to put the other one under a pen name because critics wouldn't pay any attention to anyone who wrote more than one book a year. That used to be more true than it is now. I don't advise writers to use a pen name these days. Stephen King and other people have proved that you can publish more than one book a year and certainly get plenty of attention and plenty of sales.

In addition, I varied my genres somewhat and I was told you couldn't do that sort of thing under one name or else you'd alienate and confuse your readers. I later decided that was completely boneheaded. Readers are after a certain kind of reading response from fiction, certain values, and if they get those values, they don't care if the fiction is varied in its nature. Berkley has been reissuing books that were originally under pen names and they've been selling very well. And I haven't gotten any letters from people who feel they've been shortchanged or something.

WT: Was it ever your preference to use

a pen name or was it always at your publisher's behest?

Koontz: It was either a publisher's or an agent's demand. I never rushed out to create a pen name thinking "Oh boy, I want to become famous under an assumed name." So it was never really by choice. However, I bought what they told me at the time — that the use of pen names was essential.

WT: Do you think that the pen names slowed the public's recognition of you and thus delayed your success somewhat?

Koontz: Definitely. Of the first three books I ever had on a bestsellers list (they were all paperback bestsellers), two were under pen names. One was Leigh Nichols and one was Owen West, and sandwiched between those was *Whispers.* And there were books like *Voice of the Night* and *Face of Fear* which I think would've added quite a bit to the impact my name had in the marketplace if they had been under my name.

WT: Why did you drop the last of your pen names — Leigh Nichols — a couple years ago? You had indicated at one time that you would keep that one.

Koontz: Well, I told myself at one time that I would stay with the Nichols name because Nichols had sold so well. But there came a point where it just seemed to make no sense to be writing a Leigh Nichols novel into which I put the same amount of effort as I put into a "Koontz book" and yet receive substantially less income from it. So that was the death knell for Leigh. Besides, no matter how modest we all pretend to be, if we're in this, we have egos and we prefer to see our achievements reflecting on our own names rather than on pen names.

WT: Dark Harvest is bringing out the five Leigh Nichols books under your name now, aren't they?

Koontz: Yes. Both Paul [Mikol of Dark Harvest] and I are very pleased with how things are going. And four of the five Nichols books were part of a package of six old pen-name books that my agent just sold to Berkley for reissue in paperback under my name. It reinforces what I tell young writers: you should always strive to do your best work because those books are like annuities — they pay off for you later if your career accelerates. But I never believed that these old books would pay off for me to the extent that they have. When we recently signed the deal with Berkley, I made more from the sale of each of the six books than I had originally made from all six of them put together. So the books have increased in value, just like an investment.

WT: What do you feel were the best things that you did under a pen name?

Koontz: Well there's *Voice of the Night,* which I'm very fond of. It's one of the most seamless things I've done. For me, it strikes a mood and maintains it almost line by line. It was a great deal of fun to write. *Face of Fear* is a totally different kind of book, but I'm very fond of that as well.

My favorite of the Nichols books, I think, is *Shadowfires,* which I really would like to have had under my name. It hurt me when I finished it, not to have it under my name. I also liked *The Servants of Twilight.*

Besides that . . . a lot of people tell me that they like the lone Richard Paige book, *The Door to December,* about as well as anything I've done. And crazy old Joe Lansdale says *Hanging On* [a comic novel from 1973] is one of my best. The man has weird tastes, but I've learned to respect him, so maybe he's right.

WT: You mentioned a couple of years ago that you planned on revising *Invasion,* a book you'd written many years ago under the name of Aaron Wolfe, and doubling its length. Whatever happened to those plans?

Koontz: It's still cooking away and may wind up being triple its original length. I thought of some really weird and totally off the wall alien stuff that I've never seen before, and I've seen and heard one Helluva lot of alien stuff. It's gotten so interesting in my mind that I don't want to do it just to revise it and get it out there. Once it's revised, you'll be hard-pressed to tell that it's the same novel or that the same material was used.

WT: You've fought the label of being a horror writer — or any other label, for that matter — for several years. Could you summarize why that is, and maybe touch upon the problems you had shedding the "science-fiction writer" label earlier in your career?

Koontz: Well, eight years after I stopped writing science fiction — and I'd published many books in those eight years — I could still expect, every time a new book of mine came out, to see a reviewer say, "Oh, here's something new by that science-fiction writer Dean Koontz, something different." And I'd been writing something different for eight years, so I'd scream every time I saw one of these reviews. It took a long time to shake the label, so I'm very wary of getting another label. Often, if you wear a label, critics in the mainstream and other publishers can dismiss you without ever bothering to read you.

And then, back around '74 or '75, after I'd been doing straight suspense for a few years, I began doing what at the time I thought was completely new. I began, with *Night Chills* I guess, taking elements of horror, science fiction and other genres and blending them with suspense and reaching for a way to tell these "blended" stories from a mainstream point of view with a mainstream style. I called them cross-genre books. I became excited about that because it seemed to offer so many opportunities to do something without falling into a formula. At that time, nobody seemed to understand what I was talking about. I was told frequently

that I had to stop what I was doing because the books couldn't be labeled and you can't sell books that aren't labeled. But ultimately it paid off.

By avoiding the label, I reach out to more readers. I like to read all sorts of genres myself, and I'd like to touch the readers of all those genres, I'd like to get my hands on them. I mean, what we're in this for is to communicate, to saturate the world with our own view of it, and the more people we can get to read us, the better.

My feeling is that while I'm a fan of horror — I was president of the Horror Writers of America — I don't want to be labeled. I don't think I do a strictly genre kind of book. And in addition, I have some strong feelings about a lot of things published under the horror label — there are some great horror writers that I'm happy to be associated with in people's minds, and then there are others whose work is lazy and sloppy. Unfortunately our genre is increasingly identified with the latter. I don't want to be immediately associated with that.

WT: It's fairly well known that you're a workaholic who often worked seven-day weeks and only cut down to six-day weeks a few years back. Have you been able to gear down to working five days a week?

Koontz: No. I've had a horrible year with my father, who's a life-long alcoholic and a very, very strange person. About 1980, he was diagnosed as a lifelong borderline schizophrenic, complicated by alcoholism, with a tendency to violence. He's been very difficult all of my life, and we took over support of him in . . . '77, I think, and have supported him ever since. In this past year, he tried to kill me, and I had to take a knife away from him, and he wound up in a psychiatric ward. I've lost huge amounts of work time because of that. Consequently, I'm working seven days a week again. But I swear to God, come this summer, I will cut back to five days a week.

WT: It would be natural to assume that your intense drive is a product of your rough childhood. Do you think that's an accurate assumption?

Koontz: Yes, I think so. I was poor and determined not to stay poor, for one thing. But it was more than that. I turned to books because they were an escape from this awful atmosphere that I was living in. I could slide into a book and utterly escape. It was the only way I could escape. And I think very early on, I developed a tremendous desire to do that for other people, to create a world they could step into that would relieve them of all they may have suffered in the real world. That drives me, and has always driven me, as much as the money. It now drives me more than anything, because the money isn't really a concern now. Therefore, that childhood really formed me and made me a writer.

WT: Your story "Twilight of the Dawn" in *Night Visions IV* had a good deal of theological musings and introspection by the protagonist. Did that story reflect some of your personal beliefs?

Koontz: I think it did. People keep saying to me, "Boy, you're a spiritual writer." I don't think of myself that way. God forbid, I'm not Jerry Falwell writing dark suspense. The character in that story probably reflects me to some extent because I went through a period of "agnosticism to atheism to agnosticism." I don't hew very closely to any particular faith, probably closer to Catholicism than anything.

I did move completely away from atheism, and strangely enough it was because of . . . a lot of the science reading I did, especially physics reading. The idea of a completely chaotic universe formed totally at random was less and less tenable.

WT: Let's switch from page to screen for a moment. The film *Watchers* was

released recently — wasn't that the third film to be made from your work (following *Shattered* and *Demon Seed*)?

Koontz: The third film and either the worst or the second worst. I'm not quite sure. It's a reeking pile of celluloid, that's all I know.

WT: I take it you had no involvement with that?

Koontz: No. If I had, I'd have to do the honorable thing and kill myself. Wait for the video. And rent it only if it's 99¢ or less. And keep an air sickness bag close by.

I knew I was in deep trouble when I read an article in which the director said, "We looked at this lead character, this 35-year-old ex-Delta-force man, and his dog, and thought *gee, isn't that a little tired? Let's do something fresh. What really excited us was the fresh concept of a boy and his dog.*" And I said, "Oh God, if they think that's a fresh concept . . ."

WT: What happened to the options on *Whispers, Phantoms, Voice of the Night, Night Chills*? And are there any other current options on your work?

Koontz: The option was exercised on *Whispers* and the film rights were bought, but nothing further has developed. I think there's been several screenplays written. I've seen two myself. Whether anything will happen with that, I don't know. People come along all the time wanting the film rights on that, and we have to keep referring them to the people who already own the rights.

Phantoms . . . the option was exercised by Steve Lane and Bob Pringle, who at this point I think have some arrangement with New World.

As far as *Night Chills* and *Voice of the Night* — the earlier options lapsed on both. But now those are two of sixteen properties that we just optioned in one large package to Warner Brothers. They're going to try to take some of this and put it together as a series of TV movies with my name above the title.

Whether this will come about or not, I don't know — though they have just made a deal with CBS for part of the package. But the nice thing about it, if it does happen, is that the agreement calls for me to be co-executive producer and have some really strong input on scripts. And to write them, if I choose to, but I probably wouldn't.

WT: Speaking of television, I think the question that we all want answered is: How in God's name did you ever wind up writing an episode of *Chips*?

Koontz: That year was one of the dark years. I would write a book and publishers would say, "Yukk, what is this stuff? We'll publish it, but we don't like it, and we won't promote it." These were books that the public would like later, but at the time they weren't being enthusiastically published. I was getting a real bleak feeling. I was looking, since we'd moved to Southern California, for alternatives and film was it. So I said to my film agent, "Let's try a few things."

First I wrote a screenplay for *Face of Fear* for Columbia/Screen Gems. They liked it a lot and had an arrangement with NBC to produce it. But within a week or two, René Valenti, who was head of Screen Gems, left to go into independent production, and the head of NBC-TV movies left as well and it [*Face of Fear*] became an orphan project.

And right about then, my agent said, "Would you like to write an episode of CHIPS?" And I thought, "Boy, this is off the wall." But I thought it could be neat because I had a particular idea to pitch. It was to be a real funny episode, and they really went for the idea. But the show wound up absolutely botched beyond belief. They left in all the jokes but they cut all the punch lines, so you've got 14 jokes building up to 14 nonexistent punch lines, and it's very, very strange.

Following that, I had a horrible experience with a pilot script for a project featuring Raymond Burr at Universal.

In fact, I had so many horrible experiences that I said, "I don't want to work in this business" and I dropped it and went back into books. Now, I'm in a position to work with people at a different level and I think I may get back into the business a little bit because the people approaching us now are much more creative and much more flexible.

WT: Your fiction is now listed as "copyright NKUI, Inc." I give up — what does NKUI stand for?

Koontz: I figured it [the copyright] was going to appear in all the books, so I wanted to find something that was intriguing. At that time I was writing both Nichols and Koontz books, and I thought it would be funny to have a grandiose corporate name, so it stands for "Nichols and Koontz United International."

I also wanted something that looked like a word in another language. "Kui" — which I tried to get first, but it was already taken — is, in fact, a Vietnamese word. And "nkui" looks somewhat like a Vietnamese word. But everybody pronounces it wrong. I was appalled to find that some people pronounce it "nookie."

WT: *Oddkins* seemed a strange step for you. Could you explain what led to the creation of that book? Was it something that came up in the wake of working with Phil Parks on *Twilight Eyes*?

Koontz: Yes, it came directly from that. I liked Phil's work so much and thought *Twilight Eyes* was such a handsome book. After *Twilight Eyes* came out, Chris Zavisa (who published the small-press edition of *Twilight Eyes*) approached me with an idea he had for a book. The "idea" turned out to be only a few lines, but it was very intriguing, having to do with magic toys. He didn't really have characters or a plot yet, and there was no conflict in it, but there was something about it that was intriguing. I was really interested in working with Phil again, so I said "Yeah, let's do it."

It was the kind of thing that you can't know how the Hell you're going to market, or who's ever going to publish it. You don't know if you're going to make a dime out of it, but the whole idea you're in love with, so you do it for the love of it. Happily, it's gone on to do very well.

WT: You seem like someone who's always striving to improve. Has there been any point in your career, discounting anything you did early in your career simply in order to pay the rent, when you felt like you didn't improve from book to book?

Koontz: Well, when I'm looking over ideas and trying to decide which book to do next, the guiding principle for me is . . . "which book will have the greatest amount of material that I've never done before, which book presses the furthest into new territory?" And sometimes when you do that, with *Lightning* for instance, you find yourself in the midst of something, that is so different it becomes staggering. Then you can lose track of trying to work that prose up better than you ever have before and to work greater depth into the story than you ever have before, because the newness of the material is such that it occupies you entirely.

Lightning, for example, was not just a time-travel story. It had the added conceit of time travel in the opposite direction from what everyone was expecting. That was brutal enough, but the thing that made the project even more appealing to me about doing the book was that it was a suspense novel that took place over 30-some years. Nobody, to my knowledge, had ever written a suspense novel that took place over such a long period of time. To follow a lead character through 30-some years of her life, and to condense periods of her life into interesting vignettes that keep the story plunging ahead and yet paint her growth as a person, was a challenge that I really wanted to tackle. I became so involved in that, that I don't know if the prose quality of *Lightning* improved from that of *Watchers.* But at least it was something new, fresh.

WT: Speaking of *Watchers,* back when you were putting the finishing touches on that book, you stated that you had ideas for your next ten novels firmly in mind. What's the queue look like these days, and specifically, what can we expect after *Midnight* ?

Koontz: The book I'm working on now is called *The Bad Place* — a more-than-one-word title! I've been searching for a multiple word title for several books now, but . . . with *Strangers,* for instance, when it finally came down to that, I had to admit it was the best title for the book. It fit in many ways. *Watchers* I wasn't sure about, although my preferred title — "Guardian" — was also one word. *Lightning* was about the best title for that book. *Midnight* was going to be called "Midnight Music," but they felt that sounded too romance-oriented, and finally I had to agree that in fact *Midnight* was a better title.

But . . . with *The Bad Place,* I finally came up with a multiple-word title they liked. And I'm having a lot of fun with it. It's got some of my kinkiest, strangest stuff in it, and the villain — I don't know, you never know until you finish — but I *think* he'll be the most genuinely frightening guy in any of my stuff since Bruno in *Whispers.* It also has one of the most *challenging* characters that I've ever had to work with. He's a major character, he's the lead female's brother, and he's a Down's syndrome victim. There are scenes from his point of view, and that's been real interesting to work with.

And after this, I've got several more lined up, but I just don't like to talk about books that far in advance. Ω

THE GREAT FEAR

by R. Garcia y Robertson

Starvation Spring

Madeleine's body was gaunt but growing. For months she had gone to bed hungry. All the old grain was gone and there was precious little new grain threshed during that winter. Next summer's wheat had slept beneath the snow, while the poor ate pounded acorns, and Madeleine heard wolves howling at the edge of the night. Every Sunday the priest told her that the Devil had his claws on the Beauvais. At night she overheard talk in hushed tones of half-eaten corpses found in the wheatfield, whose slashed throats showed that *loups-garou,* werewolves, were running with the packs.

During cold nights her only comfort had been a cat, the one called *La Blanche,* who would creep in and sleep between Madeleine's thighs, but be gone before dawn. By spring sowing, her hunger was a gnawing erosion that kept sleep at bay. Lying in bed, Madeleine heard her father say that they should eat the cats.

Mother yelled back that father was a fool and drunkard. "Young girls cannot eat cats. You bring bad luck just by saying that." Her mother's spittle sizzled in the hearth, driving the Devil away.

Her brother and youngest sister stirred. Madeleine rocked them back to sleep, letting them know that the "little mother" sat between them and noises in the night. Singing lullabies to her siblings, she looked down at *La Blanche.* The cat lying between her legs showed no concern at the prospect of being cut open and stuffed with garlic, or served in an onion stew. Instead *La Blanche* stretched, yawned, flexed her claws, then inspected the pads of her feet. Madeleine held out a finger for a lick from a raspy tongue; then she watched *La Blanche* get up, arch, and reclaim her place, becoming once more a pool of white fur on the coarse blanket.

She heard Father pound on the plank table by the fire. "Why not eat cats? Will my girls sup only on grain-fed goose and suckling pig? Beggars are living on boiled grass, and not living well, I might add. Before the harvest is in we will be eating rats, and grouching between bites to find them so thin."

Madeleine looked up, fearing a fight. She saw her mother's hands balled hard against hips, and heard her answer back. "When my mother's mother was a girl, in the Old Louis's time, there was a famine greater than this one; a winter when the seed froze in the ground and the Seigneur's apple trees were shattered by the wind. Then a family in Crèvecoeur boiled a cat in the stew, and all sat down to sup on it, including their virgin daughter."

Father folded his arms, brows pulled into tight dark furrows. "I had heard of some sense coming from Crèvecoeur, but never believed it before."

With a note of triumph Mother crossed herself. "The poor girl ate that stew, and then had kittens. Just like the Blessed Virgin, only it was a litter."

Madeleine heard a thick fist hit the table again. "Woman, I want to hear no more stories from the Montagne." Mother came from up near the border with Amiens. "In the Montagne they are lucky to raise even kittens. They eat no meat, just cheese stinking of cow piss, spread on bread so coarse that you can pick up the loaf by the chaff left in the flour." With two fingers pressed together he pretended to hold an imaginary loaf over the empty table.

Madeleine saw her mother lean forward, pressing balled fists against the table boards. "We can lock the oat seed in the ground, then if need be go on the road and beg."

"Will my horses beg beside me?" Father's tone was sarcastic.

"The horses will eat straw and tree bark."

"And if the horses die?" Father's voice

rose.

"Then we shall surely eat them," answered her mother.

"What, and risk having colts?"

By now Madeleine had learned to sleep through shouting, and she did not wake again until *La Blanche* left. The white cat never stayed during the day, coming by dead of night and going before dawn. With sleep in her eyes, the little mother slipped from the warm, crowded bed to draw water and start a fire. Father brought in wood. Madeleine saw by his rumpled shirt he had not slept. In the cold half-light she avoided his eyes. He pulled on his big cloth coat, dyed with oak bark, mumbling over his shoulder that he was off to see the bailiff. Madeleine breathed freer through the rest of her morning chores.

By noon her father was still not back. Mother told Madeleine to get some of the oat seed and grind it into meal. "If your father can break his fast with the bailiff then the rest of us can fill our bellies."

Madeleine felt strange robbing from the seed grain, so she ground the meal herself, a task that she usually passed on to her younger brother. He was becoming more of a man, less willing to take orders from the little mother. When she smelled the cakes baking, Madeleine took guilty pleasure in conspiring to feed the family. In that way she was already a woman.

The children were stuffing their mouths with oat cakes when they saw a large coach and four rolling up the high road that split the field. Madeleine led them in a charge past the hedge, down to the dusty road. There they knelt in a ditch full of weeds, with purple foxgloves and dry nettles, smudging their faces and trying to look poorer than they were. When the carriage drew even with them, Madeleine called out, saying, "Give us a *sou*. We have eaten only husks and belt leather since Sunday mass."

Most carriages spun past, but this one stopped. Madeleine guessed they would get something good tossed to them, for the coach had a fat driver and four well-fed horses. The black door swung open, exposing an inner lining of red velvet. Madeleine was shocked. The man who stepped out was the Seigneur, and the woman he helped out was the Mademoiselle de Corcy; a pair so far above her they might have come down from the moon.

The Seigneur was scrupulously shaven, with a sallow complexion and deep-set eyes. His coat was black and silver, with wide lace at the cuffs. Black garters with red rosettes supported white silk stockings. He carried a silver and ebony cane in one hand. It frightened Madeleine to see how fast he moved but she was even more scared by the woman. Mademoiselle de Corcy had the dark eyes, curved lids, high cheekbones, and fine chin found in the old families. Thick black hair hung in heavy coils over skin soft and white as well-handled ivory. The corners of her lips were pulled back in private amusement.

Madeleine had heard many names for the Mademoiselle. "Black Widow" or the "Witch" were the most common. Madeleine knew other names even more explicit, that men used when they supposed women were not listening. She knew from their tone the men envied the Seigneur, an envy in no way tinged with respect. Out of his hearing the Seigneur was called Onan, after the son of Judah who had bedded his brother's wife. Mademoiselle de Corcy was the Seigneur's sister-in-law, his brother's widow, but the name had a double meaning. Onan in the Bible had not only seen his brother's wife naked, but had gotten no satisfaction from her.

The children broke off their begging. Before Madeleine was the man who held the *ban* and *banalités,* the right of low justice, the right to a mill and wine press. Her parents paid him for the privilege of keeping pigeons, raising rabbits, and going to market. Heavy as her family's payments were, she knew they were a tiny part of what the Seigneur collected in rents, tithes, and the harvest of his own domain. In her imagination only two people were more powerful than the Seigneur. One was King Louis, and the other was the woman at the Seigneur's side. Madeleine feared the Widow de Corcy more, because the Witch's fingers rested on her soul.

The Mademoiselle looked down the line of dirty children, directly at Madeleine. "What were they saying?"

"They were saying that they had no bread," replied Onan.

The Widow patted the dust from her gloves, made a face, and said, "Then I suppose we must make do with cake." This joke, attributed to the Queen, was already old at court, but Mademoiselle was referring to the oat cakes. In their haste the children had forgotten to hide them.

The smaller beggars shuffled behind Madeleine, heads hanging down, hair hiding their faces.

"Come, come," said the Seigneur, "which of you is the oldest?"

"Yes," said the Mademoiselle, touching her glove to sharp white teeth. "The one called Madeleine?"

"Is that her name?" The Seigneur looked the children over. Madeleine stood stupefied. She did not need to answer, since the two adults were already studying her.

"A bit dirty," said the Seigneur, "and small." She felt little and bony, standing by the road in a thin shift. On bare feet Madeleine was a full head shorter than him, and Onan was not a tall man.

"Actually, her skin is very fair under that dirt," said the Mademoiselle. "She is a starved foal, who would be quite pretty, if her parents would only feed her. Give her the *sou* and help me back into the carriage."

Onan did as he was told; first lifting the Widow into the coach, then turning to Madeleine. The girl had not moved. Onan reached down, took her right hand, opened it and placed the *sou* in her palm, then curled her fingers back around the coin. His movements were firm and simple. Madeleine had not wanted him to touch her, but she was unable to resist. To her his hands seemed infinitely stronger.

The carriage spun off, throwing more dust on the children. Madeleine watched it dwindle into the distance, leaving only the empty road. Now the dark lane seemed even more sinister to Madeleine, cutting across the fields, connecting the ground at her feet to the great mystery that lay beyond the horizon. She had seen villagers pressed to repair or rebuild the road, but no one Madeleine knew used it, except to beg and roam when their was no food at home. Its rutted surface swallowed up the poor and homeless, the young men who went off to war. The road was home to scavengers, smugglers, highwaymen, and the petty brigands who stole eggs from under hens or milked other people's cows. That new year's she had seen a body lying in the ditch by the road, black and twisted, with eyes pecked out by crows, too thin and frozen for starving dogs to eat.

Her brother and sisters asked to see the *sou*, but Madeleine trudged back to the house without speaking. She felt too disturbed to relish their successful begging, too worried because mighty people knew her name. It gave them more power over her than she had suspected. She knew that witches could cast spells with only a name.

Late that afternoon her father returned, hanging his black coat on the door and avoiding his daughter's eyes. "Wife," he said, "you may eat our oat seed in peace. The Seigneur has given us a loan, enough grain to see us through to the harvest."

He heaved his tired body down on the stool by the plank table. There was no happiness in how he said it. Madeleine felt the same chill as when the Seigneur and Mademoiselle said her name and looked her over.

"What is the interest?" asked her mother. "What does Onan take?" The biggest portion of anything was always called "Onan's share."

Father waved a heavy hand. "It is a rate that we can live with. If the crop in the field comes in as good as it looks, we can pay him off with the harvest. For now he is calling it a gift, so there will be no tax on the interest."

"A gift?" she looked wary. "Did you sign a paper?"

"Of course I signed a paper. Onan has a passion for papers." He traced a stubby finger over the deep wood grain on the bare table.

"You signed on a loan that does not legally exist?"

"Yes," he said, "because it is bread in our mouths. Onan cannot make the paper public without exposing himself to the tax."

"You signed your name to fraud. That paper will lie in his library to be used against us or our children. When you are under the soil and our son is a man, who will know what taxes have been paid?"

"Enough, woman, I did what I had to. There will be no payments until after the harvest, and no interest if we give back the gift in full."

"And Onan wants nothing now?"

"Did I say that?" He hunched his shoulders and looked at Madeleine. "He wants her, to work in his house until the harvest. He will feed her and clothe her, more than we could do without the loan."

"Oh my God," said her mother. "Madeleine is just a child, and my only help around the house. I do not trust Onan."

Father leaned forward, looking into his gnarled hands. "Do you think I trust Onan? Any man who eats as he pleases and stays thin is a monster against nature. With the loan we too will eat until the harvest, without selling a furrow of land."

"What about the Witch? She can make a mare drop her foal and dry up a cow's milk with a word."

"Then thank God Madeleine is not a mare or a cow," said her father. "*C'est fini,* woman, she is also not a son."

Madeleine ran straight out of the house, past the vegetable plot and earthen well, down to the wheat field. Everything she saw made her sad, the sky, the towering clouds, the endless acres of wheat. The field went on in all directions, unbarred by fences, nothing dividing it but the road. The field's boundaries were natural ones, folds in the land, the fallow and the oat fields.

She sat still among the tall shoots. The seed had lain in the frozen ground throughout the famine winter, giving birth to new life in the midst of hunger. These shoots were the living promise that everyone would one day eat. Countless people had ancient claims to the field, but not a furrow belonged to Madeleine, so she laid claim to it all. She stretched her sobbing body out among the other young plants, feeling for the power in the earth. Digging her fingers into the ground she cried, because she did not want to leave her village, her family, this spot in the field. Madeleine could feel the great mystery rushing towards her, the impossibly wide world that was at the end of the road. She knew that when she got up, when she went back to the house, the thing that she feared would happen. The world would claim her and carry her away.

Except for shaking she did not move. At vespers she head the village bells. Madeleine knew how at seventeen Joan of Arc had heard the Saints' voices in her village's bells, calling on a peasant girl to free France. At nineteen Joan had been burned as a witch, across the border in the Diocese of Rouen. Madeleine was only fifteen and she did not want to free France. She could not even free herself. All the village bells said to her was, "Come to prayer, come to prayer."

Madeleine prayed where she was, begging the Saints and the Virgin to let her stay at home. When she did hear voices, it was not the Saints, but her parents calling for her. Still she did not go in, though it was now cold and dark.

It was *La Blanche* who finally found her. The white cat padded through the wheat, sniffing as she went. She rubbed up against Madeleine, nudging her towards the warmth of the house. When Madeleine would not move the cat stepped back and stared at her, as if to say, "Must we spend the whole night in the cold?" Madeleine got up, picked up the purring *La Blanche* and walked home for the last time.

That night the coach came to get her and the fat driver was drunk. Madeleine tried to sit inside, but the driver leaned down. "Oh no, come up and ride along with me. There is no red velvet for you."

She climbed up beside the driver, clutching her bundle of clothes to her breasts, pulling her dress down as far as she could. While Madeleine struggled to hide her calves, *La Blanche* leaped up to the open coach window, then jumped down onto the red velvet. The driver smiled at the girl's attempted modesty, then whipped the horses, carrying them both off into the night. Twice the driver stopped the coach to piss, saying that if Madeleine was cold she could warm herself on the cushions with him. Both times she braced herself, preparing to bolt off into the darkness. The man seemed too drunk to risk a tussle, so *La Blanche* rode in solitary comfort.

The driver spun the carriage past the tall manor, around to the dark stables. As soon as he stopped, Madeleine slipped down and ran towards the lights of the manor house. Cursing the drink that made him so slow, the driver got down himself to unhitch the horses. *La Blanche* leaped up to the coach window, then dropped to the ground, trotting off towards the pool of light that surrounded the big house. Halfway there the white cat stopped, turning to meow distinctly, "Merci, monsieur." The man was too lost in wine to hear her.

The Open Road

A fat, sleepy cook took Madeleine into a red-tiled kitchen hung with polished copper pots. The woman had thick round arms and skin as creamy white as the plastered ceiling. She heated water on the stone hearth, saying, "The Seigneur says you must be bathed at once." While the water heated the cook gave Madeleine wine to drink and served her bowl after bowl of potatoes and milk. Madeleine had not tasted potatoes since Christmas, and could never remember being allowed to eat her fill of anything.

Naked and half drunk, she eased herself into the warm water, admiring the round white curve of her distended belly. There was no haste to the bath. No one had used the water before her, no one would use it afterward. It seemed a delicious sin to have water heated just for her. The cook scrubbed her all over, scraping away the soil and smell of the village, giving advice as she worked. "You will of course respect the Seigneur's slightest wish, but it is the Mademoiselle that needs watching. She is *la chatte* that makes the mice jump. Certainly you know her story."

Madeleine told the cook that she knew no one's story, except her own.

"What a calf," said the cook, "did they feed you nothing but fairy tales? I will have to watch you. Mademoiselle was married to the Seigneur's brother, but her line is far older. She is the heiress to an ancient and empty title, with no lands, no *banalités,* no one knows where her money lies. Her great-grandmother was burned alive for witchcraft, and better her line had ended there. She is a great scandal, living with her brother-in-law and never setting foot in chapel. Do nothing to displease the Mistress, not even by mischance."

The girl stood up and water streamed off her thin body. The cook laughed as she toweled her down. "What a bony calf, when we have fattened you up, you will strip even better." Madeleine blushed, but her mind was on meals to come.

The house was grander than Madeleine had ever imagined. She went about with her head down, doing the work she had done at home: fetching wood and water, spinning wool, weeding the garden. When her chores did take her into the main rooms of the manor, Madeleine would walk past huge framed mirrors made from thick cut glass. At first she mistook the mirrors for doorways that led into other rooms where a very different girl was going about similar tasks. She was always startled to discover that the shy stranger was her. Madeleine had seen herself before, in still ponds, polished metal, or panes of glass, but her reflection here was different. Before she had been gaunt, and skinny. The girl in the manor house mirrors had rounder hips, fuller curves, and large luminous eyes.

The more she ate, the more her body assumed a new and pleasing shape, filling out starched and pressed servant's dresses. At night she would lie naked beside *La Blanche,* feeling to see if she was what she saw in the mirror.

She enjoyed having her own bed almost as much as being fed, until she found out why she had been fattened and left to sleep alone. One night Madeleine awoke in blackness, when *La Blanche* straightened up. At first she thought it was near morning, because *La Blanche* always left before daylight. Then the floorboards creaked, and she felt the weight of someone on her bed. There was no latch on her little room. She could tell by the draft that the dark door was open. Before she could cry out, there was a palm pressed on her lips. She recognized the firmness in this grip. These were the same fingers that had forced a *sou* in her palm by the side of the road, folding her hand over the coin.

"No noise, girl, no noise at all, there is no need for that." The Seigneur's voice was civil and polite, but with the promise of violence behind it.

A hand was at her hips, pushing up her night shirt and stripping back the bed clothes. Madeleine knew very well what was happening. She had heard the sounds her mother and father made in the night, and she had seen it done by dogs and barn animals. She wanted to fight, but felt paralyzed by fear and surprise. The man on top of her had so much power. Not just strong hands and a stern voice, but behind him stood servants, bailiffs, law courts, and the gendarmerie if need be.

She felt loathing and shame at being alone, not at home in her own bed. The man who had her showed no shame. He was brutally efficient, as though he knew what he wanted and had done it many times. Madeleine ached to cry out, but could barely breathe. She felt her legs being forced apart to make way for his stiff blunt instrument.

There was an animal howl, and then a scream. Neither came from Madeleine. Onan leaped off her, *La Blanche* on his back, her claws raking him, her sharp little teeth sunk in his rump. He whirled and cursed in the narrow room, banging against the walls, but the persistent cat clung to his nightshirt, her rear legs spinning and scratching wildly. Onan put his hands down to protect future Seigneurs and bolted out the door.

For a moment Madeleine was crying alone in the dark. Then heavy feet drummed on the stairs and the cook came running, holding a lit candle and a gleaming cleaver. "Calf, what has happened? Was it a nightmare? Are brigands breaking in?"

Hiding her tears in the sheets, she said, "No, it was the cat."

The cook glanced about, her candle flame casting wild shadows. "What cat?"

"The white one," said the girl, *La Blanche.*" The big woman shook her head. "Little calf, you were dreaming. All the cats come begging at my stoop. We have grays, blacks, and an orange tiger, but there is not a white cat on the manor."

Madeleine lay awake until morning, afraid to sleep, shamed to know why she had been brought to this bed. *La Blanche* did not come back. Abandoned even by the cat, she had an earnest talk with God, asking for the Seigneur to forgive her and have pity on her family.

She hoped most to be sent home, but when morning came the only change was that Onan did not sit for breakfast. Another girl delivered food to his bed. At midday Madeleine got the call the cook had warned her about, the call to attend the Mademoiselle.

Her first thought was to run off without wasting a moment, but there were terrors on the road too; brigands and highwaymen, troops of soldiers. Full of dread, but feeling too cowardly to flee, Madeleine found her mistress instead.

Mademoiselle de Corcy was pacing before an open gallery that ran the length of private apartments. A dressmaker from Beauvais was scurrying back and forth on his knees, trying to pin the hem on her black gown. She fixed Madeleine with an intense gaze, then let her attention wander over the wooded park beyond the open windows. This cutting inspection and look away made Madeleine feel small and ignorant, which might have been intended. Then with a toss of her head Mademoiselle took charge of the interview. "I see

I shall have to keep you with me. Your normal duties are at an end. You will attend only to me, sleeping on my couch or at my bedside."

Madeleine was certain that Mademoiselle de Corcy knew what had happened in the servants' quarters. She knew the Mistress did not want her for her work, which was clumsy and farm-girlish. Punishment hovered over her, all the more awful because its form was not revealed. Tension made the Mademoiselle's words and gestures languid, slow to the point of irritation. The Witch wandered off onto another subject, looking out the windows. "Midsummer's Eve is near. Do you know anywhere better to be than Paris on Saint-Jean's night?" Madeleine had spent every Midsummer's Eve of her life at home, and could not say whether that was better or worse than Paris.

"No, I suppose you would not know, but in any event, the Seigneur and I shall be leaving for the city at once."

Madeleine stood there amazed by the power of prayer. God had not just listened but acted. Instead of punishment she saw liberation. Onan and the Witch were leaving. Bowing her head, she said she would miss them both. Lying had never been so easy at home, but here it seemed so natural; just say whatever someone wanted to hear.

The Mademoiselle turned so quickly that pins tinkled out of her hem. Her smile lifted, parting her lips further and showing a set of sharp white teeth. "Oh, I doubt very much that you will miss us."

Madeleine had not planned to miss them in the least, and her stomach gave a guilty heave when she heard the Witch repeat her thoughts.

A gloved finger tapped against Mademoiselle's lips. "Besides my dear, you are coming with us. I would not think of parting with you."

Madeleine saw the great open road yawning before her, and beyond it the horrible horizon. She could not believe

it, but Mademoiselle was already giving instructions for the trip. With patient emphasis the Witch showed her a yellow carpetbag. "Keep this bag with you until we reach Paris. Sleep with your head on it each night, but never open it. If you lose the bag or let anyone open it, then you are lost as well."

She nodded, clutching the carpetbag and watching the brisk preparations with horror. In the time it took to hem the black gown the coach was stowed with wine and baggage. Madeleine crept up onto a velvet seat, next to Mademoiselle and across from Onan, hiding as best she could behind the big carpetbag.

The air in the jolting coach was magnetized with unspoken conflict. She could see tension in the way Mademoiselle and Onan sat. They held their bodies stiff, never touching, the way her parents did after a fight or when a lamb died. Whenever Onan spoke the air grew crisp, but he never said a word to her, treating Madeleine's seat as vacant. The Mademoiselle kept everyone on edge with her energy, taking cat naps during the dull stretches, but always waking with renewed enthusiasm for the trip. She seemed to care for nothing but being in Paris by Midsummer's Eve.

At night they slept in country inns with Madeleine curled on the floor at the foot of Mademoiselle's bed, her head resting on the yellow carpetbag. In Île-de-France she passed by pastures that produced beef and brie for Paris. Herbs grew by the banks of slow streams. Peas and beans ripened in the summer sun. Vagabonds without the will to live lay in the dirt at the roadside.

On the day of Midsummer's Eve they approached the city. First Madeleine saw long lines of people. The road into the capital was choked with artisans, traveling mountebanks, peasants and laborers looking for work. Everyone was after the food stripped from the countryside and carted into the City. A company of infantry was marching south with their wives and women.

While Onan cursed and tried to clear the road, Mademoiselle leaned out of her window and began to flirt with an officer named Elie, wearing the uniform of the Queen's Regiment. From the way Mademoiselle talked Madeleine assumed he was a Marshall of France, but he admitted that he was only a half-pay lieutenant living in the capital. After a pleasant exchange he ordered the infantry aside, pushing people and bundles into the ditches, so the carriage could splash by.

Even with the throng parted Madeleine still could not see the city. All she saw was a vast wooden wall stretching east and west into the blue haze. Louis XVI had ordered a many-gated wall built around Europe's largest city, to force everyone entering or leaving to pay the customs tax. Mademoiselle de Corcy leaned out the window and was again waved through. She was noble and immune to taxation.

Inside the wall Madeleine saw neither city not country, just the gray Rue Saint-Martin running straight through the green desolation of the faubourgs: past farm buildings, taverns, inns, gambling dens and pleasure gardens. Pigs rooted by the roadside, and behind the shops were small vegetable plots, stock and slaughter pens, laundry yards and dumps.

In this strange semi-rural landscape Madeleine saw people too destitute to live in Paris proper. Peasants who came to the faubourgs and could go no further mingled with the city's human waste; the unemployed, the debtors, the felons, the hopeless lunatics and the incurably diseased. The air was thick with the stench of rubbish, outdoor tanning and smelting, and the acid works. Madeleine had never suspected that Paris would smell worse than her village, but Onan and the Witch must have known, because they were already breathing through nosegays and perfumed handkerchiefs.

Halfway down the Rue Saint-Martin Madeleine passed a second gate, more imposing and made of stone. Past the Porte Saint-Martin, Madeleine was plunged into a maze of buildings and streets, colored by a living kaleidoscope of people and costumes. Parisians swaggered about in mad outfits made from military uniforms and the cast-off clothes of the rich. She heard the clatter of hooves, of hand-carts, hackney coaches, and wooden shoes. Women's high voices hawked meat, bread, wigs, remedies, their washing, and themselves.

In the narrow lanes between Beaubourg and the Lombard Quarter the coach could barely move. A heavy jolt threw Madeleine against the Mademoiselle. Through the window she saw a two-wheeled washing cart collapsing, tipping white linen into the mud and litter. Women screamed and cursed. A virago with massive arms began to beat on the coach with a heavy wooden washing bat, demanding payment for a broken wheel and soiled washing.

Mademoiselle straightened her dress and put on her gloves. "It seems we are in the city," she said to Madeleine. "Come, we will walk to my apartments."

When Madeleine emerged from the coach she saw Onan and his coachman pushing and shoving with some large women. She was shocked to find that now the Seigneur had no magic. The crowd pressed around him, siding with the women. Interested bystanders started prying paving stones out of the street, and Onan's rapier hung useless at his side. It was suicide for a lone aristocrat to brandish the *arme blanche* against a Paris mob.

Mademoiselle searched through her purse and produced silver *livres,* big coins, not little *sous*. Each one was worth half a day's wages. As she gave these to the women, jeers turned to cheers. When she closed her purse the washerwomen were bowing, pushing open a lane for the lady and her maid.

Leaving the coach behind, Madeleine found the crush of people on the Rue Saint-Martin appalling. Trained dogs did tricks in the street. Old soldiers displayed their wounds and sold their stories. Vendors offered mirrors, flowers, magic lanterns, caged birds, and pornography. Never in her worst nightmares had Madeleine thought that the end of the road would be like this.

The summer sun boiled out the City's every essence. Sitting in the stink where the Great Sewer fed the Seine were dramshops, cabarets, cafés, and bistros. Despite the stench Madeleine was dizzy with hunger. She stumbled behind her Mistress over the *pont* at the end of the Rue Saint-Martin and onto the Île de la Cité. Notre Dame towered over her, seeming to cover half the small island, a massive reminder that there was another world waiting. Crowded around the great House of God were luxury shops, gold smithies, and enameling works; serving a city that boasted as many master jewelers as bakers. She saw stone gargoyles frowning down on the money changers, ready to vomit rainwater on both rich and poor. She smelled food and started towards the cool cavern of the cathedral. Priests were feeding the poor on the steps, and the homeless slept in the shade of the huge Gothic arches.

Mademoiselle de Corcy caught her servant, saying with her half smile, "No, that is not for us." Madeleine mumbled an apology and let Mademoiselle lead her over another *pont* and onto the Left Bank.

Here Mademoiselle sat Madeleine down at a table of a street café and told her to eat. Madeleine had never ordered food at a table. Even in the inns on the road she had eaten in the kitchen with the servants. A young man with boyish curls saw her confusion. With deft self-assurance he pulled up a chair and offered to order for her. Taking her silence as assent, he gave incisive orders to the serving woman and then engaged Mademoiselle in conversation. Madeleine watched in wonder. He was clearly bourgeois, a young man of leisure, with lace at his throat and wrists. Every action was impudent and willful, which Mademoiselle seemed to enjoy. He said his name was Saint-Just, and soon lost Madeleine in a torrent of opinions about poetry, philosophy, and the Estates General sessions at Versailles. She was left watching his Cupid's bow lips and their constant motion.

The serving woman returned with coarse Breton crêpes, cooked in garlic and onions, on a platter with cheeses, and lumps of pâté. Madeleine found the food delicious, even liking the strange hard cheeses so different from her native Camembert. As the hungry girl ate, her gaze followed the bright crowd of people passing along the river.

There was a touch on her arm. She started, expecting to see the young man's hand on her. Instead it was the Witch. "This, my dear girl, is Paris."

Saint-Jean's Night

The Paris apartments of Mademoiselle de Corcy were on the western tip of the Île Saint-Louis, high above the Seine and filled with light. Tall windows framed Notre Dame and the Left Bank. The Île Saint-Louis was an island in the Seine tied to the city by twin bridges: the Pont Marie and the Pont de la Tournelle. Madeleine wished she could study the light, the view, the river and its bridges; instead she helped lay out masks and costumes. She asked to spend the evening in the apartments, watching the Saint-Jean fireworks show and bonfires from the balcony.

Mademoiselle waved her wishes aside, handing her a black ribboned mask. "Wear something peasant, you do that well enough. Playing peasant is not entirely passé. Your costume will pass as something old enough to be new."

She helped the Mademoiselle become a black widow, adding white powder to already alabaster skin, curling hair into dark ringlets, and blackening long nails. The Widow wore her new black silk gown. Her only spot of color was the slash of red paint across her lips.

At dinner Madeleine saw Onan dressed as an Ogre, wearing furs, curving goat horns and a leather mask. He said nothing about the coach, the washerwomen, or their entry into Paris. Costumes and flickering candles gave even the dinner an evil air. The food itself was an inoffensive whitefish in cream sauce, and *filet de boeuf Richelieu* with *foie gras,* jeweled aspics, truffles, tomatoes, and stuffed mushroom caps, followed by sweet gossamer deserts. Such a sparkling meal made Madeleine feel graceless and incompetent, coming from a family that argued over eating the cats.

After dinner, servants carried them off in sedan chairs, pushing through the mob at the Place de Grève, past the hollow stalls of the Corn Market, and into the Palais-Royal. Mademoiselle explained to Madeleine that the fireworks would be in the Place de Grève by the Hotel de Ville, "A very common place, used for public announcements, branding criminals, and hanging holidays. All the best entertainers will be at the Palais-Royal: jugglers, poets, actresses, the better sort of beggars, lawyers and police spies — everyone in the theater trade."

Madeleine watched masked young men dance and caper, free for a night from social distinctions. Drunks banged their bottles on the sedan chairs. On a normal day Paris consumed a gallon of wine for every adult and child above the age of ten years. On special nights the city became completely drunk.

She saw a grand esplanade and a

promenade garden, ringed with colonnades and arcaded galleries. "This," said Mademoiselle, "is the Palais-Royal, the capital of Paris, and a city within a city." A dozen different vices went on in the open air. Drinking, gambling, brawling were all underway. Women offered themselves beneath the wooden arches, or sat in upper-floor windows with their skirts up, calling to men below. Couples in costume passed open boutiques displaying studied silks and furs, portraits and engravings, whips and chains.

Mademoiselle led them into a cafe called the "Caveau," a political club where Madeleine was introduced to a torrent of smiling strangers. One couple in particular was friendly in the ardent way Parisians adopted with utter strangers. Camille Desmoulins had long waving hair and pretty, childlike features. He insisted that Madeleine call him Camille. It was the first time any of her betters had ever demanded any address save a title. His wife, Lucille Duplessis, was beautiful and unmasked. She too wanted only first names. Both Camille and Lucille seemed solicitous precisely because Madeleine was poor and one of the "little people." This social inversion was an attitude that Madeleine could barely comprehend, as upside-down as indoor bathrooms and making love in the streets.

Words and phrases made sense to Madeleine but Parisians would string them together in incongruous or incomprehensible ways. She heard that this morning King Louis had appeared before the Estates General in all his majesty, employing the full panoply of a *lit de justice*. The King declared the acts of the Estates General null and void, then dismissed the assembly. Instead of obeying their King the bourgeois representatives had stayed in their seats. Madeleine could not imagine such folly. These men were saved from their foolishness by the Duc d'Orleans and other charitable nobles who turned back the guards sent to clear the hall.

Onan dived into a verbal duel with a friend of Camille and Lucille's, a somber lawyer from Arras with a white wig and black eyebrows. The Seigneur defended the King's right to do exactly as the King pleased. If the King were not supreme, than a Seigneur was no better than a bourgeois and they all might as well be peasants. The lawyer found this common sense insufferable, accusing Onan of taking part in aristocratic plot to put the King before the nation.

Mademoiselle led Madeleine away from the café, saying, "It is useless to cross words with a lawyer. If the man could not argue, he would not be a lawyer."

Madeleine hesitated, then said that none of the lawyer's arguments had made sense.

"Hush, he has quite a reputation. His name is de Robespierre. He defends the victims of gross injustice, which of course makes his cases easier to win."

Madeleine asked, "How is this all possible?"

"The Palais-Royal is protected by the Duc d'Orleans," said the Witch. "The same noble who saved the Estates General today. Even the Lieutenant-General of Police has no power here, though his agents are everywhere in the crowd."

"Are they spying on us?" Madeleine felt incriminated by everything around her.

"Oh yes," said Mademoiselle, "and enjoying themselves. Police agents are peculiarly addicted to vice, since the job has few other attractions."

She led Madeleine into the Cafe de Foy, where the talk was not about politics, but was no less extravagant and confusing. At once the Witch attached herself to a masked officer in the uniform of the Queen's Regiment; who might have been the helpful Lieutenant Elie who had cleared the Paris Road for them that afternoon.

Madeleine heard a Harlequin telling

an actress dressed as an Amazon that a letter had come to France by air from America; a letter signed by President Washington. Madeleine had heard of America, a far-off land discovered by France but stolen by the English. Its inhabitants were multicolored savages, some red, some white, and some black.

The Amazon expressed amazement that a letter could come all the way from America by air.

"Well," her escort explained, "the letter came to London by ship. From there Dr. John Jeffries of Boston took a coach to Dover and ascended in Monsieur Blanchard's balloon. The balloon came down south of Calais, and Dr. Jeffries and the letter came to Paris by carriage."

"Then only the hop across the channel was by air," said the Amazon.

"Yes but the letter entered France by air, which proves the principle. Besides, the channel crossing was the most dangerous part. The balloon nearly came down in the sea. Dr. Jeffries put on a cork life vest and offered to jump overboard, even though he had paid for the balloon."

"Americans are naturally generous," said the Amazon.

Madeleine turned back towards Mademoiselle, and found that the Witch and the masked officer were gone. She was shocked, struck with pure disbelief. Madeleine knew that the Witch was capricious and unpredictable, but the girl never imagined she would just be abandoned in a place like this. Before that night Madeleine had never even imagined that a place like the Cafe de Foy in the Palais-Royal existed.

She got up to go, determined to find Camille and Lucille in the Caveau. Halfway to the door she stopped. In her anger at the Witch's wickedness she had forgotten the Ogre. Onan was at the Caveau. She remembered his horned mask and the way his cultured lips twisted as he argued with de Robespierre. Without Mademoiselle's evil counterweight, Onan might do anything. Here in this city Madeleine supposed that the Seigneur could do as he pleased, knowing that she could never find her way home. She rightly suspected that Paris could easily swallow up girls from the country.

Alone, afraid, and forsaken, Madeleine heard a familiar voice from above and behind her. Turning about, she saw the self-assured young man who had ordered crêpes and cheese for her that afternoon. At that moment Louis Antoine Saint-Just looked to her like a drunken angel. He had soft, almost feminine features, and was standing on a table just outside the cafe, waving a bottle and reciting a poem he had written. Here was the first person in Paris who had shown kindness to the her. She dropped her mask and let the angel see her face.

The poem was a long one of twenty cantos, many of them were pornographic, and Madeleine could only understand bits and pieces. The poem attacked the King, Queen, courtiers, generals, and religion, while advocating the "pursuit of happiness," raping nuns and the other rites of love. When the poem was done Madeleine thought she had been hasty in unmasking, but Saint-Just leaped down off the table, reintroduced himself, and asked how Madeleine was finding Paris.

"Right now," she admitted, "Paris is confusing. I am lost and I would like to return to my Mistress's apartments on the Île Saint-Louis."

"Your Mistress," said Saint-Just, "you mean the Witch with the half smile and the dark eyes? Nothing could be simpler." He inspected his bottle, exchanged it for one that was almost full, then opened a path through the crowd, leading Madeleine away from the Palais-Royal.

His quick steps suggested that she would soon be safe in Mademoiselle's apartments, but instead Madeleine found herself on a drinking tour of the Tuileries Gardens. When she heard distant fireworks, she knew the Place de Grève and the Île Saint-Louis were far off and behind her. She tried to get more specific directions from Saint-Just, but the young man shook his head, "Tonight we are at home anywhere in the city. Have a drink and tell me what you think of my poem."

Madeleine took a fortifying drink and gave the bottle back. "It seemed to mock religion and glorify death."

"Why thank you, few critics have understood it so well." Saint-Just waved his bottle in the general direction of Notre Dame. "Religion favors the rich. Only death is democratic, treating everyone alike."

Her father had told her tales with similar morals around the winter fire, but it did not give Madeleine more confidence in her guide. "Do you think that nothing is sacred?"

The young man pushed an unruly lock of hair out of his eyes and tapped his chest with the bottle. "My dear, I despise everything, even this dust that forms me and speaks to you." He leaned against her. "But I do not despise women. I was raised by women, by my sisters and widowed mother. They cared for me until I ran off with the silver spoons. Mother had me dragged back from Paris and locked up under a *lettre de cachet*. Now I am free and back in the city where anything was possible."

As the bottle emptied, Madeleine needed more support from Saint-Just's stubborn grip. They crossed the Pont Royal, entering the Faubourg Saint-Germain, a dark left-bank area inhabited by soldiers, invalids, and women of the night. Madeleine was stumbling, but she took courage because they were headed upriver, towards the Île Saint-Louis. In the Théâtre Français, Saint-Just found a fresh bottle at a tavern near the Cordelier's Club and charged it

to his mother. Then he guided Madeleine into an alley. He held her while he pulled down his pants and urinated against a wall, taking drunken pride in directing the stream where he willed. Madeleine watched as he shook himself dry, sobering somewhat for this simple but important task. Then he pushed Madeleine up against the same wall and said that the "pursuit of happiness" demanded that they make love right in this dirty ally. "We are both enlightened individuals," he assured her, "and will not mind the circumstances."

Even with all the wine she had consumed, Madeleine still cared very much about the circumstances and wanted to do no such thing. She struggled, but it was hard to say no to the young man's peremptory demands. Pinned against the wall, Madeleine heard heavy footsteps. A broad-shouldered woman entered the alley, filling the narrow space, holding a bottle of her own. By her stance and the hour of morning she had to be a prostitute; not the refined courtesan or hard working tart who sold herself in the Palais-Royal, but a part-time worker with a sweaty day job as well.

"Here, boy," she said, "you can afford to pay. Forcing young girls steals food out of the mouths of honest whores."

Saint-Just seemed paralyzed by this vulgar assault, losing his modeled self-assurance. The woman was quick to see weakness. Encouraged by his indecision, she stepped forward and clipped the drunk young man on the side of the head with her bottle. Saint-Just collapsed against the hard wet wall.

Madeleine watched as the woman went through Saint-Just's coat, traded bottles with him, then straightened up. "More full than his pockets," she said peering into the rounded glass. "Come on, girl. This boy will be good for nothing until morning. We can still have some fun."

The prostitute was free with Saint-

Just's wine. Despite her obvious capacity, she also passed out on the street. Madeleine slumped down beside the woman's warm bulk. Fireworks boomed across the river.

The girl was awakened by a gentle nudge and a raspy tongue on her cheek. Madeleine looked up into the night and saw *La Blanche*'s white form. "Madeleine," the cat meowed, "come with me."

Madeleine was shocked to see *La Blanche* in Paris, and almost as surprised to hear the cat speaking.

"Madeleine," she meowed, "come with me."

The girl swayed to her feet and followed the cat through the dark morning over cold cobbled streets. With *La Blanche* leading they went past Notre Dame, over the Pont de la Tournelle, to Mademoiselle's apartments on the Île Saint-Louis.

The Pimple on Paris

When Madeleine awoke on Midsummer's day *La Blanche* was gone. All that remained of the evening, night, and morning was a staggering headache. She lay back on the empty bed wondering, had *La Blanche* really talked to her last night? Could her cat even be in Paris? That Madeleine had been in the city for less than a day was itself unbelievable.

Unable to answer any of these questions, Madeleine looked for Mademoiselle. Every movement made her head ache worse, but the girl peered past the couch she slept on into Mademoiselle's bed. The Witch was asleep, sprawled stark naked across her bed, small pale breasts rising and falling as her breath whispered in and out.

Keeping her head as level as she could, Madeleine rose and went to her morning chores, moving around that slim white form. Her mind was filled by *La Blanche*. Of course the cat was special,

but she had never suspected how special. Twice now the cat had come to her aid, and now was speaking to her. Was she caught in some pact with a devil that she could not remember making? That thought was disturbing and frightening. The only devils she knew were the Witch and Onan, and she would not believe that *La Blanche* was that evil.

That next night she waited in hope and fear for the cat to appear. If the cat came back, should Madeleine attempt a conversation? Would thanking *La Blanche* imperil her soul even more? Her worries were for nothing, because *La Blanche* did not come.

Days turned into weeks, and Madeleine gave up waiting. If the cat was in Paris, she would not sleep with the girl the way she had at home. Madeleine missed the simple magic of sleeping with a warm body curled between her legs. She no longer cared if the cat could talk, and doubted that *La Blanche* was in Paris at all. Saint-Jean's night faded into a drunken memory, in which anything or nothing might have happened.

By her third Friday in the city Madeleine was familiar enough with the markets to do morning shopping. On her way to the Corn Market a file of French Guards overtook her. These troops terrified her. They were supposed to keep order in the city, but barely two weeks before they had provoked a riot. No one knew when they would use their muskets, and all they seemed to care for was free drinks at the Café de Foy.

Madeleine stepped aside to let them cross the Rue Saint Martin. Then a strange and horrible sight brought back Midsummer's Night. The ranks of French Guards parted for several carts filled with bound women. Madeleine saw the soldiers hurl insults and garbage at the passing line of tumbrils. With their hands tied the women could not protect themselves, but they did manage brutal and inventive replies. Seeing Madeleine with her mouth open, the soldiers laughed. One of the cart drivers called down, asking if she wanted to ride along as well.

To hide her confusion Madeleine asked an old scissors seller what was happening. The crone spit in the gutter. "These are the whores who have not paid the police. They are being taken to Salpetrière hospital for *triage*. Those who pay up will be freed, the better sort will be left at Salpetrière, and the most diseased will be hauled to Bicetre, the prison-asylum for the insane."

Madeleine looked back at the carts, her gaze caught by a young woman with wild auburn hair and big brown eyes. The young whore did not call back at the men, but stood up straight in the jolting cart. Her mouth was a single hard line, and she held her head high, as though she could see over the gabled roofs to the green fields beyond. Madeleine was sure the woman had been at the Palais-Royal on Saint-Jean's night, then she realized what made the young woman seem most familiar. The bound prostitute was wearing Mademoiselle's Black Widow dress, the costume that Madeleine had not seen since the Midsummer fête at the Café de Foy.

Madeleine raced through her marketing, propelled by fear and fascination. Seeing Mademoiselle's Black Widow dress on the back of a Palais-Royal prostitute was a small look into a larger mystery. It made Madeleine want to know more. She ran back to the apartments and found them empty. Under the pretext of cleaning, Madeleine made a careful search of Mademoiselle's rooms. She looked to see if the Black Widow dress was really missing, and for anything that would tell her more about her mistress's secrets. The usual places turned up only the usual things. The closets and chests held clothes — but not the Black Widow dress. The bureau and dressing table held toiletries. The bed and curtains hid nothing.

Madeleine's search ended with the single unused furnishing, a huge ebony cabinet with gilt and bronze trim that sat in the back corner of the room. It was a heavy piece from the last century, serving no purpose except to impress. Mademoiselle never asked for anything from this cabinet, nor did she order Madeleine to store anything there. The girl tested the door and it swung silently open. Sitting alone in the back of the cabinet was the yellow carpetbag that Mademoiselle had made Madeleine watch over all the way to Paris.

Madeleine knelt down and touched the clasp, feeling only a finger's width away from the Witch's secrets. Here was the one bag that Mademoiselle had not unpacked, and never seemed to open. The clasp separated in her hand. She could see fabric inside the bag.

"You knew you were not supposed to do that."

The metal in Madeleine's hand became slippery with sweat. She looked over her shoulder and saw Mademoiselle's long form framed in the doorway. The Witch's eyes were narrow, hooded by heavy lids. She strode into the room.

Madeleine knelt hunched over the bag, her hands holding tight to the clasp to keep from trembling. A cool white arm reached down and closed the clasp. "You were supposed to guard that bag but never look inside."

The girl nodded, not trusting her voice.

The Mademoiselle stepped back, touching a thin finger to her white teeth. "If you wish to learn my secrets, we will start with the simpler ones. Stand up."

Madeleine did not move.

"I can call the Seigneur. You would move for him."

Madeleine stood up. She was scared enough without having to face Onan.

"Very wise," said the Witch. "We do not need to involve Onan yet."

It shocked Madeleine to hear Mademoiselle use the villagers' secret name for their seigneur. She wondered how she had ever hoped to keep anything from the Witch.

Mademoiselle touched the back of the cabinet and it pivoted inward, revealing a curtained and recessed chamber. "Here, come with me." She took Madeleine's hand. The inner room was dark and windowless, much larger than Madeleine imagined possible. Light from the bedroom showed her that the ceiling was mirrored. A second scared Madeleine stared down at her.

There were several wooden chairs in the chamber, arranged around a covered metal tub studded with lightning rods. A lock and chain hung from the heavy tub. Mademoiselle lifted the chain and said, "Give me your hand."

"No." Madeleine looked at the lock and put her hands behind her back.

The Witch smiled. "I was beginning to think that no one had taught you that word. This will not hurt much. You may trust me on that."

"I trusted you before and you abandoned me in the Palais-Royal."

"So I did," said the Witch, "and you survived. Someone is watching over you. Even the Palais-Royal on Midsummer's Eve did not swallow you up."

Madeleine kept her hands behind her. "You cannot make me. You are not above the law."

"You are right. I will not force you. We can go before a magistrate instead. A magistrate will assume that a servant girl sneaks into her mistress's bag thinking to steal. You must not blame him, that is just the way a judge thinks. I can assure you that the contents of that bag are important enough to put you in La Force prison until your hair turns gray."

"I did not mean to steal."

"I know. I think you meant to learn, but knowledge without price is worthless. This room may be bleak, but it is paradise compared to a damp cell with vermin for companions."

Madeleine held out her hand. The Witch locked the hard chain around her limp wrist, then stepped away. "I am leaving you here. The curtains are heavy and the walls are padded. No noise will enter or leave the chamber, so feel free to cry and scream. Let yourself go and you will learn things."

The Witch left, taking light and sound with her. Madeleine could only feel the hard chain connecting her to nothingness. She yanked at the chain just to hear the harsh clash of metal on metal. It was cold comfort. When Madeleine tired of standing she groped about and found a chair. Nothing happened. No one came for her. The silence and blackness were solid. She beat her feet on the floor, carpets buried the sound of her stamping.

More time passed. Madeleine's thirst and hunger grew. She knew that only the Witch could free her. In panic she imagined Mademoiselle and Onan packing up and leaving Paris. Who could question them? She would be just another country girl, swallowed up by the great city. She heard herself crying in the dark.

Time stopped. The world shrank down to a rough wooden seat, cold iron chains, and her own slow breathing. She thought she slept, but sleeping and waking were difficult to distinguish in noiseless darkness.

Madeleine heard soft music played by wind instruments. *La Blanche*'s white face hovered in the black chamber. She followed the cat home. The wheat was taller, people were working in the fields. These sights and sounds were comforting, but sure signs of madness. Madeleine felt herself sway. She pictured herself being hauled to Bicetre prison-asylum in a jolting cart.

Suddenly the door flew open and the chamber blazed with light. Madeleine was blinded. She closed her eyes, covering them with her fists. This vision was the most real yet. Voices crowded around her, and she smelled food.

"Here is the afflicted girl." She recognized Onan's voice. Trying to open her eyes, she saw only the Ogre's horned head. She shut her eyes, surrounding herself with darkness, screaming to drive off the voices. Strong male hands stroked her belly and hips. She thought these must be the asylum attendants and started to struggle, but the hands were soothing, as strong as Onan's but tender and caring. Their touch actually made her feel less afraid.

Madeleine opened her eyes. The man holding her waist was not an asylum guard, but a gentleman. He twice her age, but had a young and ardent smile. His voice was strong and sympathetic. "How do you feel?"

Madeleine blinked, but could not speak. Bewilderment replaced fear and anger.

The man kept holding her and asking kind questions. Candle light streamed through the hidden door. The curtained room had filled up with men and women in silk and lace. She was surprised to see Lucille Duplessis smiling down at her, while Camille Desmoulins was congratulating the man who held her. The gentleman took Camille's praise with sincere generosity and a touch of juvenile vanity.

Mademoiselle stepped out of the crowd and unlocked Madeleine's hand, saying in a solicitous tone, "Do you still feel like screaming?"

Madeleine shook her dazed head.

"She does not feel like screaming," the Witch announced to the crowd. "And can you speak?"

"*Oui,*" was all she could whisper.

The gentle folk applauded politely, as if that one word were a minor miracle. Mademoiselle would not let go of Madeleine's hand, instead she motioned with her free hand. "Everyone form the circle." The kind, handsome Marquis took Madeleine's other hand, and soon

she was part of an open circle around the metal tub. The man and woman at the open ends of the chain each touched a lightning rod.

Energy surged through her body. She gasped, trying to pull away from the tingling, but the Marquis and Mademoiselle would not let go. The rushing current became a purr. *La Blanche*'s voice rang in her ear, "Madeleine, you are with me." Hearing *La Blanche* calmed her. She let herself sway with the current, one link in the chain of people.

When the chain broke there was more applause. Mademoiselle led everyone back through the cabinet into her bedroom. The bed was gone and a buffet of caviar, champagne, lemon juice, sour cream, chopped egg, and pheasant mousse was spread on small tables. They ate off mother-of-pearl spoons while the men discussed living electricity, magnetic currents, repelling and attracting fluids. Women fluttered around Madeleine, saying how happy they were for her. Lucille Duplessis kept laying hands on her, asking if she really felt well.

These kind gentlepeople left Madeleine a great mess to clean up. She polished silver and mother-of-pearl, then scrubbed pheasant mousse out of the rug while servants brought the bed back. Returning from seeing her guests off, the Witch tossed herself down on the coverlet, waving the men servants away. "Oh, stop cleaning, Madeleine. You were wonderful. Without you the party would have been nothing."

Madeleine looked at the woman, trying to see if she could be serious.

"No, it is true." Mademoiselle rolled over and propped her chin on her hands. "I told them that my serving girl was having fits and seeing things. Look at you now, completely cured and back to work."

Madeleine stood up and glared. "You lied."

"Did I really?" The Witch's tone made

Madeleine uncomfortable. "Then tell me truthfully how you found your way home through the city on Midsummer's Eve, and what sent you going through my things?"

Madeleine said nothing.

"Truth is not so simple, is it? So remember, the truth could easily have us sharing a ward in Bicetre."

"Does that mean we must lie?"

"Perhaps," said the Witch, "but we certainly must go about with our eyes open, not expecting ignorance and innocence to protect us. The worst crimes are committed by people who think they are doing good."

She lay back and patted the bed. "Come sit beside me, you must have questions."

Madeleine sat down cautiously, as far from her Mistress as the little bed would allow. "Was that witchcraft?" she asked, very much afraid that the answer would be yes.

"Oh no," Mademoiselle yawned. "That was merely mesmerism, animal magnetism. You can feel it by rubbing the fur on a cat and then touching metal. Speaking of cats, did you feel your familiar?"

La Blanche was the last thing that Madeleine wanted to discuss with the Witch. The cat was her only protector. She did not want to discover that *La Blanche* was a devil also.

"Do not be coy with me. You know who I mean, the one who has been watching over you."

Madeleine looked down, "Yes, I did feel her."

"Good," the older woman closed her eyes, "Tomorrow I will give you another lesson."

"What day is tomorrow?" By now it seemed a week since Madeleine had entered the hidden chamber.

"Tomorrow is Saturday, and today is still Friday." She yawned, as though such simple discourse made her tired. Madeleine watched the Witch fall asleep, then she snuffed out the candles and retired to her couch.

Even without *La Blanche* to wake her, Madeleine was up before her mistress. Onan was up as well, no longer an ogre but still demanding breakfast. She served him strawberries and fried apples. When he was done he sat back with the soiled dishes in front of him. Madeleine considered waiting, then reached in to take his plate away. Onan's hand caught her wrist. Though she had half dreaded it, the actual act came as a rough surprise. She smelled his unwashed body as he drew her closer.

"Look at me," said Onan. Madeleine looked up his arm to his unshaven chin, and found that the Seigneur was smiling. "I hope you will see," he said, "that there is a great difference between the Witch and me. I was perhaps crude, but you could have satisfied me with a little mutual pleasure. Her, you will find much harder to satisfy."

He let fall her wrist, sitting back again as if to say, "See, I need nothing."

Madeleine took the dish without a word, walking to the kitchen and feeling her wrist. The seigneur's touch was always so sure, so confident. His fingers made everything else seem like a girl's fantasy, as if he alone knew what was real.

In a short time the Mademoiselle was also up, briskly arranging Madeleine's day. "Your second lesson will be in seeing the future. We must go to Versailles for that."

Madeleine was glad to be leaving the city, but her future seemed too vague and frightening to warrant a look.

"Oh, do not be so alarmed," said the Mademoiselle. "I have only your education in mind. I am not doing this just to see you suffer."

A carriage whisked them off to Versailles. The coach carried Madeleine along the very route she had walked with *La Blanche,* past the Théâtre Français and through the Faubourg

Saint-Germain where the soldiers were camped, then out a gate in the customs wall onto the open road. Between Paris and Versailles the terrors of the road were tamed. Gendarmes kept the homeless moving along and more soldiers guarded the Sèvres and Saint-Cloud bridges. Madeleine almost felt secure, much less afraid of Mademoiselle now that it was daylight and they were out of the city.

Versailles was a little city dominated by a single building, the huge and sprawling Grand Château, bigger even than Notre Dame or any House of God Madeleine had ever seen. The Witch said she was not welcome in the Château, and took Madeleine to hear speeches at the Estates General. This torrent of words meant nothing to Madeleine until she heard the same firm and gentle voice that had soothed her the night before. Looking up, she saw the man who had held her in the Witch's curtained room. He was pleading for something called "The Declaration of the Rights of Man and the Citizen."

"Who is he?"

"That is the Marquis de La Fayette. You have been in Paris just over a fortnight and already you have been fondled by a Marquis."

Madeleine blushed, but the Mademoiselle brushed her modesty aside. "You will have to drop that peasant prudery. Paris has no use for it. The rich do not need modesty and the poor cannot afford it."

"He is making demands on the King. How can the King allow that?"

"When the Marquis was nineteen he sailed to America to fight for President Washington. After facing British bullets and red Indians, I doubt that the Marquis is much scared of Louis. More to the point, the Marquis de La Fayette is worth three million *sou* a year, almost nine thousand *sou* a day. Do you know how much money that is?"

Madeleine said she could never imagine such a sum.

"That is three million *sou* more than the King is worth," said the Mademoiselle. "A bourgeois named Necker has gone over the King's accounts and discovered that France is bankrupt."

"How can the King be bankrupt? He collects the taxes."

"No, the King collects no taxes. Louis sold that privilege to his bankers long ago."

"Then what will happen?"

The Witch crooked her finger. "That is what I came to show you." She led Madeleine out into the sunlight and greenery that surrounded the Grand Château. "Here were can look into the future. Tell me what you see."

As best she could Madeleine described the formal garden, with its geometric walks, fruit trees, and beds of flowers; a floral tapestry so large that it included a canal and two small palaces.

When she was done the Witch asked, "Did all these plants just grow this way?"

"No they were planted, trimmed, and tended."

"And who did that?"

"King Louis, I suppose."

"King Louis and twenty million gardeners," said the Witch. "What you see is France as she is, confined, controlled, laid out with compass and ruler. Now look at her as she will be." Mademoiselle led Madeleine off the neat walks onto dark forest paths, where trees had no obvious order and shrubs grew all about. The only building was a small white columned temple overgrown with ivy, set on a wild isle in a pond choked with lilies.

"This is just a wood," said Madeleine.

"No, this is called an English garden. Here every weed is free to grow as it wills, and to strangle its neighbor if it must. Do you suppose that the King of England is rich?"

"Until I talked to you I supposed that all kings were rich."

"England has a national debt as crushing as ours, but the English do not seem to care. They are happy to buy and sell little pieces of that debt, as though it were gold or diamonds."

"The English are known to be mad," said Madeleine. She had never seen an English person, but was only repeating what everyone in the village knew.

"Yes, but their madness allows them to make money out of disorder, to build factories and steam engines out of chaos. One day France will follow." As they walked the woods opened up and Madeleine saw a mill pond, surrounded by rose cottages, grape arbors, and large but simple houses. She could smell a barnyard beyond. "What village is this?"

Mademoiselle sat down and ran a stiff green blade of grass through her thin, nailed fingers. "This is where the Queen comes to play peasant. Even she knows the old ways have played themselves out. The Old Louis's Grand Château is built on an inhuman scale. Ever since he built it the Royal Family has been building smaller palaces to live in. This village is their final retreat. The Queen pretends to be a peasant and the King pretends to be a watchmaker, and wild woods where only the strongest survive encroach on their fantasies."

The Witch stood up, swinging her arm in a circle large enough to include the village, woods, formal garden, and the progressively smaller palaces. "What do they call all this in the Corn Market?"

Madeleine hesitated.

"No more peasant modesty," said the Mademoiselle. "What do the market women call Versailles?"

Madeleine giggled. "They call it the pimple on the ass of Paris."

"Exactly," said the Mademoiselle. "It cannot last. It will all fall down, perhaps tomorrow, perhaps in a hundred years, but the fall will come."

The Night of 14 July

She did not have to wait a century to see the future. The collapse came the next day. It was Sunday and Madeleine spent the morning hearing mass without her Mistress. When she emerged, the markets were filled up with news. Necker had been dismissed. Huge placards proclaimed that peaceful citizens should stay indoors, and that there was no cause for alarm. Madeleine knew that if there was no cause for alarm, then there was no cause for placards on the street corners either. She went at once to the Palais-Royal, where her mistress was bound to be.

She found the Mademoiselle outside the Café de Foy, and heard a different story. "Sabres are just across the Tuileries Gardens. Royal dragoons and hussars are mustering at the Place de Louis XV." Madeleine could feel fear and indecision in the cafe crowd, but when she looked for troops all she could see were Sunday strollers in the gardens.

Then Camille Desmoulins burst out of the Café de Foy. He leaped onto the same table that Saint-Just had read his cantos from on the night of the Midsummer fête. His hair was wild and instead of a wine bottle, Camille was waving a pistol. "Friends," he shouted, "shall we die like frightened hares? Like sheep bleating for mercy, where there is no mercy, but only the whetted knife? The hour has come for swift death or deliverance. To arms! To arms!"

Madeleine saw Lucille looking up at him, her pretty face proud and sublime, her head held high like a sacrament. Mademoiselle seized Madeleine's arm, her nails making sharp contact. Madeleine suddenly felt she was seeing the future again. Lucille looked a little older, with her face more tired and drawn, but she was wearing the same proud smile, though a great silver blade hung over her head. Mademoiselle broke the spell, shouting Madeleine's ear, "If we are to arm the city we will need more than Camille's little pistol."

"But where could we get weapons?" Madeleine hoped that the impossibility was self-evident.

"Where there are soldiers," said the Witch.

Madeleine looked about. As usual there were French Guards lounging about the Cafe de Foy, but they were unarmed drinkers. Mademoiselle seized a partly sober soldier and told him to take her to his barracks. He agreed and staggered off at the head of the women. Halfway to the barracks they saw a company of French Guards coming to meet them with leveled bayonets, driving a crowd before them.

Violence hung over the small intersection. No one knew what would happen, least of all the company sergeant, a confused and sheep-faced fellow hiding behind his whiskers and authority. Their drunken guide sobered and vanished when he saw the guns. The crowd began to melt away down the alleys. Mademoiselle linked arms with Madeleine and stepped out, saying, "Women to the front. The French Guards will not fire on the women of Paris."

Madeleine was dragged forward by the Witch's energy, though she knew the statement was far from true. In the market Madeleine had heard how the French Guards put down bread riots, shooting women and men alike. A stout woman with gray in her hair took Madeleine's other arm. More women pressed her from behind, forcing her towards the leveled steel. Madeleine tried to recoil, then felt the animal magnetism that had run through the mesmeric circuit. It was flowing from the Witch through the female chain.

The baffled sergeant ordered the women to disperse.

The Witch's voice sounded full of the self-assurance that came from generations of command. "The French guards will not fire on French women. You must march to the Tuileries, where foreign regiments are killing your comrades, murdering Frenchmen." Madeleine knew that this last was a lie. She had just come from the Tuileries and seen nothing but peaceful picnicking.

The sergeant could not meet her stare. He lowered his sword, saying her order made as much sense as any he had heard today. The crowd cheered and surged forward, swallowing up the soldiers. The French guards, now Parisians in uniform, marched to the Palais-Royal.

Madeleine walked arm in arm with the Witch, worried about what the sergeant would do when he saw he had been lied to. But when she reached the edge of the Tuileries Gardens, she saw steel flashing in the fading light. Prince de Lambesc's King's German cavalry, big men riding bigger horses, were charging into the crowd. Madeleine stared in amazement as the Germans' sabres rose and fell, slashing at both rioters and Sunday strollers. The air was filled with thrown bricks and bottles. The sergeant and his French Guards shouldered the women aside, pouring a ragged volley into the Germans. The cavalry fell back, having come to France to be paid in silver, not in lead.

Night did not end the madness. That evening from the apartment balcony Madeleine saw smoke and fire rise all around the city as the people in the faubourgs burned down the wooden customs wall that ringed Paris. Mademoiselle was still out on the streets, and for the first time Madeleine felt safer with Onan.

The Seigneur stood beside Madeleine, brought closer to her level by the magnitude of what had happened. He talked to her the way a wise and wealthy uncle would. "Madeleine, you must now see the danger. In this city the Mademoiselle is destructive to herself and others. I want to convince her to come home, back to the Beauvais. You must want to see your village and family."

Madeleine was amazed to hear her Seigneur speaking of her wants and needs. The world was turned upside down indeed. She managed to say, "Yes, I miss my family very much."

"Good, all I need is to have a quiet talk with the Mademoiselle. We need a time alone, when she is not surrounded by mesmerists, masons, balloonists, the Gallo-American Society, the Friends of the Negro, and all her Palais-Royal crowd."

His vehemence made Madeleine nervous. "What could I do?"

He looked down at the girl and smiled, seeming to put his anger in check. "Just let me know when the three of us can be alone. I promise you will find your home even better than you left it. I can cancel your family's debts, and return you to your parents free of any obligation."

Later, when she went over the day in her mind, Madeleine was stunned by how much had changed between her and her Seigneur. No longer aloof, he seemed a man aware of his rights and powers but willing to be fair. His attempt to rape her in Beauvais seemed merely a social miscarriage, an unfortunate aspect of their former relationship. She saw a whole new world opening up.

For two full days Madeleine had no chance to act on Onan's request. The Witch was a whirlwind of activity that Madeleine could hardly keep up with. Mademoiselle held meetings, listened to extravagant proposals, gave speeches to women, and did everything but sleep.

By Tuesday morning Madeleine was watching from their rooftop while concerned citizens of Paris poured musket fire into the Bastille, a great pile of stone that rose above the city chimneys less than a mile from their apartments. Mademoiselle appeared below with Lieutenant Elie in tow, and ordered Madeleine down from the roof, and the three of them set out for the Place de la Bastille. There the crowd was trying to take the fortress using fire hoses, axes, burning straw, and a pair of ornamental cannon that had belonged to the King of Siam. A sailor and wine merchant acted as gunners. The Bastille's walls were a hundred feet high, and immensely thick, so Madeleine thought the mob might just as well go home.

As they arrived, some men were struggling with a woman. Mademoiselle wanted at once to know who the woman was.

A man who was holding her said, "She is the daughter of the fort's commander. We are going to burn her in front of the fort if the gates do not open." The terrified woman insisted that she was not remotely related to the fort commander. The chief pyromaniac dismissed her pleas as self-serving.

For the first time Madeleine saw the Witch shaken. She demanded that the men release the woman at once.

The men refused, saying women did not understand military tactics. "Look, we at least are doing something. If the fort commander even thinks this is his daughter, then the effect will be the same."

Mademoiselle screamed at them, "How do you know the commander even has a daughter? The fool in the fort might be impotent for all you know."

They were still arguing when the French Guards arrived with real cannon. These cannon captured the men's attention, and Mademoiselle was able to wrestle the woman free.

With Madeleine at her side, she helped Elie position the cannon before the main gate. The guns drew a hurricane of fire down from muskets in the fort's embrasures. Already the entrance court was strewn with a hundred bodies, some of them still moaning, but the Witch seemed to stand in a charmed circle. Madeleine clung to her mistress, and Elie went about his task undisturbed by the rain of musket balls.

When the guns were in position, but

before they could fire, a white flag appeared at the gate. Lieutenant Elie went forward to take the fort's surrender. There was more debate over this, since it had all happened too fast for those who wanted to hear their own cannon roar. Madeleine, however, was glad beyond belief to see the shooting stop, but the Witch dismissed her fears, patting dust off her gown with a gloved hand. "I doubt they were firing silver bullets. The only death I really fear is fire. Now let us go home. I need some rest." For the first time since Sunday she seemed tired.

As soon as Mademoiselle was in her room asleep, Madeleine alerted Onan. "She seems so swept up in what is happening, that I do not think she will ever want to leave."

"Oh, quiet persuasion works wonders," he said, dismissing her servants, sending them off to celebrate the city's victory.

When the Witch awoke, Madeleine was startled by the Seigneur's methods of quiet persuasion. Soon he was shouting, "Have you no regard for our position? You play Palais-Royal trollop, dallying with salon lions and garret scribblers that no one could take seriously. Then you riot with street women, fools, and criminal traitors." Madeleine had never seen Onan's face so flushed as he waved a finger at the Witch. "You make to much of your abracadabra, thinking it will protect you. Remember the fate of your great-grandmother. You can end things the same way she did."

Mademoiselle was a white pillar of ice. "My great-grandmother was burned at the stake in the same square where Joan of Arc was burnt before her, with half of Rouen watching. We do not know where your great-grandmother was, perhaps selling onions to the crowd, certainly no one but the pauper house priest thought her passing worth recording."

"Enough," said Onan, throwing up both his hands. He went to a bronze and ebony cabinet and produced a paper. "I hoped it would not come to this, but here is a *lettre de cachet* with your name on it. You will be in protective custody until you come to your senses. As you can see, the signatures and seals are all in order."

Mademoiselle laughed, tossing dark hair out of her eyes. "Do you plan to put me in the Bastille? Such letters are a few days out of date. The poseurs and fools that I have been boring you with are now in charge of Paris. La Fayette commands the National Guard. Trying to arrest me with a letter from the King will only land you in La Force prison."

"Perhaps it would," said Onan, snapping his fingers. His fat coachman and butler appeared, flanked by two burly men in hospital uniforms. "These men are attendants from Bicetre hospital, in my temporary employ."

Madeleine stood paralyzed with terror, but the Witch did not flinch. "You would not dare put me in Bicetre."

"No, even Bicetre is no longer safe. I am taking you back to the Beauvais."

He waved his hand. With professional indifference the two attendants stepped forward and seized her arms. When she started to protest one of them shoved a bar gag into her mouth, then both of them worked a leather hospital jacket over her arms and shoulders, buckling the long sleeve ends behind her back. Madeleine watched with mounting horror as the men worked with clinical efficiency, expressing no excitement. It was their job to restrain women.

While her body struggled in their grip, the Witch's eyes blazed at Onan from above the gag, but the Seigneur ignored her and turned to Madeleine. "I thank you for your assistance. My sister-in-law is an evil woman, from an evil line. She is unchristian, and you have seen how she has behaved here in Paris. She remains a woman and needs female care, especially since she will be in restraint. Attend to her, but answer to me. Your family will profit as I have promised."

Madeleine was half expecting a hospital jacket for herself as well. Shaking, she said she would do her best.

Their flight from Paris was smooth and swift. From atop the coach Onan guided them across the Pont Marie, then by back streets around the black towering stonework of the Bastille and the Porte Saint Antoine. Once they entered Popincourt, the carriage rolled straight up the Rue de la Roquette, past Bicetre itself.

"Passports." Lanterns swung in the night when they reached the charred remains of the la Roquette gate.

Onan stepped down to assure the sleepy National Guardsmen that everything was well. He had not only passports, but also a hospital order confining his afflicted sister-in-law to his care. Madeleine remembered her father saying that Onan had a passion for papers. He made no mention of a *lettre de cachet* from the suspect Royal Government. La Fayette's men looked into the coach and saw only a serving maid, two large hospital attendants hunched up on a seat, and a woman in restraints with wild black hair half covering her glittering eyes. Every Friday cartloads of bound women were brought to Bicetre for detention. The Guards waved them through and off into the night.

For Madeleine the trip home was as bad as the trip out three weeks before. Once more she cowered with the carpetbag in her lap, as silent and helpless as her gagged mistress. Before she had been carried along by events. Now it made her even more sick to remember how she had helped shape them.

On the trip home they avoided the country inns, stopping only to change horses. No one at the post houses saw any suspicion in their haste, since Paris was in a state of insurrection and flocks of brigands filled the roads.

The Great Fear

Despite her new and cordial relationship with the Seigneur, Madeleine felt as much a prisoner as the Mademoiselle. When they returned to the manor she was not allowed to visit her parents nor to communicate with the village. The Witch was kept behind a thick locked door, and twice a day Madeleine passed meals through an overhead transom, exchanging them for the chamber pot which she emptied and returned. Madeleine begged forgiveness for her part in Mademoiselle's imprisonment, saying she had no idea the Seigneur would be so harsh. The Witch laughed at her innocence, and said, "Keep my carpetbag safe and wait for my instructions, all will be well." Madeleine could not believe that.

Only Onan could open the door. Once Madeleine saw him go in using a large iron key. Creeping up, she listened to their interview through the transom. They argued about the Widow's money, which Onan claimed that the *lettre de cachet* assigned to him.

Mademoiselle informed Onan that he might as well fish for gold in a privy, as expect to get anything out of her.

"Do you still dare to insult me?" Onan's voice had a violent edge.

"Is it possible that I am being obscure?"

"Remember, Witch, I know your fear and can make it happen."

Their argument terrified Madeleine. Between them there was now no pity, no dissimulation, no self-control. She knew this was a relationship stripped of all pretense, since nothing stood between them, not the Church, not custom, not the bonds of marriage. They did not argue like lovers, but like brother and sister, which they were by holy writ. Having sinned so much, nothing seemed to stand between Onan and his threats.

Nothing but Madeleine. She was determined to free the Witch, to undo what she had done. She went at once to the carpetbag. Madeleine was not sure how she would use the magic inside, but she had to know what it held. When she opened it she found first a dress, not a silk Black Widow gown but a sturdy traveling dress. Beneath the dress were underclothes, and beneath the underclothes were bundles of papers. Each paper was engraved with strange words and symbols. Madeleine knew enough letters to know that the language was not French, and that she had no hope of reading these papers. If these were the Witch's most prized secrets, they were very ordinary secrets and of no use to her now.

This defeat threw Madeleine back on her own resources. She decided to cache the carpetbag near to the Witch's prison room, then somehow get the key that would open that door. Domestic duties allowed her to search almost everywhere for the key. After several days of searching she concluded that Onan kept the key on his person, even at night. Though she thought it through a dozen different ways, there seemed only one sure means of getting to the key. She could think of only one thing to barter for it.

She spent a whole evening alone on her knees in the chapel, smelling the dust and old incense, asking the Saints and Virgin if she should sacrifice chastity for the sake of her mistress. She would not sin for her own sake. Correctly viewed, Onan's bed would be just a softer version of Joan's stake and St. Catherine's wheel. When the Saints and Virgin sent no answer by morning Madeleine took it as mild consent.

She started paying more attention to both herself and the Seigneur, making sure she was washed and groomed, and that she smiled at him. The contrast between a sour mistress and a sweet obedient serving girl is one that any man is sure to notice. While Madeleine made herself pleasing the village made

its own plans. The wheat had ripened all summer in the field. The heads of wheat were heavy and golden, but growing with then was the fear that this harvest would never be reaped, because the seigneurs and speculators would profit more from another famine.

Madeleine's mother walked all the long way to the manor, but got no farther than the back door and the kitchen. She was not allowed to even see her daughter, but the Cook fed her potatoes and tales from Paris. Her return to the village drew talkers and listeners, each talker with a bit of news. In Clermont brigands had been seen leaving the forest to steal the wheat. There were more brigands in Bray. In Picardy the crops were being burnt in the fields. Onan had quarreled with the Witch, so no one need fear her curses anymore.

When Madeleine's mother spoke, the circle of voices hushed. Here was real news spoken by someone they knew, a face they could study and a voice they could judge, someone whose flesh and blood had been to Paris. "The Seigneur's cook says that my daughter saw Germans in Paris, attacking people at the Tuileries and led by a Prince of the Blood. The French Guards and the people of Paris drove them from the city, but there is chaos in the capital and no one can be trusted, least of all the Seigneur." Her listeners pictured the shy, sensible girl that the Seigneur had taken from the village. The one who spoke with authority to the younger children, and was already half a mother.

Madeleine's father listened, then strode past the tall stalks to the shed where his tools were stored. He came back into the sunlight carrying his largest scythe and a small black whetstone. Planting the curved butt of the scythe in the soft ground, he began to whet the blade, making a slick whine as the stone whisked back and forth.

People looked at him. "Why are we

still talking?" he asked.

They watched the blade grow brighter. "Why are we talking, and not doing what our grandfathers would have done if they could have, or their grandfathers before them?"

His wife stared at him over the sharp shining metal, her eyes as hard and bright as his. "Burn the library," she said.

People looked at the grain ripe in the field, calculating what the world would be like if all the wheat went to them, then they went home to get their scythes, their axes, their pruning hooks, even their pikes and shotguns.

In the manor that evening the shy sensible girl that the village remembered spent hours in front of a mirror. She tried on Mademoiselle's gowns, testing different make-ups and ways of doing her hair, testing her smile. When Madeleine saw that stranger in the mirror, the one that Onan would want, she knew the magic was done.

Over hors d'oeuvres the Seigneur was surprised to see one of the Witch's gowns come walking into the room, filled out by an attentive young servant. With wine and food her attractiveness grew. Over the sherry Onan was intrigued. With the dinner wine he was aroused, and by the time the desert brandy arrived he was ardent.

He reached past the brandy and took her hand, to keep her from disappearing with the desert tray and chocolate truffles. His touch gave Madeleine the thrill of knowing that her magic had worked, that she had done it all right. When his grip tightened, she felt fear. Madeleine had meant to submit, to martyr herself for the Mademoiselle, but that had been fantasy. Her Seigneur's hand was the real thing. There was an authentic tremble in her voice when she asked him to be generous.

"But of course," said the Seigneur, drawing her closer. Onan found it easy, even pleasing, to be generous when he was having everything he wanted.

"I am afraid," said Madeleine. "Promise that you will not send me away. I do not want to spend the night alone."

Onan assured her that sending her off was not his thought at all. When they got to the bedroom Madeleine asked if she might have some brandy. Even martyrs deserve an anesthetic. Onan drank with her, and the warm liquid relaxed and encouraged them both.

As Onan undressed her Madeleine felt this was happening to someone else, only the rough shock of his hands on her bare skin made it seem real. She kept her gaze fixed on his face, managing a worried half-smile. When he removed his shirt she saw the heavy key, hanging from a thong around his neck. Onan removed that too, looping it over a bedpost. The girl made herself look away, ignoring her objective.

The firm grip on her naked shoulder appalled her. As Onan lead her towards the bed she thought, "I am nothing. Why does he even want me?" Stripped of Mademoiselle's gown, the magic should be gone. "Please," she asked aloud, "put out the light." Onan looked her over, then complied, sniffing the candles one at a time, turning his lair into a soft cave. Madeleine tried to concentrate on what she would do afterwards, how she would find the key in the dark without disturbing Onan. What happened between now and then could not be worse than losing a tooth. With her mind set on that, she lay still in the dark, feeling his touch and hearing nothing but the hammering of her heart.

Then there was another hammering, not her heart beating inside her, but the sound of axes shattering glass and splintering wood. Onan cursed and leaped off her. From beneath them came a horrible crash, howls of rage, and the pattering of frightened servants' feet. A mob was breaking in below.

Madeleine rolled over, took the key, fell out of bed and scooped her borrowed

gown off the floor. Since returning from Paris she had gone over the bedroom a dozen times with a dust rag, so finding her way without light was simple. She could hear Onan fumbling about, cursing after her like a Corn Market porter. Though he was just as familiar with the room, his mind had been focused on his own pleasure. Madeleine was up and out the door before he could catch her or light a candle.

Smoke poured out of the library wing. Hundred-year-old tax rolls, land claims, lists of dues paid and unpaid, all burned briskly. Many villagers could not tell a dangerous document from a book of poems, so to be safe they tossed everything on the pyre. Soon drapes and wood-paneled walls were burning too.

Madeleine first found the carpetbag where she had cached it, then stumbled down a smoky corridor by the dancing light of the library fire. When she reached the Witch's gaol she stuck the key in the lock and started to turn it. Metal rasped on metal. The bolt drew back.

A firm hand in a lace cuff seized her wrist and twisted the other way. She looked up the arm and saw Onan, fully dressed and in command. If only she had not gone for the carpetbag.

"No," he said, "this is one burning the Witch will not miss."

The girl struggled to turn the key, but Onan tightened his grip, twisting until the pain made Madeleine sob and let go. He pulled the key out of the lock and hurled it down the dim hallway to meet the flames eating their way up from the library. The key tumbled end over end and vanished into the growing inferno. With a satisfied grunt Onan picked up a heavy ebony chair, not the lighter mahogany then in style, and tossed it through the tall glass windows that lined the hall. Yelling a cheery goodbye through the open transom, he followed this piece of Louis XV furniture into the night.

Still clutching the carpetbag, Madeleine sank in a shaking heap, beating against the heavy door with her bare fists. She could not hope to move it. Down near the floor the air was cool and breathable, but already she could not see the transom through the smoke and tears.

The fire marched down the hall. Flames tore down the window curtains and smoke billowed out through the broken glass, but Madeleine could not bring herself to leave the door. She curled her body closer to it. Her first attempt at martyrdom had been a failure, but the approaching fire seemed sure to do better. All around her the splintered crystal was turning blood red in the fire light. The girl only wished she could speak through the door, and say her own goodbye.

Madeleine's lungs began to fill with smoke, she coughed but could not clear her head. A small body pulled at her sleeve. Looking down she saw *La Blanche*, tugging at the silk fabric with sharp little teeth. The cat dropped the sleeve and said, "Madeleine my dear, we must go."

She tried to push the cat away, but *La Blanche* was not leaving without her. The determined feline bit through the fabric and into her flesh, sinking small teeth into Madeleine's wrist. The sudden pain of that bite cleared the smoke from her head and made the burning world more real. Madeleine got up and staggered after the cat, dragging the carpetbag behind her.

La Blanche led her through the broken window. Crying, choking, and nearly retching, Madeleine knelt on the cool dark lawn, feeling the waves of heat from the flaming manor. *La Blanche* kept nudging her, saying "Madeleine, follow me," so the girl tottered to her feet and followed the cat towards the fruit trees that lined the lawn and garden.

When they reached the tall black

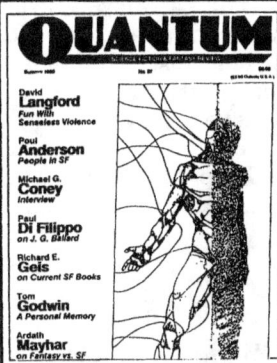

grove the cat stopped and started licking her paws. Madeleine recognized this little feline ritual of leaving. Like a cat licking butter off her paws, *La Blanche* was cleaning the old home off her feet. When she was done, she stretched, raised her head, and began to grow.

Rising through the silvery moonlight, the cat stood up, her form shifting from feline to female. In a moment Mademoiselle stood stark naked where the cat had been. Aside from the sable triangle of fur between her thighs, she might have been carved from bone or ivory. Her arms were folded beneath sculpted breasts and her alabaster face was framed by black curls. Curved eyes looked down at Madeleine, and the old half-smile was on her lips. "Well," she asked, "are you going with me?"

"Going where?" asked the girl.

"Back to Paris, of course. There is nothing more to keep us here." The

---

The Tome

"The Dark Works of Great Minds, and the Great Works of Dark Minds"

Coming soon, the Manley Wade Wellman tribute, featuring the first reprinting of "When the Lion Roared," his first known published story. Also work by Hugh B. Cave, David Drake, Karl Edward Wagner, Janet Fox, Jeff Osier, Mark Rainey, John B. Rosenman, and many, many more.

Sample copy #3.50, 2 issues $6.50, one year (4) $12.00, check or M/O only to David N. Wilson or William H. Backer, 454 Munden Ave., Norfolk, VA 23505

Don't miss a single issue!!!!

---

manor was now a roaring bonfire, bathing her bare skin with rose light even at some distance. "Open the bag," said the Witch.

Madeleine complied, and Mademoiselle removed the dress, but made no attempt to put it on. Instead she touched the cryptic paper etched with a strange language. "This is all we will need to travel on," said the Witch, "several thousand *livres*, drawn on the Bank of London."

If the Witch had produced a broom and candle, saying they would fly to Paris, Madeleine would not have been more amazed. She had never seen or heard of money made out of paper.

"Why?" was all the astonished girl could ask.

"Because great things are happening in Paris and we can be a part of them. Miracle and wonder are ahead of us: a new age, not just in Paris but in the whole world. Imagine the cities, the events, the danger and gaiety."

Madeleine looked back at the burning manor. The old certain world was crashing into embers, and Mademoiselle seemed to care less for her loss then Madeleine, who had lost nothing.

"Of course you could grow old in this village," said the Witch, "and never know the world beyond, but I believe there is more to you than that. I chose you from all the others to discover my secrets. Now you bear my mark, but you are still free to choose."

Madeleine looked down at the tiny teeth marks on her wrist. Mademoiselle stood naked against the night, but it was Madeleine who shivered. "I am afraid."

"Of course you are," said the Witch, "but there is no need for fear. There is no mystery. We live, and we die. What really matters is how we do it, for that is what we leave behind."

Mademoiselle stood for a moment more, a white pillar in the cold moonlight, then she pulled on the traveling dress. Ω

www.ingramcontent.com/pod-product-compliance
Lightning Source LLC
Chambersburg PA
CBHW060750180626
46818CB00002B/520